B

Ans	_____	
ASH	_____	
Bev	_____	
C.C.	2/07 _____	
C.P.	_____	
Dick	_____	
DRZ	_____	
ECH	_____	
ECS	_____	
Gar	_____	
GRM	_____	
GSP	_____	
G.V.	_____	
Har	_____	
JPCP	_____	
KEN	_____	
K.L.	_____	
K.M.	_____	
L.H.	_____	
LO	_____	
Lyn	_____	
L.V.	_____	
McC	_____	
McG	_____	
McQ	_____	
MIL	_____	

M.L.	_____	
MLW	_____	
Mt.Pl	_____	
NLM	_____	
Ott	_____	
PC	_____	
PH	_____	
P.P.	5/08 _____	
Pion.P.	_____	
Q.A.	_____	
Riv	_____	
RPP	_____	
Ross	_____	
S.C.	_____	
St.A.	_____	
St.J	_____	
St.Joa	_____	
St.M.	_____	
Sgt	_____	
T.H.	_____	
TLLO	_____	
T.M.	11/07 _____	
T.T.	_____	
Ven	_____	
Vets	_____	
VP	_____	
Wat	_____	
Wed	_____	
WIL	_____	
W.L.	_____	

BLAZE

***Also by JoAnn Ross
in Large Print:***

Out of the Storm
Out of the Blue
Out of the Mist
Magnolia Moon
River Road
Blue Bayou
Confessions
A Woman's Heart
Southern Comforts
Untamed

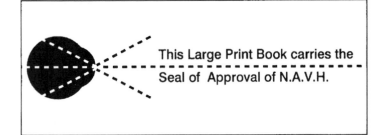

This Large Print Book carries the
Seal of Approval of N.A.V.H.

JOANN ROSS
BLAZE

WHEELER
PUBLISHING

Published in 2006 by arrangement with Pocket Books,
a division of Simon & Schuster, Inc.

Wheeler Large Print Hardcover.

The text of this Large Print edition is unabridged.
Other aspects of the book may vary from the original edition.

Set in 16 pt. Plantin by Minnie B. Raven.

Printed in the United States on permanent paper.

Library of Congress Cataloging-in-Publication Data

Ross, JoAnn.
    Blaze / by JoAnn Ross. — Large print ed.
        p. cm.
    ISBN 1-59722-166-X (lg. print : hc : alk. paper)
    1. Arson investigation — Fiction.   2. Pyromania —
Fiction.   3. South Carolina — Fiction.   I. Title.
PS3568.O843485B57 2006
    813´.54—dc22   2005029081

To Jay — again and always

As the Founder/CEO of NAVH, the only national health agency solely devoted to those who, although not totally blind, have an eye disease which could lead to serious visual impairment, I am pleased to recognize Thorndike Press* as one of the leading publishers in the large print field.

Founded in 1954 in San Francisco to prepare large print textbooks for partially seeing children, NAVH became the pioneer and standard setting agency in the preparation of large type.

Today, those publishers who meet our standards carry the prestigious "Seal of Approval" indicating high quality large print. We are delighted that Thorndike Press is one of the publishers whose titles meet these standards. We are also pleased to recognize the significant contribution Thorndike Press is making in this important and growing field.

Lorraine H. Marchi, L.H.D.
Founder/CEO
NAVH

* Thorndike Press encompasses the following imprints: Thorndike, Wheeler, Walker and Large Print Press.

Acknowledgments

A thousand thanks to the many people who helped make this book happen:

For providing hugely helpful technical details and answering my questions, I'm indebted to jewelry artist Nancy Gatland, of British Columbia; Carlene Augustine Barthé, Public Affairs Coordinator for the New Orleans Fire Department; retired New York City Fire Department Deputy Chief Vincent Dunn; Kathy Buckman and all the folks at UPV, Inc., of Upland, California; and retired Division Fire Chief Jack Jarboe, of Grace Industries, Inc. During the long months spent writing, photographs from firelinephotos.com — taken by International Fire Photographers Association president and District Chief of the NOFD photo unit, Chris E. Mickal — kept me "in" the fire scenes. Any mistakes or incidences of creative license in *Blaze* are solely my responsibility.

A very special, heartfelt thanks to fellow author and friend Patty Gardner Evans, of the gloriously devious mind, for all the night-time brainstorming sessions and for never once saying, "You want to do what?!"

Man is the only creature that dares to light a fire and live with it. The reason? Because he alone has learned to put it out.

— Henry Jackson Vandyke Jr.

God gave Noah the rainbow sign;
No more water, the fire next time.
African-American spiritual

one

The Flamemaster had been watching the building for weeks, studying her, learning all her secret quirks. Even in her youth she hadn't been all that attractive, and despite the recent face-lift, the passing of years still showed. She reminded him of a dowager who'd fallen on hard times, then gotten an extreme makeover from a quack plastic surgeon.

A couple approached his vehicle, the woman's stiletto heels clattering on the crumbling cobblestone sidewalk.

The Flamemaster scrunched down in the driver's seat so they wouldn't see him. Not that he was in danger of being discovered; they were so blissfully oblivious to anything or anyone around them, they could have been strolling in the peaceful, moss-draped environs of Admiral's Park on a Sunday morning, rather than risking this industrial waterfront neighborhood.

The man leaned down and murmured a soft something in the woman's ear; she laughed silkily in response. They paused, staring into each other's eyes, like some love-struck couple in a diamond commercial.

As their lips met and clung, The Flamemaster imagined a formally dressed couple in a gilded hotel room. The man opens a black velvet box, revealing an iceberg-size diamond glittering like ice on black satin. The woman instantly falls to her knees and attacks her companion's zipper.

Two carats or more, the deep voice-over advises as violins soar. And she'll damn well have to.

He chuckled at his little joke.

A purple cloud drifted over the sliver of moon, casting the couple in deep shadow. The only light was from the faint yellow flicker of old-fashioned gas lamps edging the pier. Music drifted from a dinner cruise ship somewhere out on the fog-draped harbor, fading in and out on the soft March air.

The guy's hands lifted her butt; she moaned and twined like a python around him. Just when The Flamemaster was looking forward to them doing it up against the brick wall, they came up for air.

The man tucked his shirt back in. She wiggled her dress, which had crawled nearly to her waist, back down to midthigh. They shared another laugh as they entered the centuries-old pink brick building.

The warehouse, abandoned for decades, had been on the brink of condemnation when some hotshot chef from New York City bought the building for a song and turned the top floor into a members-only harbor-view restaurant and dance club.

Tonight a throng of ultra-hip *Friends* clones with Gucci chips on their shoulders had packed into the loft on the warehouse's eighth floor to celebrate St. Patrick's Day with Guinness, overpriced shots of Jameson Gold, and lethal cocktails with names like the Dirty Mick, the Belfast Bomb, and the Blarney Stone Sour.

Paddy's Pig might be the hottest nightspot in town, but all the money the Yankee had poured into the project hadn't transformed the sow's ear of a building into anything resembling a silk purse.

The trendy pink and green neon lights and the floor-to-ceiling glass windows that had replaced the eroding brick was like dressing a bag lady in a designer gown; it couldn't change the fact that she was still as ugly as homemade sin.

He'd be doing the city a favor by getting rid of it.

Hell, the mayor should present him with a good citizen's award. A medal for beautifying Somersett.

The Flamemaster flipped open his cell phone and keyed in 625.

When he hit Send, the call triggered a remote-control device deep inside the building's wine cellar. There was a burst of white light and a faint popping sound, like a lightbulb bursting.

The retro-eighties heavy metal band rocking the building drowned out the sound. A waiter ran in and pulled a bottle of champagne from its slot. With his station full, and more people jammed into the bar waiting for a table, he'd been on the run all evening. Which was why he didn't notice the tiny orange flame flickering behind a row of fruit brandies.

The fledgling fire fed lazily, climbing up the wooden wine racks, twining around the studs, licking at the rafters.

Outside, observing from a public parking lot a safe block away, The Flamemaster's pulse picked up a beat.

An orange glow flickered, changing to bluish white as the heat soared.

Bottles began to expand and break, like fireworks over the harbor during Buccaneer Days; missiles of heavy green glass slammed into pine studs that were weeping dark, flammable pitch.

The Flamemaster took his eyes off the building just long enough to glance down at the sweep hand on his watch. It wouldn't be long now.

Expectation rippled up his spine.

The neon-lit walls shattered; deadly shards of window glass rained down like guillotine blades. Debris fell from the smoke-filled sky. A black lacquer table hit the sidewalk, sounding like a rifle retort before shattering into pieces; a trio of chairs followed, their metal frames twisted like pretzels.

Sirens wailed in the distance as a woman, her long hair on fire, her skirt blown up over her face, landed on the side-walk with a deadly thud, bounced into the gutter, then lay still. Screams rent the night as others followed, tumbling through the gaping hole where the glass walls had once stood, legs pumping wildly, arms wind-milling on the way down to the pavement.

A red ladder truck, followed by an en-gine, had just careened around the corner, emergency lights flashing, air horn blasting, when the explosion ripped through the block.

The Flamemaster's vehicle rocked from

side to side as a tidal wave–like force rolled beneath the tires. The night sky brightened, as if lit by a thousand suns. An instant later a dense cloud of acrid black smoke rolled down the street, engulfing everything, including the responding vehicles.

As the rigs' Jake brakes squealed, The Flamemaster drove off in the opposite direction, away from the hell-like conflagration that had turned the warehouse into a pile of stone and twisted metal.

This had definitely gone better than last week's rehearsal, which had been aborted when sprinklers drowned the flames as soon as the temperature hit 165 degrees. (Who'd have guessed a damn strip joint would've been built to code?)

Unfortunately, tonight the firefighters hadn't even arrived at the scene, let alone set up an interior attack line, before the charges he'd so meticulously set throughout the building triggered.

He'd have to work on his timing.

Oh well. The Flamemaster shrugged. Practice makes perfect.

If it was true that the third time was the charm, his next fire would be perfect.

two

Tess Gannon had known Daniel McGee all of her life. She also intended to spend the rest of her life with him.

If she survived getting married.

"Planning Desert Storm had to have been easier than this," she muttered, as she flipped through the latest stack of magazine articles on theme weddings her mother had insisted she read.

"We could just say the hell with the bells and whistles and caterers and bands and elope," Danny suggested.

Tess didn't need a wedding ring to confirm their love, but her biological clock had begun ticking louder this past year and they were both old-fashioned enough to want to be married when they became parents.

"There's nothing I'd like better."

She frowned at one of the beautifully staged photographs. Would anyone really want a wedding cake made to look like a sandcastle? And wasn't decorating it with real seashells just inviting a guest to break a tooth?

"But I also don't want to break Mom's heart."

Bad enough that she'd followed in her dad's big black boots and become a firefighter against her parents' wishes. After earning a degree in fire and safety engineering technology from Eastern Kentucky University, she'd returned home to South Carolina, promptly aced both the civil service and physical firefighting exams, then fulfilled a lifelong dream of joining the Somersett Fire Department.

Having had a quickie "shotgun" marriage of her own, Mary Gannon had been fantasizing about her only daughter's wedding ceremony since Tess was in the cradle. As much as Tess hated all the hoopla, she didn't have the heart to deprive her mother of that longtime Cinderella dream.

"I thought it was supposed to be the bride's day," Danny said, proving himself to be as clueless as most males when it came to female rites of passage.

"Ha-ha-ha. That just goes to show how much you know about weddings."

Not that she was completely caving in.

Instead of the traditional formally dressed couple, the miniature bride and groom who'd be topping the tiered white wonder of a cake would be wearing fire-fighting gear, right down to their shiny yellow helmets. Having found the pair on eBay, Tess had opted to wait until the last minute to spring it on her mother.

"I know a helluva lot more than I did six months ago."

And a lot more than he undoubtedly wanted to. "And you've been a wonderful sport."

Better than she'd been. Tess couldn't count the times he'd leaped in to play referee when she and her mother were about to be gored on the horns of a serious disagreement.

And hadn't he addressed half of the two hundred and fifty invitations? Though secretly Tess was a little concerned the post office might not have been able to decode Danny's scrawling handwriting enough to actually deliver them.

Feeling a burst of fondness, she leaned over the table and gave him a quick, friendly kiss. He tasted of coffee and Big Red gum.

"I've gotta run. See you tomorrow morning."

"Just about the time I'm leaving," he said without rancor.

"I know." She sighed. Somersett firefighters worked twenty-four-hour shifts with a day on the job, a day off, a day on, then four days off. Assigned to different stations as they were — with Tess working the A shift and Danny working the C — their individual rotations had them both off at the same time only a handful of days a month.

"I'm going to work on getting my schedule changed," she promised. Right after she decided whether she was going to have the reception band play "I'll Be Your Everything" or the old Nat King Cole standard "Unforgettable" for their first dance as man and wife.

She'd wanted Kenny Chesney's "The Good Stuff," but her mother had put her foot down, insisting that it'd be unlucky to have a song about a wife dying for a bride and groom's first dance. With the wedding a mere four days away, she was running out of time.

Suspecting that actually being married was going to be a snap compared to this wedding planning stuff, Tess scooped up her car keys.

"Don't forget, you're supposed to choose the groomsmen's gifts."

He rolled his Bambi-brown eyes and groaned.

Ha! "It's a lot easier to be blasé about decisions when you're not the one stuck with making them, isn't it?"

So far just about the only thing her mother had made Danny do was select the groom's cake. Having already figured out it was easier to go with the flow, he'd instantly accepted his future mother-in-law's suggestion of chocolate. Then had it frosted in the University of South Carolina's team colors of garnet red and black.

Which, while not the least bit flattering to her attendants' sea-foam green dresses, at least wasn't nearly as bad as the groom's cake shaped like a retriever her aunt Dixie's duck-hunting third husband had chosen for their wedding last month.

"How about I give the guys gift certificates for lap dances at that new place that opened across the county line last week?"

"How about not. And it's interesting that you'd know about it so soon."

"We got called to a fire opening night, but the sprinklers had pretty much taken care of things before we arrived." Another waggle of brows. "Guess those girls are really hot."

Tess shook her head and refused to return that sexy, rakish grin. "I doubt either of our mothers would approve of strippers as gifts. Mom made up a list of suggestions."

She retrieved the three-by-five card from her purse and handed it to him.

"Money clips?" he asked. "Pocket watches? Silver flasks engraved with our wedding date? Who thinks up this stuff?"

"Mom says they're traditional."

"They also sound like something a girly groom would buy. When was the last time you saw a firefighter with an engraved sterling silver flask?"

How about never? "Do you have a better idea?"

"Sure. I'll get each of the guys a box of cigars."

He wadded up the paper and tossed it into the wastepaper basket across the room, showing that seven years after graduation, he still had the moves that had made him the top-scoring high school forward in South Carolina.

"Problem solved." He touched a finger to his tongue and made a mark in the air. "You can cross one more item off your to-do list, sugarplum."

"Cigars are okay," Tess decided. "So long as no one smokes them inside at the reception."

She might have been dragging her feet about all this wedding stuff, but there was no way she was going to let a bunch of drunk firefighters light up stink sticks anywhere around her lovely tulle, pearl-studded Vera Wang knockoff wedding dress.

As she drove to the firehouse, Tess decided that wedding hassles aside, she was a lucky woman. She was in love with a fabulous guy who loved her back, she had the exciting career she'd always dreamed of, and by this time next year, if everything went according to plan, she'd be a mother.

Life couldn't get much better than that.

three

Hell night began three hours before midnight with a wispy zephyr of smoke wafting from the roof of an old cotton mill in the harbor district. The acrid odor that would linger over the city of Somersett for days wasn't initially noticed beneath the sweet fragrance of honeysuckle and Confederate jasmine perfuming the soft South Carolina air. Unaware that her life was about to unalterably change, Tess was losing at poker in the rec room of Somersett's Harbor View fire station.

"Call." Even knowing the odds against drawing on an inside royal straight, she tossed a chip into the center of the chipped Formica table one of the ladder guys had liberated from a Dumpster.

The scent of lasagna lingered from tonight's dinner; coffee, which was bound to be thick as swamp pluff because Brian Murphy had made it, dripped through the Mr. Coffee. Across the room, two of the guys were playing a popular firefighting computer game while *Backdraft* was setting the TV screen on fire for the third time this week.

Despite the action scenes, which didn't begin to resemble real life — no one could run through that much flame and survive — firefighters never got tired of watching the movie. Tess remembered reading it was also on most arsonists' top-ten must-see lists.

The first alarm sounded at nine p.m.; when the big old metal bell began clanging, every head in the room swiveled toward the speaker bolted onto the wall above a *Penthouse* calendar. Miss April was decked out in a pair of shiny yellow boots, a black nor'easter rain hat, and a come-hither smile.

One tone signaled a minor emergency, along the lines of a cat in a tree or a medical run. Two meant something more serious.

"Engine 9, Ladder 8 for a possible fire at 1517 North Harbor Drive."

Play continued.

Muscles untensed, nerves relaxed.

She'd been hoping Dispatch would call her Engine Company 3. Fighting a fire was always preferable to playing poker. The fact that she'd grown up at the station, where she'd been an unofficial mascot during childhood, probably contributed to her being more accepted into the testosterone-driven, smoke-eating fraternity than a lot of women firefighters, but Tess nevertheless felt the need to play the damn game to prove that she was one of the guys.

Unfortunately, not only did she lack the patience required, she'd never been any good at bluffing.

"Probably another damn fool calling in a false alarm," Brian drawled around a fat, unlit stogie.

First-responder calls often proved to be false alarms, more so on April first. Especially during Third Watch, which was more than the name of a TV show. The last shift of the day, Third Watch was always the most active.

Along with the false alarms, they'd also been called to three Dumpster fires in the past two hours, set by kids whose embarrassed parents had already turned them in to the fire marshals.

Play continued.

Less than three minutes after the first alarm, the speaker squawked its two tones again. "Engine 8, Engine 24, Ladder 4, Engine 7, Rescue 1, report to a confirmed working structure fire at 1517 North Harbor Drive."

A whisper of fear stirred in the back of her mind. Rescue 1 was Danny's truck and in firefighter's parlance, *confirmed* meant that a police officer or firefighter on the scene had corroborated the initial report.

Rescue suggested there were people thought to be inside, and although Danny was supposed to be having dinner with her folks tonight, he'd called earlier to say that he'd been called in to replace Mark Lambert, who'd gone home with a case of food poisoning.

"Lucky dog." Jake Hardy, who was both Tess's mentor and godfather, flashed a harvest-moon smile from beneath his bushy gunfighter's mustache. His billed black cap announced A FIREMAN AND HIS RIG — IT'S A WONDERFUL THING. "They've been getting all the good calls this week."

Tess had no problem running into a maw of smoke and fire herself, but she always got a knot in her gut when she heard her fiancé go on call.

When he'd first joined the department, Danny had landed in an engine company. Engines carried five hundred gallons of water, hoses, nozzles, and assorted couplings, while trucks carried aerial ladders, power saws, ropes, fans, and other tools. Her father, who was definitely prejudiced in the long-going trucks versus engines debate, insisted that ladder guys could vent until doomsday, but the fire wasn't going to die without the engine guy's water.

The rivalry was long-standing: engine guys liked to rag laddermen with the label *firemen's helpers,* while ladder company firefighters insisted engine guys couldn't locate their asses with both hands and would never find their way to any fires if they didn't have trucks to lead the way.

Last year Danny had switched to Rescue, a role that, Tess reluctantly admitted, fit him to a T.

Rescue guys were the cowboys of the department: rushing into the flames ahead of the hoses like John Wayne, armed with only an ax and a Halligan — a short crowbar with a hook on the end used to break through walls and windows — searching for people who might be trapped.

Fire was more than a job to Tess. It was a way of life she'd grown up with. But to Daniel Michael McGee, it was an obsession, calling to him the same way a bottle of whiskey called to an alcoholic, a line of white powder to a coke addict.

There was no hesitation in Danny. There were times he reminded Tess of her father, although from what she'd heard, the word *impulsive* had never been in her father's vocabulary, while Danny was constantly getting called on the carpet for his free-lancing ways.

Still, while some men might feel con-flicted about marrying off their only daughter, there were times when Tess be-lieved her father had pushed for the mar-riage because with her brother Joe having crossed that thin blue line to become a cop, and Mike, the family's former bad boy, taking Holy Orders (which just went to show that either God had one twisted sense of humor, or miracles really were possible), Captain Doyle Gannon viewed Danny as the firefighter son he'd always wanted.

"You gonna call or fold?" Jake's gruff voice cut into her introspection.

Although she'd memorized them, Tess looked down at her cards again.

Then sighed.

"Call."

She tossed a chip into the center of the table. It was important to be a good fire-fighter. More important to be a lucky one, which Tess had, knock on wood, always been. She kept hoping a bit of that luck would follow to poker. It never had, but as she threw in another chip, she reminded herself that there was always a first time.

"And raise you a dollar."

"Shit on a stick," Brian growled, discarding his cards facedown onto the table. "I'm gonna have to fold."

Tess grinned. It was the first time she could remember successfully bluffing. Maybe tonight was her lucky night.

The speaker squawked again just as she began to scoop up the chips she'd won.

Three tones this time.

Which meant that there'd be lots of flame and smoke, along with oceans of steaming water backlit by fire and flashing lights! To any firefighter worth his or her shield, a three-tone alarm was like winning the Powerball jackpot.

"Engine 53, Engine 21, Engine 13, Ladder 12, Engine 15, Ladder 5, Engine 3, Ladder 6, report to a fully involved structure fire at 1517 North Harbor Drive."

"Let's rock and roll, boys and girls!" Brian hit the edge of the table as he leaped up, scattering colorful chips like confetti.

"It's a big one." Tess couldn't recall so many trucks ever having been called to a single fire in Somersett.

There had been one conflagration back in 1974, when some hippies, who'd been using an abandoned hotel in the north part of town as a flophouse, had tipped over a candle while mellowed out on Mexican pot. The resultant fire had taken the lives of five firefighters, one of which had been Danny's father, but that had been before she'd been born.

"Fire enough for all of us," Jake Hardy confirmed happily, sounding like a six-year-old kid the night before Christmas.

The trucks, polished to gleaming red and shiny chrome, were parked nose out in the first-floor bays. Tess's bunker pants were on the apparatus floor near her engine, rolled down and stuffed into boots.

After five years in the department, she had the moves down pat — left leg, right leg, yank up the pants, pull the padded suspenders (and yes, they were red) up over her shoulders, jump into the backseat of the truck where her jacket was waiting, sleeves already threaded through the harness of her air tank to save time.

Twenty seconds after they'd been called, the red aluminum doors rumbled upward and the diesel engines roared to life. Since the firefighters on Engine 3 had managed to get on board first, Tess's rig was the attack truck, leading the others from the station as they tore over the apron outside the station, sirens screaming.

The traffic light turned red; Brian, who

was driving, pulled on the air horn. The blare sent cars scattering over to the curb to get out of the way of the screeching, flashing convoy.

As they tore up Harbor Front Avenue, swinging wide to make the curve at Harbor View Drive, bumping over the old trolley tracks, Tess looked into the rearview mirror, where the sight of the red lights and wail of sirens gave a quick, extra boost to her already-high-running adrenaline.

four

The smoke was hovering like a thick black cloud near the ceiling, leaving a good six feet of breathing room, when Danny and his partner, John Tyler — nicknamed Ty since there'd already been two Johns at the station when he'd joined the department — entered the old mill. There weren't any visible signs of flames.

"This'll be a lead-pipe cinch," Danny predicted. "Won't even need our masks."

Smoke from a newly ignited fire rose to the ceiling. When a fire continued to burn, the gases banked down and heated up the entire space. Danny had experienced worse heat than this just living through a Somersett summer.

"What floor is our victim supposed to be on?"

"Eighth," Ty reported.

"It figures."

A small army of homeless had obviously been using the mill as an unofficial shelter. Skirting around moldy mattresses, discarded fast-food bags, and empty beer and whiskey bottles, Danny headed toward where the prefire plans the first responders' lieutenant had brought to the scene showed the stairwell to be.

By the time they'd reached the fourth floor, a feeling that something was wrong had begun to niggle at the back of Danny's mind.

"This is almost too easy," Ty muttered, echoing his thoughts.

Danny keyed the handi-talkie in the hand that wasn't carrying his Halligan. "This is Rescue 1. We're in the stairwell, on the way to the fifth floor, Chief. Any further report on our supposed victim?"

"Negative," the response crackled. "All Dispatch received is an unconfirmed report that there's a person trapped on the eighth floor."

Trapped?

"No health problems? Like drugs, or a heart attack or anything?"

"Negative."

Danny and Ty exchanged a puzzled look. The shoulders of Ty's heavy black turnout coat lifted as he shrugged.

"Any sign of flames on the roof?"

"Negative, but we've got a crew from Ladder 8 up there in case we need to vent."

"Is the reported vic male or female?"

"Sorry. Don't know that, either."

"Five bucks says it's a chick," Ty said.

"In a dump like this?" The only women who'd risk even going inside the abandoned old mill were bag ladies, addicts, or five-buck hookers. Or a combination of the three. "I'll take that bet."

The two men had been betting on anything and everything since they'd met on a baseball diamond in the seventh grade. They'd been on opposite teams — Danny played shortstop, Ty catcher — and in the bottom of the ninth, Danny had won the game by sliding into home plate.

The resultant collision had broken Ty's leg. Danny had gone to the hospital to apologize, given him the game ball, and bet the injured player fifty cents that the foot-to-knee cast would earn him a lot of sympathy from the girls at school.

Which it had.

They'd been friends ever since, and so far Danny was about ten dollars ahead in the betting pool.

They'd reached the fifth floor. Danny pulled off his glove and put the back of his hand against the steel door. It was cool.

"Guess we'll just keep going and look around when we get there."

The stairs creaked beneath their heavy

boots as they trudged up another flight. The weight of the PPE — personal protective equipment — that supposedly made firefighting safer than in the old days added up to about sixty pounds, which made just moving forward a challenge.

Six. Seven. Eight.

"Bingo."

Danny pointed toward the wisp of smoke seeping around the eighth-floor door frame, slipping into the stairwell like a wraith. Unlike the others, this door was warm to the touch. He pulled up his mask, tightened the straps, opened the valve, and felt the familiar rush of cool air on his face.

Knowing that the fire could be lurking behind the door, waiting for a breath of air so it could come roaring out to kill in an explosive backdraft, he stood to the side.

"On three." He held up one gloved finger.

A second.

A third.

Then both men ducked as Danny pulled open the door.

Black smoke roiled out.

Looking onto the eighth floor was like looking into the blackness of a tomb. But there were still no flames.

The lack of visibility wasn't unexpected.

One of the things movies never got right was that most firefighting was done in blackout smoke conditions. Since that reality didn't make for very exciting viewing, special-effects guys always went for blinding orange over a sea of black.

It was important to always take the time to know — and remember — where you came into a room and how to get out. After that, firefighters were trained to know where they were at all times, by seeing with their hands rather than their eyes.

The floor was a warren of small spaces, which, in the dark, could seem as huge as University of South Carolina's Williams-Brice football stadium.

Danny led the way, crawling down the hallway, his breathing behind the mask sounding like Darth Vader as he used his left glove to follow the wall, counting off right turns as he swept circles in front of him with his free hand.

Each time they'd leave a room, Ty would put a strip of white reflective tape on the doorway so other teams who might follow would know the spaces had already been checked out.

They were in the fourth room when Danny heard a sound, like a rafter splitting

37

overhead. He looked up just in time to see the beam coming down toward his head. His helmet, made of high-impact plastic, wasn't strong enough to deflect the blow.

Orange stars, like sparks, swirled in front of his eyes.

"Aw, shit," he said just before he passed out.

five

"Everything was real peaceful when we first arrived," one of the ladder guys reported to Tess's captain as her crew jumped off the rig. "Then all hell started to break loose. It was like there were crazed pyros running around inside with lighters, torching anything that was standing still. The tar's bubbling on the roof. Axes weren't working, and we stalled a damn chainsaw up there, but Ladder 3 showed up with a K12 that seems to be working."

A K12 was the ultimate ladder company weapon — a power circular saw that could chew through beams and nails. It was effective. And dangerous. But it was imperative to vent the building to allow some of the heat to escape.

Like with many old industrial buildings, only the top floor had windows. Tess couldn't see anyone, victim or firefighter, backlit by the flames. "What have you heard from Rescue 1?" she asked as she latched her jacket.

"They're up on the eighth floor, searching for the victim." One floor higher than the

Somersett aerial ladders could reach.

As one of the windows shattered, deadly shards of glass raining down on the firefighters standing on the ground, Tess shuddered, hating the idea of Danny being up there.

"He'll be okay," Jake, who'd followed Tess off the engine, assured her heartily. "Rescue guys always get out."

It was what Danny always said. The truth was, they usually did. But she'd certainly gone to more than one firefighter's funeral growing up.

Like every other firefighter she knew, Tess was hugely superstitious, which was why she'd bought her fiancé a St. Florian — the patron saint of firefighters — medal for his twenty-ninth birthday.

Knowing that she'd only endanger herself and her crew if she allowed frightening thoughts of what could happen to take hold in her mind, Tess focused on what she was here to do as she jammed her scraped and burned yellow helmet over her short hair and cranked it tight.

She checked all her fasteners one last time; flames and heat were evilly clever about finding the slimmest gap to slip through. Then she pulled on her Kevlar gloves.

It was time to dance with the dragon.

As she entered the abandoned cotton mill, Tess had to squint against a fire that glowed so brightly it was like looking directly into the sun. The ceiling, walls, and even the floor were ablaze.

The internal engine on the pumper revved; the heavy hose stiffened and twisted in their hands when the water began pulsing through.

The plan of attack was to put the wet stuff on the red stuff. But every time she and Jake tracked down the fire-belching beast where it was hiding, it fought back like a boxer, weaving, bobbing, striking back.

They'd no sooner shove it one way when it'd whip around, growl, and begin throwing balls of flame nearly as large as a pumper engine from a different direction.

Impossibly, the flames flared higher; the ceiling became so hot that the water Jake was spraying up became heated and showered back down on them as boiling steam.

Acting on impulse as much as training, Tess dropped to her knees. The steam and smoke had gotten so thick, all she could see were the boots of two firefighters from Engine 22 who'd gone in ahead of Jake and her.

The visibility dropped to zero. Tess held tight to the hose to keep from turning the wrong way and getting lost. She could vaguely hear the clink of air tanks, the shuffle of heavy boots.

Why the hell wasn't the captain calling in one of the ladder guys with a fan to clear out some of the smoke?

She crawled blindly through the steaming water and black smoke, the flames they were chasing so hot she could feel the sizzling heat through her turnout gear.

The air only flowed into her mask when Tess inhaled, something she'd gotten used to, but that had been a frighteningly claustrophobic feeling her first few fires. Her nostrils were streaming, making her envy the men with thick mustaches. Civilians tended to believe firemen wore mustaches to look macho; in truth they wore them as snot blotters.

That, along with being able to pee against the side of a building at a fire scene, was one of the advantages of being a male firefighter.

Jake tripped over some trash on the floor, his curse muffled by his face mask when the stumble caused him to drop the hose.

Tess dived for it, struggling for control as

it twisted and writhed in her gloved hands like an anaconda. She'd just managed to pin it between her arm and shoulder when the fog steam suddenly stopped coming out of the nozzle.

six

"Hey, Danny! Come on, buddy. You've got to help me here."

Ty's voice was edged with something close to panic. He was trying to pull his partner from a pile of what felt like bricks and lumber and not having all that much luck.

Bells were ringing in Danny's ears. "What the hell happened?"

"Don't know. I think part of the firewall caved in. Knocked you out."

That explained the bells. And the sledgehammer pounding in his head. And the spooky fact that he couldn't seem to move his legs.

"There's not supposed to be a firewall here," he said, thinking back on the prefire plans he'd glanced at when he'd first arrived at the scene.

"The damn building's over two hundred years old," Ty reminded him. "There's probably a lot of stuff that's not on the plan."

Good point. Danny lifted himself up by his hands and tried to wiggle free. Pain shot through him.

"I don't want to borrow trouble, but I think my legs are broken," he said.

"Shit, shit, shit!" Ty began flinging away bricks with his left hand. His right arm hung loosely, and crookedly, against his body. "Don't worry. I'll get you out of there."

He shouted to be heard over the screeching of the K12 up on the roof.

"You're hurt, too," Danny pointed out. His mask began to vibrate against his face, warning him that he had about five minutes of air left.

Damn. He must have been unconscious longer than he'd thought.

"Even if I wasn't loaded down with all this PPE crap, you'd never be able to drag me down eight flights of stairs. We're going to have to call for backup."

Firefighters saved other people. The idea of needing saving himself was flat-out embarrassing. Christ, he'd probably still be getting ragged about this screwup when he was in a nursing home for octogenarian firefighters!

"You're going to have to go show the guys how to get here," he told Ty.

"No way." Ty shook his head. "Not only is it against regulations, there's no way in hell I'll leave my best friend alone in a goddamn fire."

In the early days, hotshots — like Tess's dad and the father Danny had never known — defined the machismo of fire-fighting. After people started realizing that such cowboy behavior was a real good way to lose valuable personnel, the industry adopted a protocol: firefighters entered a building in pairs and the cardinal rule was that you never, ever abandoned your partner.

"You said it yourself." The alarm kept vibrating, reminding Danny that every word he spoke used up precious air. "This damn place doesn't match the plans. We'd be putting the rescue team at risk by having them wander around up here looking for us."

A frown as black as the smoke surrounding them darkened Ty's face. "There's always the PASS."

A personal alert safety system, a bright yellow device about the size of a pack of cigarettes, was required to be attached to every firefighter's turnout coat. The PASS was designed to trigger a piercing alarm that could cut through smoke whenever a firefighter didn't move for twenty-five seconds.

Since they could set off a false alarm, most firefighters bucked regulations and kept them turned off. There was also a panic button that could be pushed to act as a beacon to rescuers.

"Okay, we'll use the PASS, too," Danny agreed reluctantly.

He'd been a smoke eater for nine years, and this was the first time he'd been forced to trigger the effin' thing. One more humiliation he was going to have to spend a lifetime living down.

He cursed, then keyed the handi-talkie again. "This is Rescue 1. We seem to have gotten ourselves into a little trouble here on the eighth floor. A wall fell on us and I think it broke my legs. And Ty's got a bum arm. We're activating our PASS systems. Ty's headed down; he can bring some guys back to my location."

"Received," Danny's chief responded. "A team's on the way up."

"Got that. And thanks." Danny clicked off. "You've got to go," he repeated to Ty.

He suspected it wasn't only the smoke and fumes that had his best friend's red-veined eyes welling up behind his mask.

"It's the best thing. Besides" — he flashed what Tess had always called his cocky-as-hell bad-boy grin — "in case you've forgotten, I'm going to outrank you as soon as I get the test scores back."

Danny had always loved his job and had never been interested in the officer ranks. But this past year, after he and Tess began talking about starting a family, he'd decided that it was time to start growing up so he could be a role model to his kids. Which was why he'd taken the lieutenant's test last month.

He held up a gloved fist. He and Ty bumped knuckles, then went through a complicated series of gestures dating back to their seventh-grade summer.

A pal was a guy who'd have a beer with you. A best friend was one who'd be puking in the toilet next to you at the end of the night. But a brother was someone who'd follow you through the gates of hell, stay right beside you, then after it was all over proclaim, "That was fucking awesome!"

Ty was the closest thing to a brother Danny had ever had. He'd walked about five steps when he turned, barely visible through the thick black smoke.

"I'll be back," Ty promised.

"Sure you will."

His best friend and soon-to-be best man would never abandon him. But, as Danny's mask continued to rattle against his face, he couldn't help thinking that sometimes fate was a damn fickle bitch.

"We need more water!" Tess shouted into her radio, afraid she wouldn't be heard over the screeching of the saw chewing its way through steel beams somewhere above them.

The hose had gone slack. They'd already pumped out all five hundred gallons on the truck, which meant that Brian would either have to find an unused hydrant, which was unlikely given how many engines were parked out in the street, or start sucking water from the harbor, which could take time to set up.

The steam hissed evilly around her; as if sensing its opponent's vulnerability, the dragon went on the attack again, hurling flames that filled the air with crackling, popping sounds.

Just when Tess was certain things couldn't get any worse, Danny's voice managed to get through the radio's static. She knew the calm tone relating problems on the eighth floor was forced.

No firefighter would call for help unless he believed his life to be in danger.

Especially *this* particular firefighter.

The mask he'd been wearing magnified what sounded like labored breathing. Doing the math, Tess knew that he had to be running out of air. Impossibly, since it had to be at least six hundred degrees inside the building, her blood chilled.

The darkness hovering over her was black as a tomb. It was also filled with poisons. As bad as it was down here on the first floor, it had to be worse higher in the building. Taking off a mask would be certain suicide.

The hose suddenly stiffened again. Bucked. Water gushed from the nozzle.

"Awright," Jake shouted, aiming into the maw. "We've got the monster now!"

The smoke was turning from pitch-black to a dark charcoal gray, which was a positive sign. But something wasn't right. Instead of trailing up toward the ceiling, it had shifted directions and was headed back into the flames.

"Jake." Tess pointed at the retreating smoke. "Look at that."

She'd no sooner gotten the words out than the dragon revealed it had one more trick up its sleeve.

She heard a rumble, like summer thunder. Saw the strange yellow glow through the haze. Watched it turn into a shimmering, wavy orange.

A roar like a 747's afterburners shook the building.

"Aw, shit!" Jake yelled.

Tess threw herself facedown onto the floor, squeezing her eyes tight as the blinding bright flames rolled like a freight train over her head.

Blast-furnace-hot heat seared through the heavy bunker gear.

"Evacuate!" the chief yelled over the radio. "We're pulling out. Withdraw to defensive attack!"

They were going to leave Danny and Ty? Firefighters never left their own inside a burning building!

As Tess reached for her radio to remind the chief of the two injured men who could be trapped upstairs, her turnout jacket burst into flames.

seven

Danny was still trying to drag himself from the pile of rubble when he heard the air horns bellow. Three series of four sustained blasts, signaling that they'd changed from offense to a surround-and-drown defensive mode.

Where the hell was Tess? Was she safe?

He felt a sucking sound, as if he were breathing through the wrong end of a snorkel. The vibrating alarm went silent as his air cut off.

Danny ripped off the mask. The surrounding smoke was so thick and oily he could have been breathing in hot tar. He lay on his belly, sucking in what little air hovered an inch from the floor.

One of the problems with modern firefighting clothing was that while it was fire resistant, it wasn't fireproof. Like ears of corn roasting in husks on the grills, firefighters could literally cook inside their bunker gear.

He bucked his hips, this time dislodging enough bricks to allow him to slide free. Moving at an excruciatingly slow pace, using his arms to pull himself forward, he managed to drag himself out of the room and into the hall.

His mouth tasted of smoke and burned chemicals. The carbon monoxide was making him dizzy. His head swam; his stomach churned.

He tilted his helmet to shield his face from the oppressive heat. The salty sweat streaming into his unshielded eyes felt like thousands of jellyfish stings.

Time ceased to have meaning. He could have been crawling through the smoke for a minute, ten minutes, or an hour.

Every so often, over the roar of the flames racing through the air ducts between the walls and over his head, Danny was able to hear the thrum of a pumper somewhere on the street below, the pounding of the water against the side of the building.

Every fire, no matter how small, was a personal confrontation with danger. But if you allowed yourself to dwell on the possibility of dying, you'd never climb on the engine. But it was always lingering somewhere in the back of your mind.

It was also what added to the excitement.

Christ, it's hot!

He was steaming inside his bunker pants like a damn lobster. And God, he was tired.

He'd learned at fire school that dying of smoke inhalation was a lot like freezing to death. You got sleepy, settled in for a nap, and the next thing you knew you were wandering down light-filled tunnels, being greeted by relatives who'd passed on, and taking up playing the harp instead of the electric Fender Stratocaster guitar that was a happy reminder of your days in a high school garage band.

Compared to ending up scorched like a marshmallow on a spit over a campfire, carbon monoxide would definitely be the easier way to go out.

Danny was thinking maybe he should just suck in a big mouthful of smoke and get it over with, when a burly man in a black turnout coat with reflective yellow flashing on the sleeves and chest came swirling out of the smoke in front of him. He felt a burst of optimism at the idea of Ty having arrived with the cavalry just in time.

"Hell, boy," the deep voice rumbled, "you're like your old man. You've never done easy."

"Dad?" Danny blinked.

Maybe God had sent his old man down to collect him. Then again, a body temperature of 105 degrees stimulated hallucinations. Danny sure as hell felt at *least* that hot.

He collapsed facedown onto the hot floor. Pain shot through his head; he tasted blood. *Shit!* Now he'd broken his damn nose.

As his heavily lidded eyes drifted closed, Danny reminded himself that flames weren't his real enemy.

Exhaustion and panic were what killed.

It took a Herculean effort, but he managed to lift his gloved hand to click his handi-talkie. His breathing was labored, but there was something he had to say. Just in case.

"This is Rescue 1."

The static and cross-talking between the firefighters outside and the command post was so loud that Danny had no idea if anyone could hear him. He hoped one very special person could.

"Hey, Tess, darlin', I just wanted to tell you . . ."

A big hit of smoke into his lungs started him coughing. With effort, he controlled the wracking cough and concentrated on keeping his mind clear.

"I just wanted to tell you," he repeated, "that I love you. And that our past five years living together . . . well, they've flat-out been the best of my life."

Not wanting her to think he was a quitter, he added, "And all our years together after the wedding are going to be even better."

Motivated by the idea of getting Tess into that big lion-footed tub the North Harbor ladder crew had helped him install in the master bathroom of the old fixer-upper they'd bought six months ago, Danny began crawling again.

You can do this. For Tess.

He'd reached the end of the hall. Hot damn, he was going to make it!

The stairwell should be a safe zone, free from the deadly smoke. Making his way to the ground with two broken legs wouldn't be easy, but hey, Ty and the rescue team were probably only a floor or so away by now.

You're almost home free!

Gritting his teeth, ignoring the blood streaming down his soot-stained face from his broken nose, Danny slammed a shoulder against the door, reached out a gloved hand, and groped for the first stair.

Goddammit!

They were gone.

Tess didn't know how she'd gotten out-side. But somehow she was lying on her back, looking up at a smoke-filled sky as one EMT cut away her charred bunkers and began slapping saline-soaked dressings on her legs while another set up an IV.

She tried to open her mouth, to ask about Danny and Jake, but her throat felt scorched, her tongue swollen, and she couldn't get the words out.

She dragged her eyes, which felt like two hot coals, toward the burning building. The morphine sulfate had just hit her bloodstream when the roof fell in, sending flames shooting into the sky.

Perhaps the drugs had her brain playing tricks on her, but an eerie silence seemed to descend and the hectic activity seemed to slow, then stop as all the firefighters watched the brick walls collapse inward.

eight

Jake Hardy was discovered in the early hours of mop-up, less than three feet from the front doorway. Tess, perhaps because she weighed less, had been blown out of the building onto the street; Jake hadn't been so lucky.

Nor had Danny. It took the body recovery team, working with cadaver dogs, three days to find him. His PASS had cheerily chirped beneath the rubble for an agonizingly long time, like a manic canary, mocking firefighters who'd begun with a desperate determination that he'd be found alive, but whose hopes were destined to become dashed when they finally came across Daniel Michael McGee's charred body thirty-six hours after the batteries in the alarm had finally given out.

Tess woke up in St. Camillus Hospital, unable to remember everything that had happened the night of the fire.

The doctors, who'd put her in a hyperbaric chamber at one hundred percent oxygen to bring down the carbon monoxide level of the blood, explained that her memory loss was a result of breathing in smoke after her mask had been blasted off her in the explosion. They couldn't tell her whether she'd ever be able to get back those lost minutes.

What *had* gotten through the labyrinth of her smoke-hazed mind were Danny's last words. Words he'd managed to rasp into his handi-talkie shortly before he died. Personal words of love spoken directly to her, never mind that seemingly every firefighter in Somersett — most of whom ignored the posted visiting-hour regulations — could hear them.

No one actually brought them up to her. But Tess knew they were being discussed outside the room, because a nurse who'd changed her saline dressings had fought back tears as she'd confessed that Tess's fiancé thinking of her at the moment of his death was the most romantic thing she'd ever heard.

The nurse was probably only two or three years younger than Tess, but her hearts-and-flowers take on love and death made Tess feel a hundred years old.

She couldn't talk to anyone about the depth of the emotional pain she was feeling. Not to Danny's many friends, especially Ty, who appeared racked with guilt as he'd run himself ragged going back and forth between the hospital and the fire scene.

Or to her parents, who'd never wanted her to follow in her father's boot-clad footsteps. Mary Gannon had always baked to relieve stress during her husband's duty hours; Tess's brothers Mike and Joe had told her that the oven in the Gannon house had been blasting away since the captain had shown up at their house to inform them that she had been hospitalized.

When one firefighter died, all suffered.

Tess nearly exploded when the doctors refused to allow her to attend the joint funeral.

"You're still weak," Mike said, backing up the medical staff.

"And on drugs," Joe pointed out.

"But you'll be fine," her mother said reassuringly, "once you get home."

Tess would rather come down with bubonic plague than return to the house she'd grown up in and have her mother fussing over her all day long. As soon as the doctors sprang her from this bed, she was going to go back to the Victorian cottage she and Danny had planned to fill with love and laughter and babies.

"Besides," her mother argued, "Danny

wouldn't want to be responsible for you collapsing in front of half the town and all the firefighters from all over the country who've come to pay respect to Jake and Daniel."

There was a reason the family referred to Mary Gannon as the Lowcountry Distributor of Guilt. But she *did* have a point. The Demerol they'd switched Tess to, after taking her off the initial morphine drip, did make her unsteady on her feet. And uncharacteristically weepy.

Ty stopped by on his way to the funeral, bringing her a stash of M&Ms, which she tried to show appreciation for.

"They pulled out and left him in there," she complained. The rattle of plastic trays out in the hall signaled it was almost time for lunch. Tess dreaded mealtimes, when the Stepford-perky volunteers in pink-striped smocks would try to encourage her to eat food that tasted like ashes in her mouth.

"I'll feel guilty about leaving Danny up there for the rest of my life," Ty said.

He dragged his left hand down his face, which, like hers, was speckled with blisters from second-degree burns. His voice was raspy from inhaled smoke; his right arm was set in a cast.

"It wasn't your fault."

Tess put her hand atop his, which was still trembling from his own physical and mental trauma. If there was anyone who might come close to understanding the survivor's guilt she was suffering, it was Ty.

"You did everything you could. You tried to get him out from beneath those bricks, and you went and got help. It was the damn chief who wouldn't let you back into the building with the rescue team."

Unlike a lot of firefighters she knew, Tess had never had reason to dislike those who'd exchanged fighting fires for cushy political desk jobs and lunches with the mayor. Until now.

The medical examiner hadn't released the results of his autopsy yet, but fire stations were a hotbed of gossip, and the report had filtered through the ranks that Danny's lungs had been scorched tarblack.

Meaning that he'd fought death right up until the end.

Which didn't surprise Tess, since she'd never known anyone who'd believed in living life to the fullest more than Daniel McGee. And dammit, he'd had so much to live for!

"He wouldn't have wanted more firefighters to die trying to save him, Tess," Ty said.

"No." She sighed. "He wouldn't."

Damn. She'd been trying to be brave, like her father always insisted a firefighter should be, but she couldn't keep a few rebellious tears from escaping. The salty moisture stung on cheeks that felt as if they'd been badly sunburned.

"Oh, God." Her voice choked. She pressed her hand against her mouth to hold back the sob. "I loved him so much, Ty."

"I know." He laced their fingers together, lifted their joined hands, and brushed his lips against her blistered knuckles. "And I realize that it's not the same thing, Tess, but I loved him, too."

"I know." Tess sniffled.

Ty plucked a Kleenex from the box on the wheeled table beside the bed.

She blew her nose. Then, since no one had volunteered the information, she asked the question that had been plaguing her mind.

"How's the investigation going?"

Something flickered in Ty's eyes. A flash of emotion that came and went so quickly that if Tess hadn't been watching him carefully, she would have missed it. "It was a damn hot fire, Tess. Hell, you can still smell the smoke in the air. It's going to take more time for the investigators to sift through all that rubble."

"I understand that. But there's always talk. What are people saying?"

"There are a lot of different theories." Seemingly unable to look her in the eye, he pretended vast interest in the television remote on the metal bedside table. "The prevailing one seems to be an electrical malfunction."

"No way."

She might not be an investigator, but Tess knew wiring was often an easy scapegoat because it was highly unlikely to find a burned structure without some electrical wire or device near the fire origin.

"There were a lot of melted wires, Tess. Which showed arcing."

"Which doesn't mean the arcing was the cause of the fire," she persisted. "It's all about cause and effect. A fire can cause arcing."

"I don't want to argue with you. After all, you're the one with the fire engineering degree. You asked what people are saying; I told you."

"And I jumped on the messenger." She sighed. "I'm sorry."

"You never have to apologize to me, Tess. About anything." The alarm on his watch dinged. "It's time to go." He stood up, looking a lot like a condemned man who'd just received a stay-of-execution phone call from the governor. "But I can stay if you'd like."

"No." She waved her hand toward the open hospital room door. That was another thing that irked her. Hadn't all those nurses ever heard of the concept of privacy? "You're going to need closure, Ty. And that's what funerals are supposed to be all about, right?"

Closure. As April rain streaked down the window, Tess wondered if there really was such a thing after you lost someone you loved.

Family and friends returned to gather again in her room after the interment.

"Brian's rendition of 'Amazing Grace' was lovely," her mother supplied. "There wasn't a dry eye in the place."

"That's nice." Whenever he'd practice his pipes at the firehouse, it sounded as if he were skinning cats.

Silence descended.

"It's always goddamn rough, burying one of our own," her father said, his smoke-roughened voice even gruffer than usual. "But you'll start feeling better, Tess, once you get back to work."

He had never minced words about his belief that women were not cut out to be smoke eaters; this was the first positive thing Tess could remember him ever saying about her work.

What she couldn't tell her father — what she could never, ever tell anyone, not even Ty — was how frightened she'd been during the mill blaze. Although she may not recall all the details of the fire, her subconscious mind still harbored terrifying memories.

Memories she'd been reliving every night, in vivid Technicolor with Surround sound, that had her waking up in a cold sweat, her heart pounding so painfully hard and fast that the first time it'd happened, she'd been afraid she was having a heart attack.

Tess wondered if the nightmares would ever go away. Feared they might not. Even if they did fade with time, the past few days had taught her that daring to predict the future was an exercise in futility.

But that didn't stop her from vowing that she was going to find whoever was responsible for Jake and Danny's deaths. And make him pay.

nine

Two years later

Belying the song lyrics about it never raining in California, a cold drizzle was falling from leaden skies as Gage O'Halloran ran on the rocky, driftwood-strewn beach.

Dolphins frolicked a hundred yards off-shore; Gage didn't notice.

A fishing boat chugged along the misty horizon, dragging its nets; Gage didn't care.

Two young lovers sat in a car parked up on a craggy cliff above the slate-gray Pacific, trading long kisses and blissful sighs; if Gage had noticed, he wouldn't have given a flying fuck.

The only thing on his mind was the low roar of the steely surf and the feel of his feet hitting the wet sand.

Once, Gage had pounded his way through the daily ten miles in an attempt to exorcise demons. Having given up on any success at ridding himself of old ghosts, he now ran because the alternative — thinking — wasn't an option.

He'd just reached the top of the trail leading to his house when he saw the taupe four-door sedan, which screamed U.S. government, parked in the lot.

Having to talk with anyone was not his idea of a good way to start his day. Having to talk with a Fed was a helluva lot worse.

The man climbed out of the Taurus. "I got lost three times on the way up here," he complained. "Ever think about putting up a few signs?"

Gage flicked a look over him as he unlocked the door. "I've got signs."

"Yeah, ones that say NO TRESPASSING. You know, they do make them with directions these days."

"I'll give it some thought." Gage disabled the alarm. "About the time you find a decent tailor."

Bad enough that Donovan Ryder bought cheap suits to begin with, but even if they'd been the best Italy had to offer, they'd still look like shit on the ATF special agent. For some mysterious reason, clothes rumpled the moment he put them on, and stains leaped onto ties and shirts like fleas jumping onto a junkyard dog.

Ryder's nickname, around ATF offices, was Pigpen; Gage had thought his recent marriage to a San Francisco assistant district attorney, who'd grown up in a twenty-room mansion in Pacific Heights, might have encouraged him to care more about his appearance.

Apparently, given the amoeba-shaped coffee stain on the front of his wrinkled white shirt, it hadn't.

Knowing that if he waited for an invitation, he'd still be standing in the rain come doomsday, Donovan followed Gage into the house and down a hall into the kitchen, where he helped himself to a mug of coffee from the carafe.

"Driving all the way down here to wander around lost in the rain seems like a lot of trouble to go to for a cup of coffee," Gage said mildly. He poured his own mug, then, seemingly mindless of his wet shorts, threw his long, lean runner's body onto a wooden chair. "Especially when you live in a town where you don't have to go looking for a Starbucks, they find you."

Donovan thought he viewed a glimmer of interest in his former partner's gaze, but then again, with Gage, you could never tell. Especially since his expression never gave anything away and his eyes were a spooky color somewhere between tarnished silver and ice. They were the color of eyes a ghost might have, which fit, in a way, since Gage O'Halloran had definitely become a ghost of his former self.

"I went to all that trouble because something's happened I thought you might be interested in."

Donovan took a sip of the coffee, which, like everything Gage had done before the tragedy that had thrown his world out of whack, was perfect. He paused a beat, waiting to see if Gage would ask the question.

Hell, of course he didn't. No agent had ever been able to use silence like Special Agent O'Halloran. Everything Donovan knew about investigation techniques, Gage had taught him.

"The Flamemaster's back in business."

There wasn't so much as a flicker in Gage's eerie pale gray eyes, but he went absolutely still.

Silence settled over them, as thick as the coastal fog clinging to the windows.

"That's impossible," Gage said at length.

"The device is the same."

"You can find ignition devices all over the Internet these days."

"True. But he's written a note to the paper claiming credit and has threatened more. With all the terrorist threats these days, they called us before they printed it."

"The *Chronicle* held back a story?" He looked understandably skeptical.

"Not the *Chronicle*. The paper's in South Carolina. Where the fires are being set."

Gage shook his head. His black hair was longer than he'd kept it back when he'd been chasing down bad guys. It also looked as if he'd been cutting it himself with the scissors from a Swiss Army knife.

"There's no way Griffith could be in South Carolina and locked up in San Quentin at the same time. It's got to be a copycat."

"Gotta be," Donovan agreed. "I just thought you might be interested."

"Yeah. Thanks."

You still couldn't tell from looking at him, but Donovan had heard that tone enough times to know that Gage's mental wheels had started turning.

Gage was looking somewhere inside himself. Somewhere deep. And, Donovan feared, somewhere dark.

"Where in South Carolina?"

Gage's voice was controlled. And soft. Knowing that was when his former partner was the most dangerous, Donovan hoped he hadn't made a huge mistake coming here this morning.

But how the hell could he keep such a thing to himself? Given all that had happened, given that they'd once been best friends.

Donovan still considered Gage his best friend. Unfortunately, ever since that day Randolph Griffith, a serial arsonist who'd terrified Californians for months as he'd set a string of deadly fires up and down the coast, had been sentenced to a life term without parole, it seemed Gage no longer wanted any friends.

"Somersett. It's a city on the coast, between Savannah and Charleston."

"Long way from here."

Donovan followed his friend's gaze out the rain-streaked window toward the white-capped Pacific. "A continent away," he agreed.

Not wanting to know how many department and governmental rules he was breaking, he took some folded papers from the inside pocket of his jacket.

"Sorry about that red stuff," he said, noticing the stain on the top sheet. "I had a jelly donut for breakfast."

"All that sugar and fat's going to kill you."

"Everyone's going to die of something. At least I'll go happy."

72

Gage didn't respond. He was reading the letter the self-named Flamemaster had written, claiming responsibility for a recent office-building fire and promising that was only the beginning.

"It's a copycat," Gage said again.

"It's the only explanation." The only one that made sense. Neither man was willing to consider that they may have bagged the wrong bad guy. "But everything about it, including the triggering device, and some of the stuff that never made it into testimony in the trial, is the same."

Gage mulled that over.

"Well, thanks," he said finally. "Though you shouldn't have risked your career to get me these."

"We're partners."

"Former partners."

"A technicality."

Gage's lips quirked in what might have been a hint of a reluctant smile. "How's Mel?"

"Great. Her baby clock's been booming like Big Ben, so we're looking for a house with a yard big enough for a swing set. And a mutt."

When a shadow darkened the ice-gray eyes that had momentarily warmed, Donovan wanted to bite off his goddamn

tongue for having brought up any reference to a family or a dog to a man who no
longer had either.

"Every kid needs a mutt." In the nearest
thing he'd revealed to a show of emotion,
Gage let out a heavy sigh. "Sorry I didn't
make it to the wedding."

Donovan hadn't expected Gage to show
up at the ceremony. But that hadn't kept
him from watching the doors at the back of
Grace Cathedral until Melinda Fielding
started walking toward him down the aisle,
looking like a princess from some fairy
tale.

"Weddings aren't exactly guy things. I
probably wouldn't have been there myself
if I hadn't been the groom. Thanks for the
wok, by the way. It inspired Mel to take
cooking lessons."

"Glad to hear that."

Another silence descended. This one
edged with an impatience that shimmered
in the chilly, moist spring air.

"Well, I guess I'd better get to work,"
Donovan said. "See you around."

"Yeah," Gage answered distractedly as
he reread the copy of the letter Donovan
had received from the ATF field office in
Charleston.

"Maybe you can drive up for dinner

sometime," Donovan suggested. "Even spend the night, since Lord knows, the house has enough rooms to house an army battalion. Mel couldn't cook worth a lick three months ago, but she's gotten real good at stir-fry."

"Sounds great." Gage's enthusiasm was decidedly forced, but Donovan appreciated the effort. "You're a lucky man."

"That's what Mel keeps telling me . . . You know, I never thought I'd get hitched, but marriage isn't turning out to be such a bad institution after all."

Open mouth, insert effing foot. Again. As Gage's jaw clenched, Donovan realized, too late, how that cheery domestic declaration might sound to a man who'd already experienced life in an institution.

"I'll give you a call when I get back," Gage said.

"From Somersett?" Damn, he hoped he hadn't made a mistake!

Gage met his worried gaze, his expression as cold as Donovan had ever seen it. Which was saying something. It was a carbon copy of when the jury had convicted Randolph Griffith of felony arson and first-degree murder.

And that was just for starters. There were still half a dozen more arson trials here in California to get through, while four other states argued for the right to be next.

His former partner didn't answer.

"Be careful," Donovan said.

It was the first smile he'd seen from Gage in nearly three years. It also didn't meet his eyes. "Absolutely."

There was a distance between them that hadn't been there before the fires, and all that had happened afterward. Donovan was trying to decide if it'd be too weird to shake his friend's hand, then decided what the hell, and gave him a quick, hard bear hug.

"Tell me you're not going to play Dirty Harry." Since he'd already risked the hug, he decided he couldn't leave without sharing his concern. "Or that guy from that movie where he went all over New York shooting punks after his wife got killed."

"Charles Bronson," Gage supplied. "The first flick was the only decent one; *Death Wish* two through five were obvious Hollywood cash grabs."

Donovan had to ask. "You don't have a death wish, do you, Gage?"

"Of course not," Gage lied.

He stood in the doorway, watching his

former partner walk back to his car, then waved good-bye.

After the Taurus's taillights were swallowed up by the fog, Gage went back into the house, placed a call reserving the first seat on a flight out of San Francisco, then retrieved a locked wooden box from the back of a closet.

Bronson's architect vigilante had started on his road to vengeance with a .32 revolver.

What worked in the movies wasn't always practical in real life.

Not wanting to turn into one of those clichéd, burned-out cops who ate his gun, Gage had locked his service pistol away after Randolph Griffith's conviction. Yet as he took it from its walnut case, the Glock felt perfectly comfortable — like an old friend — in his hand.

ten

It was the second big fire in two weeks. The pyro who was calling himself The Flamemaster had promised there'd be more. Was this his work? Only time would tell. He could write all the damn letters he wanted, but only a solid investigation would put the guy behind bars.

As she drove up to the scene in the fire engine–red sedan, Tess took in the people sitting on the curb. They were numbly staring at the smoking brick building that had only yesterday been their home.

The Red Cross was on the scene, handing out cookies, lemonade, and vouchers for local stores that would allow the now homeless people to begin to replace some of their lost belongings.

A team of firefighters, their faces blackened with soot, their turnout coats drenched and filthy, were spraying the charred ruins of the apartment building, putting out hot spots.

"Could be a tax fire," her partner, Bobby Jefferson, suggested as she cut the engine. Income tax fires were popular around this time of year, when landlords decided it was cheaper to have their investments torched than pay the taxes on any income.

"Isn't this the place that got on the five o'clock news last week because of a tenant strike?" she asked as she struggled into the ugly yellow-green jumpsuit that always made her feel like a chain-gang prisoner. Or a giant lime.

"I think you're right." Bobby winced at the ear-splitting screech that rent the smoky air as a crane lifted an I beam from a pile of twisted metal. "There've also been a lot of drug busts here in the past year. Want to bet the place has an insurance policy on it big enough to choke a Clydesdale?"

"Wouldn't surprise me at all."

It was an old ploy. Especially in this area only a few blocks from the river, which, like so much of the city, was undergoing regentrification. Burn out the troublesome low-rent tenants, then rebuild to attract the DINKS — double-income, no-kid couples who'd rather spend their evenings rubbing shoulders in this week's trendy club and dining on overpriced organic veggies than charring T-bones on a grill in the burbs.

Bobby rubbed his jaw as his gaze swept

the scene. "Lucky everyone got out."

"Yeah." Tess glanced at a young woman weeping in the arms of a dark-haired young man. She was pregnant and looked as if she were going to pop any minute. "Real lucky."

Tess wondered if her girlfriends had given her a shower. Imagined all the pretty little pink or blue infant outfits that were now little more than ash.

There were times, and this was one of them, when she wondered if coming in after the fire wasn't, in its own way, almost as tough as being there when the place was ablaze.

No, she decided as she absently bent down and patted one of the orange kittens in a box a teenage boy had brought up to the car. Investigating fires didn't come close to being surrounded by flames and smoke.

Although she'd never admit it to anyone, after the mill fire, staying out of burning buildings suited her just fine.

Still, unable to turn her back on a career she'd worked hard for, she'd used her degree in fire science to get appointed to the arson investigation team. She'd been working the hot squad for the past two years, and although learning to focus on the why and how of a fire, rather than just concentrating on extinguishing it, had been a bit of a transition, she loved her job.

She imagined it was a bit like being a medical examiner; though instead of conducting autopsies on charred cadavers, she conducted them on burn sites.

Tess was the first woman fire investigator in Somersett's history. Bobby was the first African-American. Neither was naive enough to think the commissioner had put them together because he thought that they were a match made in fire investigation heaven. The simple truth was that there weren't a lot of qualified applicants for a job that, despite all the *CSI* razzle-dazzle stuff people loved to watch on TV, didn't involve sirens and flashing lights, wasn't going to make you look like a hero, and paid less than the "sanitary engineers" who collected trash from the back of big blue and white city garbage trucks.

There was another reason for their hiring no one would admit out loud: thanks to those pesky equality laws that kept popping up like sand gnats, the city couldn't turn down two qualified job applicants due to gender. Or race. Or even, in Bobby's case, sexual persuasion.

A former fire marshal from Columbia,

Bobby had gotten a nasty spiral leg fracture after falling down a flight of stairs while investigating a two-alarm hotel fire. His alcohol level had been tested at the hospital; when it'd come in at more than twice the legal limit, he'd been canned.

To hear Bobby tell it, that was, literally, his lucky break. He came out of the closet, started attending AA meetings, working his way through the twelve steps as he dried out. Then, seeking a fresh start, he moved south to Somersett, where a second cousin, who'd just made captain, did some lobbying and got him a job on the hot squad.

The funny thing was, because nobody had expected them to be all that good at their job, the bar had been set so low they couldn't help but climb over it. But they'd done more than climb. They soared. Even the commissioner, who still hadn't gotten it through his head that in the twenty-first century employers weren't supposed to call a fire investigator "darlin'," had to admit that Gannon and Jefferson had closed more cases in their two years together than the fire marshals they'd replaced ever had.

Of course, as Bobby had pointed out to Tess, that wasn't real difficult, since he'd taken over for George O'Hara, a thirty-year burned-out veteran with emphysema who'd retired on a disability check and was now living on a boat down in Margaritaville, spending his days catching fish and his nights at Key West bars sucking in cigarette smoke while spinning exaggerated tales of his firefighting days.

It had been even easier for Tess. She'd replaced an ego pyro, a former department captain who'd set a string of fires over a five-year period so he could be credited with saving the victims. He was now doing ten to twenty at Lee Correctional Institute in Bishopville.

"Hey, firelady," the kid with the box said. "Wanna kitty?"

Tess shook her head. "Sorry. I don't think so."

"The firemen, they saved 'em."

"Yeah, they do that sometimes."

She felt a little tug in her heart as she remembered Danny braving flames to rescue a mother tabby and her six kittens. They'd been hiding in the bathtub, the first place all firefighters knew to look.

"That make them lucky kitties."

"I suppose it does," Tess agreed.

"You take one, maybe it bring you luck," the young entrepreneur suggested slyly. He lifted one up by the scruff of the neck.

"This one same color as your hair. Got your name on it, firelady."

Tess almost laughed. But since it'd be hugely inappropriate under the circumstances, she bit it back.

"Good try, kid."

The kitten was cute, a marmalade-colored ball of fur with gold-coin eyes opened to tiny slits and a velvet button for a nose, but kittens turned into cats, which would be a responsibility Tess didn't want to take on.

Being the fire police wasn't like her firefighter days when she worked those twenty-four-hour shifts with lots of days off in between. Back then she'd arrive in the rig, sirens wailing, and put the wet stuff on the red stuff.

Then, after killing the beast, she'd return to the firehouse, dry out the hoses, polish the engine while waiting for the next alarm, and the blaze would be easily forgotten.

Investigating the cause of a fire could take days. Sometimes even weeks. A case she'd caught her first week on the job had dragged on for months until the Colorado Springs police arsonist guys had caught a professional "problem solver" torching a restaurant.

It had taken some good old-fashioned sleuthing and a bit of lying — like telling the guy there were witnesses who put him at the scene. But like with a lot of pyros, once he'd confessed to that first blaze, information about former fires, including the rib joint in the Courthouse Square historic neighborhood that'd been bedeviling Bobby and Tess, had come streaming out his mouth like water from a two-and-a-half-inch hose.

"We've got company," Bobby murmured as a black Porsche with a rental-car sticker on its rear bumper pulled up at the curb, parking illegally on the other side of the yellow fire-line tape.

A long pair of legs clad in jeans swiveled out. At the end of those legs were a pair of black wedge-heeled boots.

"If it isn't the Marlboro Man," Bobby said.

Rather than one of those snap-front denim shirts favored by Toby Keith wannabes down at Denim and Diamonds, the man wore a black T-shirt that fit like a glove over a lean, defined runner's body. Over the shirt he was wearing a summer-weight sport coat, which even Tess, who knew nothing about men's fashion, could tell was expensive.

"Italian," Bobby murmured.

Tess glanced over at him.

"The jacket," Bobby elaborated. "If it's not Armani, I'll eat my helmet."

Since most of her partner's paycheck went toward clothes, Tess took his word for it.

The Armani-wearing cowboy ducked beneath the fire-line tape and headed toward them, walking like a cowboy from the movies — hips swiveling, boot heels clapping on the sidewalk.

"Be still my heart," Bobby murmured. He put a hand against his chest. "We're talking John Wayne with 'tude and great taste in clothing. I suppose it'd be too much to hope for that he's gay."

"I wouldn't count on it." Granted, Bobby, who could give Denzel Washington a run for his money in the hunky-looks department, was proof that appearances could be deceiving, but this guy, despite the Italian sport coat that nearly had her partner drooling, was the least gay-looking man she'd ever seen.

"Besides, your heart belongs to another, remember?"

Bobby had been in a relationship with John Thomas, a Somersett cop, for the past nine months.

"Just because I'm monogamous doesn't mean I'm dead," Bobby countered. "No harm in looking. And that cowboy's one hell of an eyeful."

"Hmmph."

Tess folded her arms across the front of the jumpsuit and forced down the irrational wish that she was wearing something — anything — else. Like a denim miniskirt and red cowgirl boots.

Then was ticked off at herself for allowing the prick of female ego.

"That yellow tape happens to be there for a reason," she pointed out. "It's to keep civilians out. So they'll stay safe."

"You want to believe a piece of yellow plastic tape can keep anyone safe, sweetheart," he drawled, "go right ahead."

Sweetheart? Couldn't he read the name tag sewn just above her breast pocket? She wasn't *anyone's* sweetheart. She was a fire cop.

Tess was about to inform him of that fact when he thrust a dark hand into the front pocket of his jeans. As the denim pulled tight against his thighs, something in her leaped to attention, just like when Sparky, the department's accelerant sniffing dog, came upon a splash of kerosene.

"If you're here for the rodeo, you're a

few months early. It's not until the Fourth of July weekend."

"Haven't ridden a bull for ten, maybe fifteen years." His western drawl brought up images of wide blue skies and land dotted with brown, long-horned cattle.

The man's legs went on forever. From the way this cowboy towered over her, she'd put his height at somewhere between six two and six three. When he came close enough for the pointy tips of his boots to practically touch the toes of her black and yellow bunker boots, Tess was forced to tilt her head back to meet his gaze.

Which she couldn't see because his darkly mirrored shades tossed back a fractured image of her own frowning face.

"Name's O'Halloran." He took a leather folder from the pocket of his jacket. "Gage O'Halloran."

Tess recognized the flashed Bureau of Alcohol and Tobacco badge immediately. He didn't look like a Fed. They usually wore blue suits, white shirts, conservative ties, and were follow-the-regulations types.

And they damn well never drove batmobile black Porsches. Tess hadn't even known you could rent sports cars at the local Hertz.

The ATF might not be as tightly

wrapped as the FBI — known to local cops who had to work with them as *Famous But Incompetent* — but she could usually spot Feds a mile away.

"Gannon," she responded, pointing to her own badge. "*Inspector.* And this is Inspector Jefferson."

The cowboy nodded, acknowledging Tess's partner.

"I don't remember calling for federal backup," Bobby challenged.

"Maybe you should have." O'Halloran pulled off the shades and hooked them into the pocket of his black T-shirt. His eyes, the color of smoke, were as hard as the strong lines of his beard-stubbled face. "Unless you're arrogant or deluded enough to believe a small, swamp-town fire department can handle a serial arsonist on its own."

He might as well have called Somersett a backwater. Possessed with a strong sense of civic pride, Tess refused to wither beneath his flinty stare.

"Somersett reported a quarter-million population at the last census. Which is probably more people than in your entire home state of Montana."

It was a shot in the dark, based on having known a guy at fire school in Kentucky who'd sounded a lot like O'Halloran.

The corner of his brooding mouth quirked, just a little. The smile, if that's what it was, didn't reach those gunmetal gray eyes. "Wyoming."

"Whatever."

"Montana's the Big Sky State. Wyoming's the Equality State. Because it was the first state to grant women the right to vote."

"Good for Wyoming."

"But I've been living in California the past ten years."

"How lovely." Her tone suggested otherwise.

The state didn't seem to fit. She'd always heard Californians were laid back; despite the laconic western drawl, this man radiated an edgy, dangerous energy from every pore.

"And I realize you Feds think you've got all the answers, but what gave you the idea we've got a serial arsonist?"

"You've got a guy who set a fire, then wrote a letter to the paper threatening more. That sure as hell sounds like a pyro to me."

"Just because someone writes a letter doesn't mean that he's what he's claiming to be," Bobby argued.

Bobby wasn't any more wild about Feds than she was. They had a tendency to take over crime scenes, call press conferences, and generally make nuisances of themselves while local investigators ended up relegated to running for coffee and sandwiches.

"There are a lot of nutcases out there," Tess said. "A lot of them write letters."

"True enough." He gave her a brief, savage smile that held not an iota of humor. The glint in his eyes suggested he wasn't accustomed to anyone arguing with him.

Tough.

"But how many of those nutcases call themselves The Flamemaster?" he asked. "And use a remote to light the sterno that kicks off the C-4, which isn't exactly the fuel of choice now that anyone with an Internet connection can get instructions to make a fertilizer bomb?"

Since the fire department didn't have the lab facilities to handle a blaze the size and scope of last week's office-building fire, Tess had handed the case over to the police. Which had been promising for days to get back to her with results.

"Let me guess." She folded her arms. "You've been talking with SPD."

"Which doesn't want to get caught on the wrong side of a terrorist attack," he said, confirming her suspicion.

Damn. If her brother Joe still worked for the department, she would have asked him to help her jump a few of the hurdles that too many orange alerts, too little funding, and not enough police on the street had created. She'd been accused, since joining the hot squad, of being impatient; Tess couldn't figure out why that was a bad thing.

"If it's any consolation, the cops don't know what they're dealing with, either," he said.

"So they sent you?"

"You could say that."

"I believe I just did."

There was something he wasn't saying.

Tess's internal alarm system was blaring to beat the band as she jammed her white helmet with its reflective fire investigator's decal on the front onto her head, pulled on a pair of heavy gloves, then grabbed her camera from the backseat and stalked off toward the smoldering building, leaving Bobby to follow with the physical evidence kit.

"I've also got work to do."

eleven

The responding units reported that the fire had begun in an apartment on the fifth floor, another thing that pointed at arson. Pros tended to light their fires on the top floor so the roof would burn off, leaving the rest of the building intact. That way the owner could collect on the insurance, kick out the tenants, then rejoin the regentrification boom, earning as much as ten times the previous rent.

Progress wasn't always what it was cracked up to be.

Someone had left the bedroom window open, which had fed the fire, quickly turning the building into an inferno. By the time the first responders arrived, the smoke was clogging the hallways, flames eating through the roof.

According to the news coverage of the rent strike, the power had been off more than it had been on over the past two months, which, in turn, had caused the majority of tenants to move out. With the building almost abandoned, the ladder and rescue guys had miraculously managed to get everyone out safely.

Everyone except the victim in room 508.

A sickly, sweetish stench, like rotten meat burned to a crisp on a barbecue grill, hit Tess as she walked down the hall.

The firefighters, occupied by hot spots, hadn't gotten around to bagging the victim yet.

The woman's charred body was lying in the center of the mattress: her legs spread, arms up, hands fisted in a pugilistic gesture that wasn't a sign of any final defensive move, but due to contraction of muscles from the heat of the fire.

"She could have fallen asleep smoking," Bobby suggested. His tone suggested he wasn't buying that possibility.

Neither did Tess. People instinctively recoiled from fire; this body was still supine.

"Or passed out," she said.

The apartment was a studio; empty bottles of Everclear grain alcohol were crowding the kitchen counter, the smell of liquor combining with the odors of burned flesh and smoke. Tess knew she'd be carrying the scent of death home with her, in her clothes and in her hair. Unfortunately, it wouldn't be the first time.

If the vic had been drunk enough, the smoke could've gotten her before the flames, which could explain the lack of response. Tess would know more after the medical examiner checked out the lungs for smoke damage.

She pulled off her insulated gloves, jammed them into the pocket of her jumpsuit, lifted her camera, and began snapping off shots of the room, shifting from the body on the bed to the surroundings, then the bottles. More and more departments now allowed digital cameras, but Tess preferred to stick to her old 35 mm rather than risk the chance of a jury worrying about computer-altered crime-scene photographs.

"Either she wasn't the tidiest person in the building, or she went on a helluva toot and ended up flambéed," Bobby said.

"That's what he hopes you'll think," a voice behind them said.

Tess glanced back over her shoulder to where Special Agent O'Halloran was taking up the open doorway. He'd exchanged the wedge-heeled shit-kickers for leather steel-toed boots. The black helmet wasn't a Stetson, but still looked annoyingly sexy atop his shaggy jet hair.

He hadn't bothered with a jumpsuit or bunker coat, which made Tess feel overcautious. Maybe the ATF didn't have strict regulations regarding uniform attire, or more likely they did, and this cowboy just ignored them. He'd taken off the pricey jacket, revealing a pistol in a shoulder holster. Although, as a fire investigator, Tess was licensed to carry a firearm, she didn't like guns and usually kept hers locked in the trunk of the car with the evidence kit.

Tess scowled at him. "Excuse me?"

He crossed the floor in two long strides to stand beside her as the three of them looked down at the dead woman. "The mattress is burned on both sides of the body."

"Wow." What kind of local yokel did he think she was? Tess shot Bobby a look as she squeezed between what had once been a stuffed chair and the bed to take a shot of the far side of the burned mattress. "Lucky for us we've got a Fed on the case. Otherwise we might have missed that clue."

"Lucky," Bobby agreed.

A body usually acted as a fire block. They wouldn't know until the lab did tests, but there was a good chance that the mattress had been lit in more than one location. Which would blow the smoking-in-bed theory right out of the water.

"A tax fire's looking less likely," Bobby

said, echoing her second thought.

"Looks personal to me," O'Halloran said.

For some reason, having this man actually agree with her about anything irked her.

"I'll go start talking to neighbors," Bobby volunteered. "See if I can get an ID. Ask about boyfriends."

"Good idea." Tess lifted the camera again to document a pile of burned rags beneath the window. There were similar piles all around the room. Either the woman never did her laundry, or . . .

A chest of drawers stood beside the bed, the knotty pine grain alligatored from the fire. She pulled open the top drawer. It was empty. As were the second and third.

"The clothes were supposed to keep the fire burning. And to make sure it spread," she mused.

"With the grain alcohol providing additional fuel."

That would be her best guess, as well. An accelerant didn't make a fire burn hotter; but it did make it burn faster. Everclear was 190 proof, with a ninety-five percent alcohol content, giving it a flash point of sixty degrees, between gasoline and kerosene. It definitely wasn't meant to be drunk straight.

"I'm guessing this isn't exactly Mr. Rogers' Neighborhood," O'Halloran said.

Duh. Tess wondered if it was the shopping carts piled with belongings out on the street, the gangsta graffiti all over the outside of the brick building, or the syringes on the stairs that had given it away.

Maybe he ought to audition for Jeopardy. I'll take Crime Scene Clues for one hundred, Alex.

"It's in transition," she said, keeping her sarcasm to herself.

"Meaning no one would give a shit if a crack house or flop joint went up in flames."

"Most people wouldn't consider it a loss."

There was what had been a cheap saucepan on the two-burner hot plate; the heat had melted off the plastic handle and twisted the metal. An empty bottle of alcohol was next to the burner. Tess leaned down and sniffed at the residue burned to the bottom of the pan.

"It's weed," O'Halloran said.

"Just because someone's poor —"

"I know my scents." He tapped the end of his nose. "A bloodhound's got nothing on me."

Tess snorted.

"Hey, it's a gift. I'll bet you fifty bucks that the vic mixed up some green dragons recently."

Tess refused to ask.

She *did* suspect her brother, the former cop, would know exactly what O'Halloran was referring to. In fact, thinking about it, although Joe had possessed a cop's distaste for all things federal, she'd bet that Joe and Special Agent O'Halloran would get along like gangbusters. They both had that "just the facts, ma'am" mentality that didn't have them giving away any more information than they had to.

A silence settled over them, as thick as smoke and even more irritating as they waited each other out. Another thing her brother had been good at, Tess recalled, remembering an occasion back in high school when he'd caught her sneaking in after curfew from a date.

Of course the fact that *he* was also arriving home at four in the morning hadn't seemed to make a difference; her date, threatened with dismemberment if he ever kept Joe Gannon's baby sister out past midnight again, was allowed to escape with a warning. Unsurprisingly, the boy had never called again.

And Joe had never apologized.

"It's a popular drink, good for using up those stems nobody smokes," O'Halloran divulged finally, his mocking eyes revealing a dark enjoyment at having one-upped her.

Tess was hating him more by the minute.

"You take a bottle of grain alcohol, pour it in a pot, heat it to just below boiling, and dump in the marijuana. Let it simmer away for twenty minutes and you end up with tinted alcohol known, among your less discriminating potheads, as a Green Dragon, which can, if you're stupid or desperate enough, be drunk straight, or mixed with pop. Out west Mountain Dew or 7-Up are the mixers of choice."

"It sounds delightful." Tess's tone said otherwise. Maybe the woman really had passed out.

Could a person be so stoned and drunk her body wouldn't react to flames? There was a cheap plastic-framed full-length mirror on the back of the bathroom door. The thin, irregular crazing lines in the glass were another sign of accelerants.

Personal, she silently echoed O'Halloran's earlier statement.

"I think we can handle this one, Special Agent. There's no need for you to stick around."

"It may look like a slam dunk. But there's always the chance the guy's changed his signature."

"It's not much of a signature if he changes it."

"When you've got a few more years as a fire cop under your belt, sweetheart, you'll discover that serial arsonists have a lot in common with serial killers; if you start trying to stick too close to the profile, you'll risk missing what's right in front of your eyes."

"Here's a little news flash for you, O'Halloran. My name isn't *sweetheart*. It's Tess to my friends. Investigator Gannon to you."

"There you go, making snap decisions again." Appearing unwounded by her tone or criticism, he was studying the iron bed frame above the victim's head. "I can be real friendly. Under the right circumstances."

"That's probably what the scorpion said when he talked the gator into giving him a ride across the river."

She watched as he took a Swiss Army knife out of his pocket and began scraping at the frame.

"You want to be the one doing the riding, that's fine with me." His deep voice was raspy with sarcasm and sexual innuendo. *"Investigator."*

She made a low sound of fury.

He ignored it and held the knife toward her. "Nylon."

"What?" She studied the melted white glob on the tip of the blade.

"Nylon melts at four hundred and eighty degrees."

Tess knew that. "She was tied up?"

"It appears so."

"And left to die?"

"Perhaps."

His gaze turned colder. Harder. Tess had never seen such malevolence in anyone's eyes. Talk about personal! There was a story there; she wished she knew what it was.

"He likes nylon. Specifically high-end, braided marine nylon."

Gage O'Halloran might be the most annoying man she'd ever met, but he was also the most confident, giving Tess the impression that he knew what he was talking about.

"This is a harbor city. There are probably as many boats as people in Somersett. Do you have any idea how common marine rope must be?"

He shrugged off her argument, dropped

the small white lump into a pill bottle from the evidence kit Bobby had left behind, and labeled it.

"It's rope and it's evidence. And whether this fire's the same guy's work or not, I'm still here for the other cases."

Tess disliked the way he'd made her sound like a wet-behind-the-ears probie. She'd been working the hot squad for nearly two years. Which, granted, might not make her a veteran investigator, but she *had* nailed the highest test score in state history at the South Carolina Fire Institute, which just happened to be the most respected fire-engineering academy in the country.

"That shows how much you know." If she'd had long hair beneath her white helmet, she would've tossed it. "So far he's only claiming one office building."

"Didn't they teach you to connect the dots in fire school? What if the first one was the strip club? Then that remodeled warehouse that had a short-lived reincarnation as a club. And don't forget the mill fire."

twelve

Something inside Tess went very still. She'd never forget the mill; especially since she still relived the flames and fear in her dreams at least once a month.

She lifted her eyes, locking onto O'Halloran's in the cracked mirror. "No one got hurt in the strip-club fire."

"Only because of the sprinklers. He was more successful with the nightclub. And the mill fire."

Tess scowled. "The mill case was ruled an electrical fire." She'd never believed that.

He was standing close behind her. Overwhelmingly close.

She turned around, refusing to give him the satisfaction of backing away.

"If ATF thinks it was arson, why didn't they get involved back then?"

Although Tess had certainly been vocal about her feelings, she wasn't prepared to admit to O'Halloran that having witnessed the fury of that fire that had killed Danny and Jake, she'd never bought the idea of equipment failure. She'd always feared that because the public had been clamoring for a reason for the two firefighters' deaths, the political powers, eager to prove they were on top of things, had rushed to judgment.

There was also the fact that two weeks after calling the press conference to declare the case closed, the North Harbor chief had received a mayoral appointment to commissioner, which allowed him to move from his cramped office between the locker room and ambulance crew quarters to a spiffy window office in city hall overlooking the water.

"ATF wasn't invited to the party back then," he said, bringing her mind back to her question regarding the federal agency's seeming interest in the mill fire.

"It's hardly a party when two firefighters die," she said stiffly.

"Bad choice of words." He looked down at her hand, which had unconsciously curled into a fist. "You gonna slug me for them?" His fingers curled around her wrist.

It wasn't exactly an apology, but he'd surprised her by admitting that his statement was out of line. She'd never met a Fed who'd admit to any failing.

"I've never hit anyone in my life." She uncurled her tight fingers. Tried to tug her hand free.

His hold tightened. "There's time to rectify that. You're still young."

"I'm nearly thirty."

"Yeah, that's positively ancient."

Although he almost seemed to enjoy the idea, Tess suspected that he wasn't that much older than she. Mid-thirties, probably, yet his eyes were spookily ancient. They reminded her of the faces of New York firefighters after the Towers fell.

Curious, she momentarily forgot about freeing her hand. "How long have you worked for ATF?"

He rubbed a stubble of dark beard. Which was another very un-Fed thing. "Long enough. Especially when you factor in that ATF years are like dog years. But enough about me . . .

"Getting back to our pyro pal, there's a lot of dissension about what actually constitutes an HTA fire. ATF can't put it in the database if a local department doesn't report it."

Her first thought was that suddenly she wasn't the only one who believed Danny's death had been murder.

Her second was that until his long, dark finger started making little circles on her palm, Tess had had no idea that her hand could be an erogenous zone.

In the first weeks after the fire, she'd missed sleeping with her fiancé. Making love to him. On those rare nights she didn't suffer nightmares of the blaze that had killed him, she'd been plagued by hot, needy dreams that had her waking up with her hand between her legs.

Still alone.

Still unfulfilled.

She'd confessed her secret to Ty's wife, Bailey, who'd invited her to lunch at the Lavender and Lace Tea Room to cheer her up. Her closest friend had arrived with a gift wrapped in hot-pink paper, but since the restaurant had been crowded with little girls dressed in Victorian costumes celebrating a birthday, Bailey had suggested Tess wait until she got home to open it.

The pebbled flesh-colored vibrator was huge to the point of obscene; it also, Bailey pointed out in the attached note, had three speeds, two temperatures, and a deep thrusting action. Bonus features included a little frog on the end supposedly designed to stimulate her clitoris, and a red plastic protrusion on the top guaranteed to hit her G-spot. Wherever the hell that was.

Tess still hadn't found it. She'd also quit looking.

After getting sprung from the hospital,

determined to track down the killer who'd taken Danny's life, she'd thrown herself into fire investigation training.

Unfortunately, arson crimes were growing exponentially. Fire was not only one of Man's earliest tools; it was one of his worst enemies. With new crimes to investigate and so many of her free hours taken up with digging through every bit of evidence she could unearth on the mill fire, along with making her crumbling old house livable, she'd totally put sex on the back burner. Then turned off the flame beneath her libido.

She'd been doing just fine, thank you very much. Until Special Agent Gage O'Halloran had shown up in Somersett with a blowtorch.

When his thumb pressed deep on the fleshy pad at the base of her thumb, a sudden heat zigzagged between them like summer heat lightning.

Unnerved by the unwanted sexual response to a man she didn't even like, Tess yanked her hand free.

"The mill fire was ruled a single incident. It wasn't seen as part of a pattern," she said.

"Even if it *was* a single event, that doesn't rule out it having been set. Arsonists don't always go on sprees."

"But they do tend to escalate. It's been a long time since the mill and there haven't been any similar cases lately. So what makes you think the mill had anything to do with these current ones?" A prospect that, dammit, admittedly hadn't crossed her mind.

He hooked his thumbs into the pockets of his jeans and looked around. "It's just a hunch."

"I may not be as ancient and experienced as you," she said dryly, "but I do know juries prefer facts to hunches."

"Then we'll have to find them some."

We? "Are you saying the ATF is planning to reopen the mill fire case?"

Could they do that? If so, the good news was that she wouldn't be the only one trying to find a way to prove there was more to the fire than the local authorities decreed.

The bad news was O'Halloran wouldn't be leaving Somersett anytime soon.

"I'm suggesting the MO is significantly close to your recent ones," he said.

"There wasn't any letter back then." If there had been, she would've found it. "No one took credit."

"Yeah." He rubbed an unshaven jaw

wide enough to park a ladder rig on. "I've been thinking about that while flying here from the coast. Maybe the guy was still working on the technical details, honing his skills, and didn't want to announce himself until he got things the way he wanted."

"The first two fires back then both used explosives." The police lab had found traces of RDX C-4, a substance used by the military and demolition companies for decades.

Despite their not having found any signs of RDX in the mill, that fire had still gotten hot enough to blow her out of the building. And ultimately collapse the steel floor supports beneath Danny. Which, despite the ruling of faulty equipment, had definitely pointed, at least in Tess's mind, to an HTA, a high-accelerant blaze.

"Why would an arsonist change his signature? And if he was a serial, why would he quit?"

None of the cases she and Bobby had tackled had pointed back to the mill, the warehouse, or the strip joint.

"Who knows?" He shrugged. "Given that your department appears to have dropped the ball on the mill investigation and taken the easy way out for political reasons, the truth behind his motive might never come out.

"Maybe the guy figured he'd done all the damage he could to one town and moved on. Maybe he got scared about the possible prison time he'd be facing after killing two smoke eaters. Hell, maybe he died in the fire."

Despite her personal animosity toward O'Halloran, Tess had begun feeling more and more vindicated that someone else could see the political motives so many others had denied. Then the rest of his response sank in.

"The only people in that building that day were firefighters."

"Firefighters have been known to turn torch. You replaced one yourself."

She was definitely a little unnerved, and irritated, that he seemed to know so much about her when she knew nothing about him.

"You've done your homework." *Why?*

"It wasn't that difficult. You've made a bit of press in the past couple years. Google kicked up four pages in a fraction of a second."

He'd explained *how*. But not *why*.

"Danny McGee never would have done anything so evil as endangering other firefighters by setting a fire. Neither would Jake Hardy."

Hating the notion that the worst days of her life were an open book to anyone with an Internet connection, Tess crouched down and cut out a piece of olive-green shag carpeting dating back to the 1970s at the open doorway.

The wall beside the frame was dark with soot, the blackest part at the floor. Fire characteristically burned upward and out-ward in a V-shape pattern from the point of origin. It then traveled across the ceiling and, if unable to continue to burn upward, would begin burning in a downward direc-tion on the walls.

If the victim had died from smoking in bed, the mattress should reveal the deepest burns. If the fire had been started in that unattended pan, there should be signs of origin by the hot plate. But the bottom of the V was by the door, another sign point-ing toward arson.

Her flash lit up as she photographed the burn and soot patterns around the door.

"He set the fire as he left," Gage stated, proving that once again they were thinking the same thing. If she hadn't found the man so unsettling, Tess would have liked that they were on the same track.

"And he didn't have to worry about her getting away," she continued the shared thought, "because —"

"He'd tied her to the bed," they both said together.

Tess wondered how long she'd have to be in the investigation business not to find such a possibility horrifying.

Suck it up. You wanted to be a fire cop.

"You're learning," he said.

"Please." She splayed her hand against the front of her jumpsuit. "If you keep throwing those compliments around, sugar, my little old southern belle heart is going to start going pitty-pat."

"Now there's an idea."

He surprised her by covering her hand with his, then trailing her fingers slowly down the front zipper track. Although the Nomar suit was designed to protect against high temperatures, the seductive touch still left a trail of heat between Tess's breasts.

"How about the rest of you?"

She slapped his hand away. "The rest of me, what?"

He tipped back his black fire helmet with his thumb. "What would it take to make the rest of that sexy body go pitty-pat?"

"God, I can't believe any man would

think that line works." But apparently it did, dammit. Because it had her wondering the same thing.

Gage O'Halloran was a strange man. Remote to the point of being cold. Which, perversely, made her wonder what it would take to warm him up.

"What makes you think it's a line?"

"Because you have no earthly idea what my body looks like, since I'm covered from head to toe in Nomex and rubber."

"Rubber can be a turn-on. Under the right conditions. And if your body comes close to matching your face, it's sexy as hell."

"The suit is padded. I might be as skinny and flat as an ironing board." Which, to her eyes, she nearly was.

"Meat's sweeter next to the bone."

"Or maybe I'm fat."

The lime-green jumpsuit had to add at least twenty pounds. She'd never — ever — expected to be hit on while wearing it.

"I've always enjoyed lush, ripe women. Soft breasts, fleshy thighs. More to sink into."

Did he have a damn answer for everything?

What the hell was wrong with her? Tess couldn't believe she was worrying about whether or not an ATF special agent would find her sexy. Worse yet, she couldn't believe they were having this conversation here, at a murder scene.

Having grown up Catholic, Tess had spent her teenage years having sex prohibitions drilled into her. No one had ever mentioned a prohibition against sex talk in front of a body, but given the Irish penchant for wakes, it had to be on some list of mortal sins.

"This conversation isn't appropriate," she insisted.

He didn't immediately respond. Instead, he was measuring her. In a blatantly masculine way that had Tess aware of every inch of hot skin and made her feel as if she were wearing some barely there froufrou piece of silk and lace instead of the ugliest piece of clothing on earth.

Even as she fought against it, every hormone in her body was on red alert.

"Found out something not all that surprising," Bobby's voice called out from the hallway.

thirteen

Tess jumped back as if escaping a flashover.

"What's that?" She hated the way her voice sounded. Shaky. And, dammit, needy.

She could feel O'Halloran looking at her, knew if she were to meet his eyes, they'd be mocking her response to his blatant sexuality.

She didn't just dislike him, Tess decided. She *despised* him.

He was so rude. So arrogant. So damn . . . male.

Needing something to do, she straightened her helmet.

"Vic was a prostitute," Bobby revealed.

"You're right. It's not much of a surprise, given the neighborhood."

There'd been a time when Somersett's red-light district had been second in the South only to New Orleans's infamous Storyville, where madams had erected gilded bordello palaces and hired jazz musicians to entertain sailors waiting their turns.

The houses of prostitution had been shut down due to demands from the U.S. Navy after World War I, but that hadn't stopped crib girls from hiring bare rooms to ply their trade by night. Some things never changed.

"Maybe one of her Johns killed her," Bobby suggested, seeming unaware of the chemistry zapping around the room. "Or her pimp."

"Wouldn't be the first time that happened."

Five years ago, back when Tess had still been a firefighter at Harbor View, a pimp had poured gasoline on one of his girls and set her on fire. The woman, who'd miraculously survived, was currently on her tenth surgery last Tess had heard, and would still have to go through life without hair or eyelashes and a horribly disfigured face that looked like a peeled purple grape because she'd made the near fatal mistake of holding back twenty dollars.

Tess sighed and wished, just for a moment, that she'd become the corporate lawyer her parents had wished her to be. Or even a housewife and stay-at-home mom like her own mother.

"Well, we're not going to solve the crime, if there is one, standing around pondering possibilities." Her uncharacteristically sharp tone earned a curious look from Bobby.

A firefighter brought up the county medical examiner's assistant, who bagged the body and took it away to the morgue, located in the basement of St. Camillus Hospital. They worked for the next hour, every so often either Tess or Bobby breaking the silence by noting some piece of potential evidence they'd discovered.

O'Halloran didn't bag anything. In fact, if the faraway look in his eyes was any indication of his thoughts, he'd mentally left the scene.

So much for him coming in like *NYPD Blue*'s late, ultra-sexy detective Bobby Simone to solve the crime.

The sun was setting outside, throwing the room into deep shadows. Turning on her flashlight, Tess thought she saw something beneath the blackened bed. Lying on her stomach, she shimmied beneath the charred innerspring mattress.

"Hand me the tweezers," she said.

"Whatcha got?" Bobby asked as he squatted down and held them out to her.

"A possible ignition device."

She plucked the cigarette butt from the filthy wet carpeting and placed it in the air-permeable paper envelope O'Halloran handed her.

So he *had* been paying attention, after all.

Aware of the way her butt was sticking up in the air, Tess shimmied back out from beneath the mattress.

"Except that it's not anywhere near the point of origin."

"It could have been a secondary device," O'Halloran suggested. "Or the water stream could have washed it beneath the bed. Good job."

If he thought he could get on her good side by suddenly making a hundred-and-eighty-degree turnaround and bestowing a compliment on her, the man had another think coming.

"That's what they pay me the big bucks for." The claim of a high salary was as false as Tess's smile. Fortunately, most days she loved her work and would do it for free.

Today, thanks to ATF Special Agent O'Halloran, was an exception.

But the cigarette butt would make it worthwhile. Especially if the lab could get a DNA sample from it.

"It's getting dark," she said. Outside the window, the sun was setting behind the twin spires of the cathedral on the west side of town. "We'll have to come back in the morning."

Although Tess thought of Bobby as an equal partner, since she'd come on the job two weeks before him, she was technically the senior investigator on the case, which allowed her to call the shots. "Early. With the UV light."

The ultraviolet light operated on a band of wavelengths between visible light and X-rays that couldn't be seen by human eyes. Certain accelerants fluoresced beneath the light, which allowed investigators to identify not only the substance but pour patterns, the shape of the containers, and pour trails leading back to those containers.

More press had gathered by the time they came out of the building, the scene brightened by the beam of light from a television news helicopter. As the blades noisily cut through the air, Tess worried that someone in the upper echelons of the department may have leaked that letter from the arsonist.

"I hate reporters," she muttered as she stripped off the jumpsuit.

It had been hot in the building, even hotter inside the Nomex, and her blue uniform blouse and black slacks, made of some kind of evil, unbreathable polyester, were clinging like Saran Wrap to her body.

O'Halloran took a slow, masculine visual tour from the top of her head, where she no doubt was suffering from helmet hair, down over her breasts, her stomach, and down her legs.

"Not too plump. Not too thin," he murmured. "Just lean-as-a-whippet perfect."

"Does calling a woman you're trying to get into your bed a dog usually work?"

"In this case it's a compliment. I got a whippet in the eighth grade. Beef prices were really down that year and the ranch was running in the red, so I'd landed part-time work cleaning out cages at the county pound after school. My first day of work just happened to be the same day she was scheduled to be put down, so I took her home.

"My dad said she was a piss-poor breed for a ranch dog, which is probably why no one in the county had adopted her, but my mom stepped in and lobbied on her behalf."

"And I'm supposed to believe that story?"

"About my mom? Hey, even Rosemary's baby had a mother."

Tess wasn't even going to go into how appropriate she found that analogy.

"God, she was sweet," he said.

"Your mother?"

"The dog. Well, my mom is, too, but I meant Ginger."

"Let me guess. You named her after that redhead on *Gilligan's Island*."

"Yeah. Sure. Why?"

"No reason."

It figured. Bad enough he'd compared her to a dog. Why should she be surprised that the Testosterone Cowboy would go for the oversexed bimbo island castaway over sweet, pretty Mary Ann.

Nor did she want to think of Gage O'Halloran coming to the aid of a defenseless, abandoned animal. It was safer thinking of him as some selfish bastard who'd crawled out from under a particularly slimy rock.

"Ah." He nodded as her question sunk in. "I was thirteen at the time. My tastes in women have matured a lot. Though" — he swept another look over her — "I'm still particularly fond of long, wraparound legs."

Returning to the mental slimy-rock image, Tess refused to dignify the remark with a comment.

Fire Commissioner Dunne was standing in a blinding spotlight, pontificating for the cameras. Which kept Tess from having to make a statement. If she played her cards right, she could slip away without having to speak with any reporters. Which, granted, was more difficult to do when driving a car the color of a fire truck, but she figured the commish was good for at least another three minutes.

The first thing she noticed, as she went around the front of the sedan, was that her front left tire was missing. Which would have been bad enough. Except the vandal had gotten the rear one, as well.

"Damn, damn, damn!" She kicked the wheel. "There are cops, firefighters, and reporters crawling all over this place. How the hell could anyone get away with stealing two tires?"

"I've seen a cop car stripped in two minutes flat," O'Halloran volunteered. "NASCAR pit crews could learn a lot from watching gangbangers."

"Excuse me if I'm less than impressed."

Bailey, who, when she wasn't designing jewelry or bestowing vibrators on her friends, was a deputy prosecutor specializing in sex crimes, had a plaque on her city hall office wall declaring that anything with tires or testicles was bound to give a woman trouble.

And wasn't today proving that to be the truth?

"And my Wrangler's stuck in the damn shop."

The manager of the dealer's service department had called earlier to tell her that they were still looking for the electrical problem that had caused her Jeep to suddenly stop running three times in the past month. Not having wheels hadn't seemed like such a big problem, since she'd intended to use the city car until she got her vehicle back.

Tess kicked the wheel again, grimacing as a pain shot from the toe of the ugly black regulation lace-up shoe to her hip. She glared up at the helicopter, which was scattering ashes and possibly evidence all over the place, momentarily wished she could shoot it down with O'Halloran's gun, then got another idea.

"I'm going to call the television station. Get all the video the Eyewitness News team's shot. The little bastards have *got* to be on it. I'll stick their gangsta asses in jail."

"Good idea," Bobby said.

"Works for me," O'Halloran agreed. For the first time since he'd shown up on the scene, he actually appeared to be enjoying himself. "Since I had the foresight to pay two of those homeboys to guard *my* vehicle, how about I give you two a ride home?"

"There's no way I'm going to leave this car here so a bunch of teenage gang-bangers can vandalize it more."

"That's okay, Tess," Bobby said. "I'll stay with it until a hook shows up to tow it to the yard, then take a cab to the station to pick up my truck."

"You don't have to do that."

"Hey, it's no big deal. My AA meeting doesn't start until eight, anyway. Doesn't make much sense to go home, then go right back out again."

The commissioner looked as if he might actually be wrapping up his speech. Being the only female on the hot squad, Tess was an appealing target for the media. She looked up at the agent, trying to decide between escaping now, while the jackals were distracted, or getting in a car with this man.

Door number one or door number two?

She opened the driver's door of the disabled car, retrieved a Snickers bar from the jockey box, and bit off a chunk.

The TV lights went off. When a blond reporter sporting big bleached hair and a bubblegum pink suit with a fringed, hand-kerchief-size skirt called out her name,

Tess made her decision.

"Let's go," she said. "Meet you back here tomorrow at five-thirty," she told Bobby.

"I don't suppose you mean in the afternoon."

"A.M.," she confirmed.

"And to think I fought like hell for this job," she heard him mutter as she ducked beneath the yellow tape.

fourteen

Neither of them spoke on the way to Tess's house, but the heat surrounding them owed nothing to the fact that even as the sun disappeared in a flare of orange and gold, the temperature still hovered around ninety.

"So," O'Halloran asked casually as he twisted the key and cut the engine, "are you going to invite me in?"

"Sorry. If you're looking for southern hospitality, I'm flat out."

He leaned his arm along the back of her seat. "Hospitality's overrated. I'm just looking to get laid."

"Well." She blew out a breath. "No one could accuse you of beating around the bush."

He toyed with a curl, his callused fingers skimming heat at the nape of her neck. "No point in wasting time playing games. I'm not looking for a relationship. I don't want any strings, or shackles, or any emotional baggage.

"What I want is you, Inspector. Lying beneath me. Naked." His caress trailed down her throat, toying with the open neck of her blouse. "And you want me. It's as simple and elemental as that."

Lying beneath me. Naked.

Oh, God, as her libido came roaring out of limbo, that's exactly what Tess wanted!

Sexual energy crackled all around them like heat lightning.

Tess, who'd once raced into burning buildings and had prided herself on being afraid of nothing, found herself oddly afraid of Gage O'Halloran.

No, that wasn't right. What she was afraid of was herself. And the edgy, out-of-control feelings bombarding her.

"I'm a fire investigator," she reminded them both, as if the words would serve as some sort of shield.

He skimmed a finger over the badge she'd clipped to the front pocket of her uniform shirt. "If you think that uniform will make a man forget that you're a very desirable woman, you're wrong, Slim."

It was as if he'd touched a sparkler to her bare breast.

Tess jerked back again, almost banging her head against the passenger window. Her back was literally against the door.

"Would you please stop touching me?"

"I like touching you." He was looking at her mouth, his hooded eyes darkening from ice to smoke. "I intend to do a whole lot more of it before I leave town."

"And when, exactly, do you expect that to be?"

"However long it takes."

"What takes?"

"To track down your pyro, of course." His thumb feathered the skin framed by the open collar. "Do all you southern females have skin as soft as magnolia blossoms?"

"I've no idea." Refusing to let him distract her, she managed to keep her voice steady even as her pulse leaped beneath the seductive caress. "I don't want your hands on me." *Liar.* "And I don't want your help with my case."

"Of course you do," he said reasonably. "Professionally, you've got a guy who gets off on turning innocent people into crispy critters. Even if he doesn't end up having anything to do with the mill fire, you'd be a damn fool to turn down any help you can get bringing him in. And everything I've learned about you says you're no fool."

"Thank you," she said with mock sweetness.

"You're welcome. Now, getting personal —"

"Oh, let's not."

"Too late. Personally, your problem is that you don't want to want me to touch you. All over."

Not wanting him to know how close he'd hit to the mark, Tess managed what she hoped was a credible laugh. "Lord, you're arrogant."

The accusation bounced right off. She might as well have been throwing spitballs against a brick wall.

"Never judge a cowboy 'til you've seen him ride," he drawled. His wolfish smile radiated male arrogance; the stubble of black beard added to his dangerously un-civilized appearance. "It's obvious that you're a hot woman in bad need of a man who'll give you a hard ride. And believe me, Inspector, I'll be the best in the saddle you've ever had."

He was infuriating. Intimidating.

And, although she'd rather throw herself off the top of the iron bridge spanning the Somersett River than admit it, outra-geously tempting.

She'd always been stubborn, though Tess preferred to think of it as tenaciousness. But along with awakening her dormant sexuality, Gage O'Halloran had tapped into her competitive streak.

"Isn't that just like a man to put the

130

focus on himself." She lifted her chin and treated him to a slow study as blatantly sexual as the ones he'd submitted her to. "I don't suppose it has occurred to you that *I* might be the best *you've* ever had?"

"Absolutely." Damned if he didn't seem almost amused by her failed attempt at intimidation. "I've always closed my cases because I believe in going with my instincts, and my first sight of you had them blaring like a fire alarm.

"Hell, I've been semihard since I ducked under that yellow tape and got hit in the gut by your sexy moss-green eyes and pink mouth."

His erection, clearly defined against the fly of his jeans, backed up that assertion.

Continuing to ignore her prohibition against physical contact, he trailed a slow, deliberate caress around her top lip. "You looked as if you'd been eating a strawberry Popsicle. Which brought up a fantasy of you sucking —"

"I get it."

An image of ripping open the metal buttons and taking him deep into her mouth flashed through her mind. Damn. O'Halloran was right about one thing.

She *was* in dire need of a man.

But not necessarily, Tess reminded herself sternly, *this* man.

"I have a thing this evening."

"Call the guy up and cancel."

"I can't."

"You mean you *won't*."

"That's exactly what I mean. I also need time to think."

"Thinking's overrated. It'll just get you in trouble."

"*You're* trouble."

He surprised her by laughing at that. A dark, harsh sound that sneakily slipped into her bloodstream. "Slim, you sure as hell nailed that one right."

Tess had only ever had sex with one man in her life. From the time she and Danny had first made love, in the back of his pickup truck parked on a shell road out in the marsh their senior year, making love with her high school sweetheart had been so sweet, so perfect, it had felt like a benediction.

But Danny had died.

And the only sex she'd had since his death required C-cells.

How pitiful was that?

"Perhaps women back in California fall into bed at the snap of your fingers," she said, clinging to some last desperate vestige of self-control. "But I'm not that easy."

"If you're looking for some smooth-talkin' southern Ashley Wilkes gentleman to court you, you've got the wrong guy."

"We're in total agreement there." Gage O'Halloran was definitely more Rhett than Ashley.

"And people accuse southerners of beating around the bush." He ran a fingertip beneath her eye, which she suspected was darkly shadowed from the long hours she'd been working lately. "Go ahead and give it some thought, Slim. I'm not going anywhere."

Tess was momentarily surprised when he pulled back and let her climb out of the low-slung sports car.

A gentleman would have walked her to the door, she thought furiously as she stomped up the brick sidewalk.

Then again, they'd already agreed that O'Halloran was no gentleman.

She felt his gaze on her as she climbed the steps, unable to decide whether to take his statement about sticking around Somersett as a promise. Or a threat.

Gage looped his hands over the steering wheel, watching Tess walk up to the door of a colorful gingerbread-trimmed house that looked as if it'd washed off the pages of a fairy-tale book.

Her ugly uniform, tailored for a man, couldn't conceal the slender, feminine curves. He'd always liked long hair on a woman, enjoyed tangling it in his fists as he drew her head back, giving him access to her throat, allowing him to control her.

And the situation.

He'd allowed a relationship to get out of control once before. With disastrous consequences. Having learned his lesson the hard way, Gage had vowed to never surrender power again.

But that didn't stop him from getting a kick out of the way those bright curls that framed Tess's face and made her eyes look huge, bounced as she marched up the walk. Or enjoying the way they'd felt between his fingers. And better yet, anticipating how they'd feel brushing against his naked body.

Fire Inspector Tess Gannon wouldn't be easily controlled. Gage could tell from the stiffness of her back and the length of her stride that he'd pissed her off. But even with those flat-heeled, rubber-soled, black lace-up cop shoes, the sway of her slender hips reminded him that beneath the black polyester was a female who'd been as turned on by him as he was by her.

"Very nice," he murmured as she escaped behind a door painted the same strawberry-sherbet color of her full, sexy lips. He was going to taste those luscious lips.

Sooner, rather than later. And that was just for starters.

It took no imagination at all to picture Tess Gannon barely clad in a pair of ice-pick heels and some skimpy bit of scarlet-as-sin lace that showed off her breasts and left her nipples — which he suspected would be the same deep pink hue of her mouth — bare.

The only problem with that fantasy was that the timing sucked. Besides, he'd always had a rule about keeping his work and social life separate.

Not that the hit-and-run sex he'd had these past years came close to resembling anything of a social life.

After the fire that had stolen everything Gage held dear, vengeance had taken a grip on his mind, driving him to work around the clock to nab The Flamemaster. Sex hadn't even been on his radar screen. After the murderous pyro was finally behind bars, he'd gone into a tailspin, engaging in nearly nonstop one-night stands with women he'd pick up in bars.

Later, when he'd begun to regain his senses, he'd realized that an inability to face the dark alone had driven him into the nearest available bed. Strangely, although he'd been walking on the razor's edge of sanity, he'd never lacked women willing to sleep with him. Which only meant, he'd decided later, that they were as crazy as he'd been.

He'd spend his nights seeking release inside a dizzying number of nameless, faceless women. His days sleeping off the surfeit of booze and sex.

After six months, one morning he'd woken up with the mother of all hangovers, unable to remember anything about the night before.

A sane man would have realized right then he was on the verge of disintegration. The problem was, if he'd been anywhere near sane, he wouldn't have found himself in such a hole in the first place.

So, instead of throwing down the shovel, he began to dig faster.

Harder.

Deeper.

It took another two months for him to end up in the drunk tank, smelling like some homeless alkie, his knuckles bruised and bloody from a bar brawl he couldn't remember, before he hit rock bottom.

He could have called Donovan to come bail him out. Despite the fact that he'd been on administrative leave from ATF since the end of Griffith's trial, Gage was not without resources; hell, he could've afforded the best criminal attorney money could buy.

Instead, figuring he deserved what he got, and finding jail a new way to punish himself, he settled for a wet-behind-the-ears, overworked public defender. The kid, who'd been in law school in Hawaii during the years Gage had made the papers, had failed to recognize either his face or his name.

Which was not the case with the judge presiding over the San Francisco night court. The same magistrate who'd signed so many warrants for the ATF special agent. Professing dismay that a man who'd dedicated his life to justice was appearing before his bench in such condition, he'd sentenced Gage to six months' community service.

The justice had rejected Gage's suggestion that he be assigned to work on a parks cleanup crew, or something — anything — that would keep him from having to interact with others. Which was how he'd ended up teaching computer skills to kids at a homeless shelter.

They'd broken his heart. Which, as the wise old judge had undoubtedly intended, had reminded Gage that he actually *had* a heart.

He hadn't been happy — he strongly doubted that would ever be possible again — but he'd been satisfied with his life.

Until Donovan had shown up at the house he'd bought after the fire and reminded Gage that a man could never outrun his past.

He unclipped the cell phone from his belt. Tess answered on the first ring.

"While you're thinking," he suggested, "you might want to keep one more thing in mind."

"Dammit, O'Halloran —"

"You might want to start looking into how your pyro knew your vic," he said, overriding her planned protest.

"What?" There was a long pause of dead air on the other end of the phone. The white lace curtains in the front window shifted, ever so slightly. "How do you figure that?"

"The Flamemaster likes rope."

"So you said," she huffed. But he'd captured her attention.

"But it's not his usual signature." It was his turn to draw out the silence between them. "He saves it." Another pause. "For people he knows." Acid roiled in his gut as memories flashed in his mind like scenes from a horror flick. "Particularly *women* he knows. Intimately."

He could feel Tess taking that in. "How do you know that?"

"It's a long story." One he wasn't yet prepared to share. "Just trust me."

Figuring he'd said enough, for now, he flipped the phone shut. He twisted the ignition key. The Porsche came to life with a growl.

As he pulled away from the curb, Gage glanced back into the rearview mirror and saw Tess standing on her front porch, hands on her hips, staring after him.

fifteen

Bailey and Ty lived in a relatively new subdivision established for young families east of town. The community boasted a leafy-green park, a playground surrounded by a jogging track, a clubhouse, a tennis court, and a sparkling blue swimming pool.

The couple could have never afforded the house on the combined salaries of a firefighter and assistant district attorney, but Bailey, who'd grown up in the wealthy Ocean Pines neighborhood on Swann Island, had not only been blessed with beauty and brains, but had inherited a generous trust fund, as well.

The suburban yard was a lush emerald green; the darkly mulched gardens were in full bloom; soft jazz filtered from outdoor speakers disguised as rocks.

"You've done a wonderful job with the landscaping," Tess said as she sat on the back deck. Low-voltage lights hidden high beneath the arched branches of the palmetto trees cast a soft light over the yard. Gleaming gold, silver, and copper-colored carp swam slow, peaceful circles in a rock-bordered pond a few feet away.

"It took me three weeks to dig that pond to Her Highness's specifications," volunteered Ty, who was blackening hunks of meat on a stainless steel grill that looked large enough to feed every firefighter in Somersett.

Tess instructed her stomach, which roiled at the smell of grilled beef after today's fire scene, to behave itself.

"You said you loved doing it," Bailey reminded him with a faint frown.

"Well, sure. But only because of the reward that came afterward."

"Men." Bailey huffed out a breath and flashed her husband an indulgent smile over the rim of her glass of soda water. "They're so easy to train. All a woman has to do is wave a little sex in front of one and he'll pant and beg for treats."

"And dig holes with a smile," Ty agreed easily.

Tess laughed at the exchange between the two and thought of how much Ty reminded her of Danny. Which, in turn, had her thinking of the other man who'd suddenly appeared in her life today.

"What's wrong?" Bailey asked.

"Nothing."

Tess dragged her mind from the memory

of the rampant lust she'd seen in his gaze just before she'd escaped into the house. She plucked a piece of pita bread from a wicker basket and scooped dip from a white earthenware bowl.

"This is great hummus."

"I picked it up at Café Corfu on the way home from the airport." She'd been away for two days in Santa Fe, at a conference of prosecutors. "So, what's up?"

"What makes you think anything's up?" Tess hedged.

"I'm an assistant district attorney. It's my job to pay attention to what people aren't saying. And you've been distracted since you arrived."

"I suppose my mind's on work. We had a nasty fire this afternoon."

"I heard about it." Bailey dipped a raw cauliflower floret into the hummus. Having flirted with the Mediterranean diet, she was back on Atkins. "Was it arson?"

"It's too soon to tell. But I wouldn't be surprised."

"That building's been nothing but an eyesore for years; it's probably just as well someone finally decided to get rid of it."

"People lived there. And a woman died there."

"I'm sorry. That was politically incorrect. And probably sounded heartless."

Tess knew her silence spoke for her.

As Bailey covered Tess's hand with her own, a pearl set in a silver oyster shell glowed like the moon. The ring was part of Bailey's Tides jewelry collection. Despite her steel-trap legal mind and sharklike professional attitude, the attorney was all woman right down to her toenails, which tonight were polished the same deep purple amethyst as her silk tunic top and flowing calf-length skirt.

Blessed — or cursed, depending on your viewpoint — with a lush, killer hourglass shape that had gone out of style with Marilyn Monroe and Jayne Mansfield, Bailey dressed like an upper-middle-class gypsy, favoring floaty fabrics in jewel-toned colors rather than the conservative clothing worn by the young matrons who'd been her classmates at Somersett Country Day.

Those same curves that had men walking into marble walls at the courthouse — the ones that made Tess, with her impossible hair and flat chest, often feel like Little Orphan Annie when standing next to her — were the bane of her best friend's existence, and, Tess supposed, explained the seemingly endless quest for the perfect diet.

"It's just that my heart stops whenever I hear Ty's gone into one of those damn old buildings historical preservationists are preventing from being bulldozed." Emotion trembled in Bailey's voice. "You, of all people, should understand what death traps they can be."

"Every time I get a call to a fire in one of them, I think how Danny died."

"That was such a tragic accident." Bailey's long hair shielded her face like a dark curtain as she shook her head.

She lowered her voice to keep it from drifting across the deck to her husband. "And, as relieved as I am that Ty survived, there are still times when I feel guilty that he managed to get out when Danny didn't."

"That would have just made it a double tragedy." Tess had certainly suffered with her own survivor's guilt. "A Fed showed up at the scene today."

"FBI?"

"ATF." Tess saw no point in mentioning that he was the most unlikely-appearing ATF agent she'd ever met. "He thinks it was arson."

"What do you think?"

"It's still up in the air." Tess dipped another piece of bread. "But he *does* believe

Danny's death was arson."

Bailey's dark eyes widened. She shot a quick glance toward her husband, who was happily spritzing water from a plastic bottle onto the grill to dampen the flames that had flared up around the thick strip steaks.

Maybe, Tess considered, if she just pushed the pieces of meat around on her plate, no one would notice she wasn't actually eating them.

"That was ruled a faulty equipment fire," Bailey said.

"Just because that was the ruling doesn't mean it was the actual cause."

"I've always understood why you were reluctant to buy the party line."

Bailey had switched into lawyer-speak mode, her words as carefully couched as if she were stating them in a courtroom.

"After all, Ty and Danny were alone on that floor when the wall collapsed. If things had gone differently, if their situations had been reversed, I'd certainly have trouble accepting the fact that my husband was lying in the cemetery because of something as simple as an electrical wire shorting out."

They'd had this argument before. Tess had always understood that it wasn't a case of Bailey not being supportive. Instead, in her own way, she was trying to help her friend get on with her life, as she had hers.

Although Bailey had steadfastly refused to talk about it, she'd miscarried the morning after the fire. The doctor had said first-trimester miscarriages were normal; Tess suspected the stress of Ty nearly being killed had been a contributing factor.

Tess had wanted to get on with her life. Truly she had, which was partly why she'd begun a new career as a fire cop. Of course, another reason had been to learn everything she could about fire investigation so she could get Danny the justice some arsonist had denied him.

She'd tried to backtrack over that day, interviewing the first responders countless times. She'd grilled the guys on the rescue truck over and over again, especially poor Ty, who if he'd been anyone but Danny's best friend, would've probably taken off running whenever he saw her coming.

"Gage O'Halloran — that's the Fed's name — is holding back a lot of information. I think he's trying to get me interested enough to share my case files. Or, maybe he doesn't really know anything at all, and just wants someone to try his conspiracy theories out on. Or . . ."

Tess's voice drifted off. Hell, how carefully had she even looked at that damn badge? Perhaps the reason O'Halloran didn't seem much like a federal agent was that he wasn't one at all.

One of the first things a fire cop learned was to check the scene for people who seemed a little too interested in events.

True pyromaniacs, as opposed to guys who'd torch a building for bucks, were actually addicted to starting fires. Unlike revenge fire starters or professionals, they didn't have any rationale for their potentially deadly acts other than whatever sick delusions — usually sexual — revolved in their twisted minds.

The word *pyromania* literally meant fire madness.

Her first month on the job, Tess had appeared on local television, asking for the public's help in apprehending an arsonist who'd been setting trash fires throughout the marsh, destroying valuable wetlands.

No sooner had the newscast aired than she'd received a call to the hotline number from a woman who suspected her boyfriend, who, according to the informant, always smelled of smoke whenever he'd show up at her apartment for sex. A court-appointed shrink later diagnosed that the man was unable to achieve an erection without setting a fire.

What if O'Halloran, if that even *was* his real name, was some pyro who'd ordered himself a fake badge from the Internet and got his rocks off by insinuating himself into the investigations he'd set?

The profile wasn't that far removed from the so-called hero firefighter-arsonist she'd replaced. But this was much, much worse, because if O'Halloran was a true pyromaniac, it could explain why he'd gotten so aroused at the scene.

"That's just sick," she muttered. It also made her own sexual response to him even worse.

"What's sick?" Bailey waved a perfectly manicured hand in front of Tess's face. "Are you okay? You've gone pale."

"I'm fine." Tess took a long drink of her wine and tried not to squirm beneath Bailey's close scrutiny.

Little wonder the other woman had one of the highest conviction rates in the county's justice system; Tess couldn't imagine many people standing up to her cross-examination.

"Is it something to do with that Fed?" Bailey's brow furrowed. "O'Halloran, did you say his name was?"

"Yes, his name's O'Halloran, Gage. And I was just wondering if he's what he's claiming to be."

"*No one* is totally what he or she claims to be."

"Some of us are. You're just jaded because you spend all your time with bad guys."

Bad guys and victims. As did Tess.

"Perhaps. A new case landed on my desk today," Bailey said, seemingly switching topics, but Tess knew better. No one could direct a conversation better than ADA Tyler. "A grandmother of three darling little kids — two eight-year-old twin boys and a four-year-old girl. She's spent the past year working as, as she puts it, their agent."

Knowing Bailey's passion for convicting sex crimes, especially against children, Tess's heart chilled. "Oh, God, don't tell me —"

"Seems the kids have star qualities," Bailey said, confirming Tess's worst suspicion. "Their little porn film is making big bucks all over the Internet."

Tess's stomach turned as a waft of sirloin-scented smoke drifted over to the table from the grill. She'd suddenly lost what was left of her appetite.

"That's beyond sick."

"Isn't it? But to look at the woman, you'd think she was the quintessential little old lady who spends her golden years baking oatmeal cookies and putting together photograph albums of her grand-babies. The pictures we took off that website are definitely not your usual granny scrapbook stuff. Which goes to my point that appearances can be deceiving."

Bailey's teeth flashed white as she bit off the end of a baby carrot; in that fleeting second she was no longer the stunningly beautiful, multitalented prosecutor and part-time jewelry designer who somehow managed to keep a house that could be a showplace on HGTV and a perfectly mani-cured yard that Tiger Woods could've used to practice his putting.

What she was, Tess knew, somewhere deep down, beneath that perfectly coiffed, perfumed, and powdered southern belle exterior, was a predator.

And wasn't it fortunate, for children who became trapped in dark and obscene existences, that Bailey Tyler brought such passion to her work?

"I don't know how you do it," Tess said admiringly. "But thank heavens you do."

Bare shoulders, kissed with the gold of a year-round tan, shrugged again. "It's my job. But I will admit to a passion. I also have no hesitation confessing that there's no way in hell I could run into a burning building like you did. And Ty still insists on doing."

Hearing his name, Ty looked up and grinned. "We're at the two-minute warning."

Bailey smiled back, and in that brief shared moment between husband and wife, Tess envied them. If things had gone differently . . .

Bailey was right. Ty could've been the one who'd died. Which wasn't anything Tess would wish on her worst enemy, let alone her best friend.

She accompanied Bailey into the kitchen. The table in the adjoining dining room, which Bailey had turned into a workroom, was covered with jewelry-making supplies. There were boxes of precious-metal clay, molds in the shape of seashells, a small blowtorch that reminded Tess of the ones chefs used for caramelizing the sugar atop bowls of crème brûlée, and colorful gemstones that glittered like a pirate's booty.

"So," Bailey said, as she took three white

plates from the warming oven, "I suppose this O'Halloran is from the field office in Charleston?"

"Uh-uh. California."

"ATF sent someone all the way from the coast because of a fire that occurred two years ago?"

"I guess they did."

"You guess?"

Tess scooped up a wicker basket of cutlery and rolled cloth napkins, studiously evading what she knew would be Bailey's prosecutorial stare.

"You had to have been there. It seemed logical at the time. Though he said he's originally from Wyoming. But you're right." She cut off the lecture she sensed was coming. "I should've checked his credentials more carefully."

She would have, if she hadn't been right in the middle of a fire-scene investigation. Which, dammit, may have been precisely what he was counting on.

Now Tess had three reasons to kick herself where Gage O'Halloran was concerned: her outrageous response to him; her oversight in ensuring he was exactly who, and what, he claimed to be; and not having found out where he was staying.

Hell, while she was sitting hoping to attempt to salvage a peaceful evening, drinking in the scent of Confederate jasmine, sipping a smooth-as-velvet pinot noir, and trying to choke down grilled red meat, the man could be on the loose somewhere in the city torching a building.

"I'll run a check on the guy first thing in the morning," Bailey offered.

"You've got kids to protect. I'll do it."

And if the man was lying to her, she'd track him down and throw his Wrangler-wearing ass in jail for impersonating a law enforcement officer.

sixteen

It could be a coincidence. Gage sat at the laptop computer in his hotel room, running the models over and over again. Sterno certainly wasn't unheard of for starting fires. And C-4 had been a terrorist's choice in weapons long before the killers had discovered that common everyday fertilizer could go boom.

It wasn't just that the plastique was immensely stable, that it wouldn't go off without a charge; it could be molded to fit any location. Any situation. His first week assigned to the San Francisco field office, he'd taken part in a joint task force arrest of two smugglers who'd tried to bring in a load of the stuff molded into the shape of Muppets and painted Elmo red, Oscar green, and Cookie Monster blue.

This guy was calling himself The Flamemaster. Which could, admittedly, be another coincidence. It wasn't such an unexpected name for a fire setter to come up with. Hadn't that company who'd taken the firefighting instruction video he'd created and turned it into a top-selling computer game named it that? Which had added to the sick irony when the pyro who'd left Gage's life in ruins had dubbed himself the same thing.

It made sense to Gage that the same arsonists who'd memorize every scene and line in *Backdraft* might have played the game that had made him the wealthiest agent in the Bureau of Alcohol, Firearms, Tobacco, and Explosives.

But it was the damn rope that grated. Gage had never trusted coincidence, and this was just one coincidence too many. Even if the Somersett Fire Department *was* dealing with a copycat, there was still no way the sicko could know about the rope, because it was one of the things investigators had held back.

One of the things only a handful of people knew. People like Donovan and him. And Randolph Griffith. Who was still behind bars in San Quentin. Gage had checked again just an hour ago.

Shit.

"I hate mysteries," he muttered as he shut down the laptop.

Somewhere in the city, a clock tolled midnight. After flying from California, fueled by gallons of airline coffee, jet lag should be setting in.

But how the hell was he supposed to sleep when his thoughts were crackling like downed electrical wires in a thunderstorm, sparking random synapses in his brain?

Snap. There was Griffith in the courtroom, grinning maniacally like Jack Nicholson's character in *The Shining* when he was going after his family with an ax.

Snap. Fast-forward to Donovan at the house, looking like a depressed executioner who dreaded accompanying the condemned on that long, last mile.

Snap. Rewind. He was inside a bedroom, watching flames spark on a cream-hued rug. Feeling as if his feet were in hardened concrete, he couldn't move to extinguish the fire that slithered across the floor to the white-on-white satin bedspread.

Snap. Griffith again, standing over the bed. The stone-cold killer glanced toward Gage, winked evilly, then turned back to the trussed and terrified woman, pursed his lips, and blew.

There was a rush of hot wind. Fire engulfed the mattress. Gage feared he'd hear his wife's screams for the rest of his life.

"Fuck." He dragged his shaking hands down his face, swallowing the bile that rose like poison in his throat.

Drenched with sweat, he left the hotel and went running along the harbor front, knowing, even as his feet pounded the cobblestones, that a man could never outrun his past.

seventeen

It began to rain as Tess left Bailey and Ty's, a soft mist that picked up as she neared town. By the time she pulled up in front of her house, the percussive sound of the rain on the roof was like the din of a dozen crazed heavy-metal drummers.

She scooped up the pie-shaped plastic container from the floor in front of the passenger seat, tucked her handbag under her arm, and with her keys clutched in her hand made a dash for the house just as the sky opened up.

She was drenched by the time she managed to unlock the front door. That's what she got for putting off doing something about that sticky lock that had been bedeviling her for the past month. She'd been tempted to just leave the house open, but feared the first time she did, some burglar would break in.

It wasn't like she had all that much to be stolen. But she knew her brother would never let her live such carelessness down.

As for her mother, well, there wasn't enough Swans Down flour in the world to handle the number of cakes her mother would have to bake to get over the idea of her daughter's home being invaded.

Her mother, who didn't seem happy if she didn't have something or someone to worry about, hadn't liked the idea of Tess spending nights alone in the house while Danny slept at the fire station.

"Why would you want to live so near the harbor?" she'd asked. "Do you know how many potential rapists and murderers from all over the world come into town on those ships?"

"I've got the best dead bolts that money can buy." Joe had shown up with them the weekend she and Danny had moved in.

"You have a perfectly good room here at home," her mother had complained after Danny's death. "Why not just come back for a while?"

Maybe because you've kept it exactly the same way it was when I left to go to college and I've moved beyond stuffed animals, a canopy bed, and Johnny Depp's 21 Jump Street *poster on the bubblegum pink wall?*

Claiming the house was close to the firehouse, Tess had held firm.

Not wanting to drip all over the floors she'd spent weeks refinishing, she stripped

159

off her clothes in the foyer. She'd closed the plantation shutters before leaving for work to help keep the house cool, which allowed her to walk naked from room to room without worrying about putting on a peep show for the neighbors.

She put the pie in the refrigerator, dumped her wet clothes in the small laundry room off the kitchen, then went upstairs. The clock was striking midnight as she pulled an extra-large PROPERTY OF THE SOMERSETT FIRE DEPARTMENT T-shirt over her head.

She brushed her teeth and washed her face, frowning at faint new lines the wrinkle fairy had left sometime during the day.

The bedroom was stuffy from the house having been closed up for so many hours. Fortunately, the shingled roof over the small back utility porch allowed her to open the window. The air smelled of rain and jasmine, tinged with the salt of sea and marsh.

Exhausted by her long day, she sank back onto the pillow, closed her eyes, and willed herself to sleep.

Easier said than done.

It grew late. The moon rose high in the sky outside Tess's bedroom window.

Neighborhood lights were all turned off. The only sounds were the rain on the roof, the lonely sound of an alto sax from a nearby blues club, and a tomcat wailing a lonely, romantic lament atop some distant fence top.

"I know just how you feel," she muttered as she tossed and turned.

She was hot and edgy. And, dammit, thanks to the man who may or may not be a federal agent, turned on.

Which was perfectly natural. After all, if people didn't have sex drives, the human race would have come to a screeching halt thousands of generations ago. Of course, civilization had come a long way since Neanderthal days.

"At least *some* men have progressed."

O'Halloran clearly being one of the exceptions. The man was definitely a sexual animal. She could easily imagine him clubbing a naked woman over the head and dragging her by the hair back to his cave.

Not that he'd need the club, she admitted reluctantly. Some women might find such swaggering, macho behavior appealing.

But not her.

It was only because she'd been without a

man so long. She was like a woman who'd spent two thirsty years crawling across a hot, arid desert, then had finally stumbled across a sparkling turquoise oasis. It was only natural, *healthy,* even, to want to take a long, deep drink.

That was the only reason she was picturing Gage O'Halloran's face as she slipped a hand beneath the hem of the T-shirt and trailed her fingers over her breasts. Her nipples pebbled, just as they'd done when he'd toyed with the zipper of her jumpsuit.

See, you don't need a man.

In her fantasy, the Wyoming cowboy was lounging in the flowered wing chair by the window, one leg stretched out in front of him, the other draped over the padded arm of the chair. The only sign that he was at all aroused the unmistakable bulge between those long legs.

He was watching her, his hooded gaze cool. Detached.

What would it take, she wondered recklessly, to get beneath that remote male exterior? She wasn't all that flattered he'd been aroused by her. After all, as Bailey was always saying, a woman had to be in the mood to want sex. A man just needed to be in the room.

What if Gage O'Halloran was in her room?

In her bed?

In her?

Lust curled at that thought; desire pooled. Heat spread like a fever.

In her fantasy, he was clad solely in those butt-hugging Wranglers, his unreasonably sexy feet bare. When she rolled a pebbled nipple between her thumb and index finger, he splayed a dark hand against the bronzed perfection of his own chest, which suddenly gleamed in the moonlight with a sheen of sweat.

Ha! Having gotten a response, Tess couldn't stop now.

Her short, unlacquered nails continued down the center of her torso; his impenetrable gaze followed.

Was he breathing harder? Perhaps. Tess couldn't tell for sure.

Her own breath quickened as she imagined him slowly unfastening the metal buttons. The corner of his mouth quirked in what could have been a smile but was probably a smirk, as he silently dared Tess to look.

She did. And stared, transfixed, as he curled his fingers around the rigid length and began to stroke himself.

A finger — his or hers? Tess was no longer sure — delved into the slick slit between her now quivering thighs. It wasn't enough. A second finger followed. A third, braided together with the others.

Her knees fell open, her heels pressed against the sheets, her back bowed as her fingers, which were a poor substitute for a penis, slid in and out.

In her fantasy, Gage had left the chair and was now straddling her, his thighs strong and hard.

A moan escaped her lips when she imagined him entering her in one strong stroke, filling all her lonely places, instantly triggering a climax.

If just fantasizing about Gage O'Halloran could leave her trembling, what would it be like to actually have sex with him?

Reality never equals the fantasy. You'd only be setting yourself up to be disappointed.

Tess told herself that over and over again.

It was, after all, very good advice. Advice a prudent woman would follow.

Unfortunately, as her mind reran, in vivid detail, every seductive thing Gage had said to her today, every wicked look, every weakening touch, Tess didn't feel the least bit prudent.

What she felt like was a hot woman in bad need of a man who'd give her a hard ride.

eighteen

It was still dark when Tess's doorbell buzzed the next morning. Thinking it must be Bobby with the car, she opened the door to find the man who'd played the starring role in her sexual fantasy standing on her porch, a tall brown cardboard cup in his hand.

"Your partner's meeting us at the fire scene," he informed her.

Although the aroma wafting from the vent in the white plastic lid was enticing, the sight of those long, dark fingers surrounding the cup caused her heart to skip a beat.

"Who died and put you in charge of the world?" she grumbled as she snatched the coffee from his hand, not at all happy to discover how thin her veneer of control really was.

"Hey, I'm just here as backup, Inspector. Consider me Tonto to your Lone Ranger."

Tess snorted at the analogy. Right before reminding herself that she'd intended to check Gage O'Halloran out more thoroughly.

"Let me see your badge again."

166

He lifted a brow, but didn't argue.

The eagle-topped cobalt and gold special-agent badge certainly looked familiar. But then again, he could've bought one from some rogue Internet site.

As if sensing her inner debate, he took a small pad and pen from the inside of his jacket pocket and scribbled down a phone number. "Donovan Ryder is the San Francisco task force supervisor."

"Who, given the time difference, undoubtedly won't show up at the office for another six hours."

"You're running this show. You want to risk giving your pyro more time to plan another fire while you're waiting around to check out my credentials, it's no skin off my butt."

Damn. Tess had been trying not to think about his butt.

His right palm was high on the doorjamb, and he seemed to be looming over her, much as he had in her fantasy. Resisting a sudden urge to drag him upstairs, Tess took a sip of coffee.

How had he known chocolate raspberry was her favorite? It was like having coffee, fruit, and a Hershey's bar for breakfast. Speaking of which . . .

"How did you get this? Koffee and

Kreme doesn't open until six-thirty."

"I don't suspect you'd believe I charmed the owner into opening up early."

"Let's see. You." She took a sip of the coffee that he'd prepared to the perfect sweetness and felt the synapses in her sleep-deprived brain kick in. "Charm." Another sip. "Nope. Sorry," she said. "It just doesn't work for me."

"Maybe you're not trying hard enough."

"Maybe I don't want to try." She locked the door and pocketed the key. "As for today, I'm not planning to suspend my investigation. Bobby and I'll go ahead and test the apartment with the UV light. If your credentials check out, you can read the report after we're finished."

"Sorry, Slim. But that's not the way it works. Like I said yesterday, you're stuck with me. For the duration. Think of me as your shadow: where *you* go, *I* go. Which, the way I see it, gives you two choices."

The index finger he held up triggered more erotic memories.

She was losing her mind! Who knew that two years without sex could destroy a brain? It was undoubtedly just stress. After all, it wasn't every day she was faced with a serial arsonist seemingly determined to burn down her city.

Of course, it also wasn't every day she met a man like this one.

One day with Gage O'Halloran and she was turning all soft and female. She couldn't be fixating on getting naked with him; she had to think like a fire cop, to concentrate on finding The Flamemaster before he killed again.

"You can delay the investigation or" — his smile was brief and savage as he held up a middle finger — "you can trust me."

Damn. The thing that really got Tess's goat was that about this situation, at least, O'Halloran was right.

Arson operated under the forty-eight-hour rule. If a crime wasn't solved in the first forty-eight hours, it might not get solved at all. Even in the most thorough of departments, evidence got misplaced or, occasionally, destroyed. Witnesses and suspects moved away, and there were always more fires, more crime scenes to investigate.

Bad enough that she and Bobby had been forced to wait yesterday for the apartment house to cool down enough to enter it. Worse yet that the firefighters, who'd only been doing their job, had chopped holes in the roof, broken windows, and poured thousands of gallons of water all

169

over her crime scene.

Waiting to check out O'Halloran's credentials would only create more delay. Since he'd already claimed he wasn't going anywhere, Tess decided the sensible thing to do would be to keep an eye on him until she'd confirmed he was who he claimed to be.

"Okay," she decided. "Let's go."

Bobby arrived at the apartment in the red sedan with two new tires just as Tess and Gage pulled up at the scene. He took a roll of black plastic, the investigation tool kit, and a handheld portable UV light from the trunk.

The fire crews had left; the building was no longer smoldering, but it was dark and gloomy inside. The lanterns on their helmets and flashlight beams provided the only light.

"Maybe we ought to have brought along a sniffer," Bobby suggested as they slogged through the pooled oil-slick puddles.

"No need," Gage responded before Tess could open her mouth. "This was a helluva hot fire; any accelerant odor's undoubtedly gone."

"Plus," Tess said, hating yet again to agree with O'Halloran about anything, "sniffers aren't as good at showing the pour pattern. And they tend to pick up false positives."

Her first week on the job she'd been given the task of operating the sniffer, which tested positive for accelerant. The following day the lab determined that the "accelerant" on the neck of the beer bottle was saliva; she'd been ragged for six months about that mistake.

The light outside the window of apartment 508 had begun to turn a pale predawn lavender. Because ambient light needed to be at a minimum to successfully use the UV light, Bobby tacked the opaque black plastic over the window.

Accelerants were usually absorbed in a fire, leaving evidence invisible to the naked eye, which was why ultraviolet light — a band of electromagnetic radiation between visible light and X-rays — had proven an invaluable fire-scene investigation tool.

Tess noted that for all his swaggering machismo, Gage accepted a pair of polycarbonate goggles designed to prevent delayed sunburn to unprotected eyes.

Lanterns and flashlights were turned off, throwing the room into darkness. "Okay," Tess murmured as she switched on the battery-operated light. "Here goes."

"Well, that settles that," Bobby said as the room all around them lit up.

The light worked on the principle that all matter is made of atoms, which are, in turn, made of electrons orbiting around a nucleus. If the electrons of many common accelerants were exposed to ultraviolet light, they'd absorb energy and leap out of their natural orbit.

As they spin out, other electrons jump in to take their place; all this movement produces energy, which beneath a UV light glows as fluorescence.

"I'm still calling the point of origin at the doorway," Tess said. "But he definitely drenched the bed."

The fluorescence was decidedly brighter on the charred mattress.

Bobby began snapping off a string of photos. "It looks as if he wanted to give her plenty of time to know what was happening."

It was a guess, but a valid one, given that there was a distinct pour pattern around a less fluoresced area in the center of the bed, where the victim had been found. Usually in a murder by arson, the victim would be drenched in accelerant, the better, the killer would hope, to destroy evidence.

Tess waited for the ATF hotshot to

chime in with his expert opinion — which he obviously believed to be far superior to either hers or Bobby's — but he failed to respond to Bobby's theory.

"Give me that light," he said abruptly.

"Why?" Her hand tightened on the red handle.

He shook his head. "Are you always this argumentative?"

"Yes. Are you always this obnoxiously bossy?"

"Absolutely." He flashed a mirthless grin. "It's one of my many charms."

It was Tess's turn to shake her head.

"Shine it over here," he instructed.

Since getting into a pissing contest wouldn't solve her crime, she trained the light onto the soot-thickened shag carpeting at his feet.

"That's it."

He pulled a knife out of a sheath on his belt and began scraping at a spot that glowed brightest of all.

"What?" She crouched down beside him, handing him an evidence container.

"What's left of a metal ring." He held out the gleaming substance for Bobby to document on the high-speed film before sealing it away.

"A ring?"

"From an aluminum can. If tests don't reveal paraffin, I'll eat my badge."

"I may just hold you to that," Tess muttered. But she was intrigued. "Sterno's a paraffin product."

"It's his signature," he said. "Along with the rope."

"Since you seem to know so much about him, I'm surprised you don't know his name," Tess said dryly.

"As a matter of fact, I do. I also know where he is."

"Duh," Bobby said. "It's pretty obvious he's here in Somersett."

"It'd seem so, wouldn't it?" Gage agreed. A bit too quickly, Tess thought. "Which would be difficult, since he's currently behind bars in San Quentin."

Tess blinked. Okay, that came as a surprise. "Then we're looking at a copycat."

"Could be," Gage agreed again. "Except there's one little problem with that theory."

"Which is?"

She was growing more and more irritated by the way he kept doling out bits of information, one damn piece at a time.

"The only people who know about the rope are The Flamemaster and the agents who finally nailed him."

"One of whom would be you?" she guessed.

"One of whom would be me," he confirmed grimly.

nineteen

Outside the draped window, a mockingbird was greeting the rising sun. Inside, a significant silence descended.

"It's gotta be a coincidence," Bobby said finally.

The problem with that idea was that Tess had never believed in coincidence. As she exchanged a look with O'Halloran, she knew that once again, she and the ATF special agent were on the exact same track.

"Maybe we'll know more after we get the autopsy report," she said.

Unfortunately, the Somersett County medical examiner was currently speaking at a conference of the International Association of Coroners and Medical Examiners in Beijing. Which meant that the victim's body was going to have to stay on ice. Literally.

"Meanwhile, I'll have a talk with the owner of the building."

From the ropes and the pour pattern, this was looking less and less like an insurance fire, but Tess had been taught to never overlook a possibility, no matter how remote.

There was also the matter of the victim's alleged profession.

"We should run the vic's arrest records. Odds are she's got a yellow sheet, so we might find a cop who knows more than we do about her associates."

Tess couldn't discount a pimp. Or a disgruntled john. The worst-case scenario was that they were dealing with a serial killer. Because prostitutes were willing to have sex with strangers for money, they were often more easily dehumanized in the killer's mind.

Also working against them was the fact they were less likely to be reported missing by family or friends. Such social isolation made hookers vulnerable, which in turn made them a common target for serial murderers. Jack the Ripper and the Green River Killer had both figured that out.

"Why don't you handle the arrest records," Gage suggested to Bobby. "I'll drive the inspector to Savannah, then we'll meet up with you at the station to compare notes."

Bobby shot a look at him. Then turned to Tess. As much as she was annoyed by the way the agent was playing top dog again, she couldn't deny his suggestion made sense.

"Funny that you'd know the building's owner's offices are in Savannah."

"I believe in doing my homework," he said mildly.

Of course, he might also know where Mannington Properties home offices were if *he* was the person who'd torched the building.

Something else occurred to her. "You haven't been taking any notes." What kind of investigator didn't keep a record of the crime scene?

"No need. You and Jefferson have been documenting everything. And besides, I've got a photographic memory."

"Right." Tess's tone was thick with skepticism. "We'll be back by noon. One at the latest," she told Bobby, making her decision to keep O'Halloran in sight for a while longer. Even if he turned out to be who he said he was, being an ATF agent didn't necessarily take him off her suspect list. "Give me a call on my cell if you run across anything."

"Sure." Bobby was obviously not thrilled with the idea of a new partner. That made two of them. "I'll check out the greasy spoon on the corner where the neighborhood hookers tend to hang out between tricks. Maybe one of the other girls will have seen something."

"Good idea." After packing away the light and camera, they left the building, headed in opposite directions.

"I don't suppose it would do any good to mention that I'm really getting ticked off by the way you insist on calling the shots?" she asked as she slid into the low-slung passenger seat.

"Nope. Because like it or not, you and I have something in common other than a hot desire to get naked together. You also don't have to believe your current cases have anything to do with mine. But the fact remains that you've got a serial pyro on your hands and the sooner you get the guy behind bars, the safer your community's going to be."

Tess could not argue with that assessment.

"So," he said, as he twisted the key in the ignition, "anyplace good in town to eat?"

He might as well have asked if the Pope was Catholic. A strong streak of native pride had her lifting her chin.

"Somersett is as famous for its Lowcountry cuisine as Egypt is for its pyramids or Rome its Coliseum. There are those who consider the blue softshell crab cream cheese frittata and bananas Foster at the Carriage Corner the closest thing to heaven."

"Good for them, but I was thinking more along the lines of a platter of burned-to-the-crisp bacon and fried eggs."

"You *do* realize that's heresy in this city?"

"You *do* realize that I don't give a rat's ass?"

Tess sighed. "Turn left at the corner."

twenty

Gage lifted his brow when her instructions took them to a pub housed in a waterfront building three blocks away.

"I know the Irish consider Guinness to be food, but it's not exactly what I had in mind. Unless you plan to get me drunk and have your wicked way with me."

"And here I've been told men can't perform when they're drunk."

"Don't worry. I've never had any problems in that regard. Drunk or sober."

Tess believed him. The mental image of him aroused nearly made her knees buckle as she climbed out of the Porsche.

"We need to get something straight," she said as they walked toward the heavy wooden door of the Black Swan pub.

"I know. You're not going to sleep with me."

He didn't sound as if he believed it. Tess didn't blame him, since she no longer believed it herself.

"One of these days you're going to have to accept the idea that you don't know everything, O'Halloran. Actually, this morning I'm leaning toward sleeping with you."

It was, she'd almost convinced herself while driving from the fire scene, the sensible thing to do. After all, everyone knew that sex was mostly mental. Once she got it over with, she could quit fantasizing about all the wicked things she wanted Gage to do to her. All the naughty things she wanted to do to him. Then, once he'd proven no different from any other male, she could focus fully on her arsonist.

"Why do I hear a *but* in that declaration?" he asked.

"Because, although it pains me to admit it, we do have something in common."

"Yeah. We both want to screw each other's brains out."

"Other than that." Tess disliked the crude description, but couldn't argue it, either. "Neither one of us is looking for a long-term commitment. Whatever happens, if and when it happens, it'll just be sex. Like you said yesterday."

To Tess's surprise, he seemed to be actually thinking that over. Had it just been a game with him? Had she lost her appeal once she'd admitted to wanting him?

And why the hell did she suddenly feel as if she were in high school?

"Works for me," he said finally as he

182

pulled open the door to the crowded pub.

A man pouring coffee for a young woman wearing a red power suit and a pair of horn-rimmed glasses looked up as they entered.

"Well, if it isn't the loveliest fire inspector in Somersett," he greeted Tess, the green fields of Erin echoing in his deep voice.

"Which isn't all that difficult, since I'm the *only* female fire inspector in Somersett," she pointed out.

"Wouldn't matter."

Tess shook her head. Grinned in a way that had Gage wondering if she and the Irishman were an item. "You've been kissing the Blarney Stone again."

It was the first time Gage had seen her smile. The wait had been worth it, even if he wasn't the recipient.

The Irishman put the carafe on the counter and drew her into a hug.

As he watched the usually prickly fire cop go easily into the embrace, viewed the guy's arms — which appeared as strong as oak limbs — enfolding her, Gage felt a short, sharp sting of envy.

"I can't believe how busy you are this time of the morning," she said when she finally pulled back. "Especially since you've only been open for breakfast a few months."

"It made sense, since I live above the store, to operate some morning hours," he said. "Business shot through the roof as soon as I put in Wi-Fi and made the pub an Internet café.

"It seems people would rather be talking online than to the person sitting across the table, which, to my mind, is a sorry state of affairs, but now that I'm buying the building from your brother, I'd not be one to pass up any additional profit."

He turned toward Gage. "I'm Brendan O'Neill, proprietor of the Swan. And you'd be?"

"I'm sorry," Tess said before Gage could answer. It was the first time he'd heard an apology escape her lush pink lips. "This is Gage O'Halloran. He's an ATF agent working with me on a case," she tacked on quickly, as if concerned the Irishman would think there was anything personal between them.

"O'Halloran." Brendan O'Neill extended a huge hand. "I knew an O'Halloran back home in Castlelough. Erin, her name was. She was originally from Washington State."

Gage nodded. "She's my cousin." He

could feel Tess's suddenly sharp look and realized she was surprised he'd offered that bit of personal information. "There are a bunch of us scattered around the world; my great-grandparents took that biblical edict to be fruitful and multiply seriously."

"Not unlike the O'Neills back home," Brendan said easily. If he hadn't been watching the man carefully, Gage would have missed the shadow that briefly darkened his blue eyes.

Secrets, Gage thought. *We all have them.* The cop in him wondered what Brendan O'Neill's secrets might be. The man who'd been to hell and back figured it was none of his business. Unless, of course, they involved the delectable Tess Gannon.

"You'd be wanting some privacy to talk," O'Neill said. "I've been doing some paperwork in that booth . . ." He nodded toward the back of the pub. "I'll just be clearing my books off the table to make room for you."

"Thanks," Tess said. Gage liked that she didn't waste time with any polite refusal to disrupt his work. Then was unreasonably irritated when she went up on her toes and brushed a kiss against the other man's cheek. "You're the best."

O'Neill laughed with an easy familiarity as he tousled her bright curls. "Now wouldn't that description better fit you?"

The table was cleared in record time. Coffee was served, menus handed out.

"This isn't exactly what I had in mind," Gage murmured as a platter of eggs Rockefeller and cheese hash went by.

"Haven't you ever heard of compromise?" Tess asked.

"Sure. I just don't believe in it."

"Look, the food's great, but not pretentious, the clientele leans more toward locals than tourists, and you can even get a serving of local color with your eggs."

"What kind of local color?"

"The building's haunted."

"Sure it is." He smirked over the rim of his mug.

"Let me guess. You're a skeptic."

"Comes with the territory." Gage didn't see any reason to mention his own ghosts. "When you're trying to put the bad guys behind bars."

"Good point. But if you were to be in the city long enough, you'd find most places come with a legend."

"Couldn't keep all those ghost tours in business without a few haunted houses," he said.

She frowned, making his fingers itch to smooth away the lines in her forehead. Which wasn't that much of a surprise, since he'd been wanting to touch her all over since he'd arrived on her fire scene yesterday. What came as an unwelcome surprise was the discomfiting desire to have her smile at him the way she'd smiled at O'Neill.

"You don't believe me." Her expression was more serious than the conversation might deem.

"About ghostly hauntings? Not really. But don't take it personally, sweetheart. I don't believe in much of anything."

"Now there's a news flash," she muttered.

"So, have you seen this alleged apparition yourself?"

"No," she admitted. "But I know people who've seen a woman dressed in rags, walking between the tables, weeping. Since this building was, at one time, the site of slave auctions, speculation is that she was forced to watch her family being split up and died of a broken heart. Others, who claim to be picking up on an intense field of negative energy, believe that she either committed suicide, or perhaps was killed when she tried to intervene."

"Well, that's a pleasant tale."

"It's not the only one. There's another ghost upstairs. She was a fishmonger who was hypnotized by an evil dentist who had an office here in the 1890s. He wanted to use her as a medium to locate buried pirate treasure, but when that didn't work out, he supposedly abused her in horrid ways until she died from an overdose of chloroform."

"And you actually believe those stories?"

"Let's just say I don't disbelieve them." She smiled. "Since the ability to maintain an open mind is important when you're trying to put the bad guys behind bars."

Gage liked the way she'd twisted the conversation to throw his own words back at him. Not many people had the guts to challenge him. Since it had been a very long time since he'd felt this way, it took him a moment to realize that he was actually enjoying himself.

A bit of white gold flashed at her throat. Curious, since she wore no other jewelry other than the enameled bugle fire department insignia on her collar and a thick, leather-banded watch, Gage reached across the table and tugged at the chain from which hung a familiar pendant shaped like a Maltese cross with a Roman soldier embossed in the center.

"If you burn me, I will climb to heaven on the flames," he quoted the centurion who'd been sentenced to death for refusing to follow his emperor's orders to persecute Christians.

"Let me guess," Tess said dryly. "You don't believe in patron saints, either."

"Doesn't seem like the guy was able to help himself all that much, since the soldiers ended up drowning him. But you're not the first firefighter I've met who felt protected wearing a St. Florian medal."

"It wasn't mine." She plucked the medal from his hand and tucked it back beneath the collar of her shirt. "It belonged to Daniel McGee."

Knowing that her fiancé had been one of the two men to die in the mill fire two years ago, Gage refrained from pointing out that the patron saint of firefighters hadn't provided all that much protection to McGee.

"Nice metalwork," he said instead. Much more intricate than the mass-produced ones he was accustomed to seeing.

"My friend Bailey made it. Her husband was Danny's partner."

The guy that had survived. Gage was

wondering if Tess had ever wondered about that when O'Neill arrived with a re-fill of coffee.

Ordering without looking at the menu, Gage ignored Tess's heavy sigh at his lack of appreciation for the supposedly famed Lowcountry cuisine. The proprietor, on the other hand, took his order of crisp bacon and eggs without comment.

As soon as they were alone again, Gage got down to business. "Okay, you know your territory better than I do. What's your gut instinct?"

Her mug paused on the way to her mouth. "Wait a minute." She held up a hand. "Did you just admit that there might be something I know that you don't?"

"It's your city. Stands to reason you'd have some idea of motivation."

"Yesterday's fire wasn't vandalism." Which was one of the five top motivations, tending to account for approximately forty percent of all arson fires.

"Vandalism's the third leg of the homi-cidal triangle, along with bed-wetting and cruelty to animals." He pointed out what he suspected she already knew. "The Son of Sam confessed to setting more than two thousand fires before he escalated to shooting people."

"True. But it just doesn't feel like vandalism."

"I agree."

"Yet another miracle," she murmured.

"Hey, I can be agreeable. In the right circumstances." He flashed her a quick leer. "With the right woman."

"Hopefully you'll find her one of these days," she said sweetly.

He had. And while she may be playing hard to get, they both knew it.

"Until we found the vic, I would've put money on it being an urban renewal fire," she said.

Her back-to-business tone dragged him out of a fantasy of pouring the maple syrup from the small bottle sitting in the middle of the table all over her body, then slowly, thoroughly licking it off.

"Any particular reason?" His voice came out an aching rasp. Gage cleared his throat and assured himself that the lust he was having a difficult time controlling was nothing more than the uncomplicated biological attraction of a male to a desirable female. "Other than it's in an area obviously undergoing regentrification?"

"I've dealt with Mannington before. The guy's got a reputation for transforming sleepy coastal towns into must-see tourist attractions. Unfortunately, whenever he starts buying up property, those towns start experiencing a lot of mysterious fires in buildings he just happened to have bought for a song."

"Buildings that were overinsured."

It was an old story. But a profitable one, which was why people were still willing to risk jail time to pull the scam off.

Tess shrugged. "Overinsured's a relative term. Thanks to being born a scion to an old-money southern family, he's considered one of the region's movers and shakers."

"What do you consider him?"

"A slimeball. And a crook who doesn't want to get his hands dirty, so I suspect he's found himself a professional torch."

"That's good enough for me."

"Wow." She lifted her fingers to her temple. "That's two times you've agreed with me in as many minutes. If you're not careful, I might start to think you're not such a prick."

"Just because I lust after your body doesn't mean I can't admire your mind." Unable to resist the lure, he reached across the table and twined a curl around his finger. "I've always considered myself a Renaissance man."

"How lovely that you're not lacking in self-confidence." Tess backed away from his caressing touch. "Mannington's obviously been trying to drive the tenants out of that building so he could tear it down," she said, getting back to business. "Which is why my first guess, when Bobby and I arrived at the scene, was that he was responsible. But tying a prostitute to the bed before burning the place up just doesn't jibe with his usual MO."

"Could be this time he hired himself a kinky torch. Or maybe a guy who harbored a personal grudge."

"Which leads us to the third motivation."

"Revenge."

"Yeah." Revenge arsonists were the easiest to catch, since they were usually in such a rage, they didn't care who witnessed them setting the fire. But they were also the most dangerous, because they set the blaze while caught up in out-of-control emotion.

"There was this woman last holiday season who was in the midst of an ugly divorce battle," Tess divulged. "She put her twin toddlers in the backseat of her Volvo, drove across town to the condo where her soon-to-be ex-husband was shacked up with his administrative assistant, doused the kids and car with gasoline, and lit them up like a Christmas Eve bonfire. The poor babies were still buckled in their safety seats when Bobby and I arrived at the scene."

"So much for the holiday spirit." Even in his self-isolation, Gage had heard about that crime that had dominated the headlines and newscasts over Christmas. "And while we're on the subject of murder, we could also be looking at a fire set to cover up a homicide," he mused.

Tess sighed. "It's occurring to me that this is not the most uplifting of occupations."

"Yeah, but with an arson occurring every five minutes somewhere in the country, being a fire cop makes for great job security."

"If you can keep from burning out." She shook her head. "I didn't mean that to come out as a bad pun."

"I know."

Conversation paused as O'Neill returned with two platters, which he placed on the heavy wooden table, then refilled their coffee cups.

"Ooh, this looks delicious," Tess said, flashing the pub owner another damn smile before he began making the rounds with the coffeepot.

Enticed by the aroma, she dug into a decadent chocolate and strawberry cream cheese–filled French toast.

Gage poked at his plate. "What's this stuff?"

"Grits. They're made from dried milled corn."

"I don't remember ordering grits."

"You didn't have to. You get them automatically down here. They're those lagniappes they have in New Orleans — something for nothing."

He took a sample taste. "Probably because no one would ever pay for them."

"Consider yourself lucky you weren't here last month when every restaurant in town dyed them green for St. Patrick's Day. And you're eating them wrong." She pushed a plate of small white tubs toward him. "Grits are essentially a butter-delivery system."

He stirred the butter from three of the tubs into the white lump of grits, then took a second bite.

"Better," he decided.

But not by much, Tess could tell by his expression.

"They take some getting used to," she al-

195

lowed, wondering if he'd even be here long enough to make the adjustment. Then wondered why she cared.

"I'll take your word for that."

He washed down the taste of the butter-drenched grits with a long gulp of coffee, then turned with more enthusiasm to the well-done bacon.

"The best way to avoid burnout," he said, returning to their original topic, "is to keep reminding yourself what they taught me during training at FLETC. That you're getting the bad guys off the street."

"And that works?"

"Not always."

"Well, that's encouraging." She pinched the bridge of her nose. "If it's the same pyro who claimed responsibility for those other two fires, he's really raised the stakes."

"That's what happens with arsonists. In the beginning, he gets off with something as simple as setting trash fires. After a while, it takes bigger and bigger blazes to give him the same sexual thrill. The engines, the lights, the crowds, all those fire-fighters and looky-loos are all showing up because of him. That idea empowers the guy. For a time."

"Until he gets to the point that he needs

to actually kill to achieve the same rush he once got from setting trash fires."

"Exactly."

"So we have to stop him." Oddly, including O'Halloran in that *we* didn't sound as impossible as when the man had first brought it up yesterday.

"Exactly," he repeated.

He'd set his jaw; his eyes were like blazing ice, hot and cold at the same time.

Eastwood was back, but this time the man sitting across the table reminded Tess not of the High Plains drifter but Dirty Harry, when he pressed that huge .45 against the perp's head and growled, *You've got to ask yourself one question: "Do I feel lucky?" Well, do ya, punk?*

"Stop him legally," she qualified.

"Of course."

Tess toyed with her napkin, a fine Irish linen that would normally seem out of place in a seafront Irish pub, but somehow Brendan made it work.

Brendan O'Neill was a nice man. A good man. A man who'd make a wonderful husband. There'd even been times lately, during the long, lonely nights, Tess had wished she could fall in love with the easygoing Irishman.

Unfortunately, while they shared a

strong mutual affection, there weren't any sparks. Certainly not the kind of chemistry that had slammed into her the minute O'Halloran had climbed out of that sexy black Porsche.

"Why is it I don't believe you about staying on the legal side of the line?"

He eyed her mildly. "Beats me."

"I don't suppose you happen to have a dictionary?"

"Not on me. Why?"

"Because I thought you might want to look up the definition of the word *partner*."

"Next time I'm in a library, I'll check out a *Funk and Wagnall's*. Meanwhile, I've always tended to work on a need-to-know basis."

"They say change is good," Tess countered. "You seem convinced my current cases are linked to the pyro you put behind bars. I think it's time you started giving me more evidence."

"If I had any concrete proof, you'd be the first to know. Right now, I'm working mainly on a hunch."

"Still, if I knew more about your closed case —"

"Okay. I'll share." He glanced down at his watch. "But it's not a short story and I thought you wanted to talk to Mannington."

"I do. But if what you know — or suspect — has anything to do with my case, I'm entitled to be in on it. And if you have any information at all on the mill fire, it would be unconscionable of you to hold it back."

Her green eyes went bright and shiny at the mention of the fire that had taken her fiancé's life, tugging a conscience Gage had forgotten he possessed, and the quiet pain — make that despair — in her voice almost had him feeling guilty for only giving her pieces of information as they became relevant to her crime.

But, dammit, he needed Tess's cooperation.

How willing would she be to partner up with a guy who'd been indicted for murder?

Especially murder by arson.

Maybe he could look up *irony* while he was at it.

He shrugged, this time to loosen the knot that had settled between his shoulder blades. "You're not going to get all emotional and teary on me, are you?"

His sarcasm appeared to work. "Of course not." But the way she rubbed at the back of her neck suggested she was feeling the same boulderlike tension. "Fire cops don't cry."

They both knew that was a lie. But he wasn't about to call her on it.

"Good."

That said, he polished off the rest of his breakfast, trying to ignore the sensation of his arteries clogging as he plowed through the butter-drenched grits.

"Okay," he said finally. "Though it doesn't make any sense, since my Flamemaster's locked up behind bars, I do believe that there's too much similarity — besides the name the guy's taken — between my old case and yours to ignore. And they both have enough in common with the mill fire that there could be a connection. In my case, when things got personal, they got real ugly. I damn well wouldn't want yours to end the same way."

He downed the rest of the coffee. "Now, as much as I'd like to hang around and play with your leg beneath the table, I suppose we ought to get going."

Their hands collided as they both reached for the check.

"Does the department give you an expense account?" he asked.

A laugh burst out of her. "God, you Feds are so removed from the reality. Here in the real world, not only do firefighters not drive around in Porsches, we're expected to buy all our own meals."

"Then breakfast is on me." Not that ATF was buying his meals anymore, but he could certainly afford a few eggs and grits.

She aimed him a sharp, level look. "This isn't a date."

"Hell, no." If it'd been a date he would've had her clothes off by now.

"Okay, then." Her lips curved in a wry smile. "Might as well get something back for my taxes."

They were back in the car and Tess was buckling her seat belt when he said, "Wait a minute."

"For what?"

"For this." He threaded his fingers through the silk of her hair, and with his eyes on hers, he slowly lowered his head.

twenty-one

On some distant level, Tess noted that he was giving her time to back away. A hundred — a thousand — feelings battered away at her as she watched. And waited.

Rather than plundering, as she would have expected, his lips brushed hers. Lightly, tantalizingly, retreating before she could respond. Or reject.

"Tell me," he demanded, his voice as rough as an oyster-shell road, "that you want this."

"I do." Her breath trembled out. Her heart was hammering in her head so loudly she could barely hear her response.

"Right answer."

He took her mouth with the easy confidence of a man who'd kissed more women than he could count. He didn't rush. His lips plucked at hers, lingering, tasting at their leisure in a lengthy exploration that trapped her in gauzy layers of sensation.

Lifting her hands, Tess framed his face. Her lips parted on a throaty moan as she poured herself into the kiss that went on and on, deeper. Darker.

Heaven help her, he tasted just as he had in her fantasy. But amazingly sexier, like a fully aroused male animal.

A harsh growl rumbled from his throat as his wickedly clever hands tugged her shirt free and slipped seductively beneath it.

"You've got two choices," he rasped against her mouth as his caressing touch had her nipples pebbling.

That's what *he* thought. Tess didn't feel as if she'd had any from the moment he'd appeared at her fire scene.

"We can go back to my hotel."

The sound of the metal zipper of her slacks lowering sounded unnaturally loud in the close confines of the Porsche.

"Or" — he slipped his fingers beneath the waistband of the cotton panties, which matched her utilitarian bra, combing a hot path through the curls between her legs — "we can go to your place."

She nearly whimpered when he teased a touch along the slick, moist folds.

"You can't say you don't want me," he said when she hesitated. "You're hot. And" — the strong fingers delved inside her — "really, really wet."

Embarrassingly wet. Which was something she'd worry about later. After she'd satisfied this edgy hunger that had her for the first time understanding how Tennessee Williams's Maggie the Cat must have felt on that hot tin roof.

"We don't have much time," she moaned.

She knew some firefighters took the occasional quickie during a shift. The mystery of why a lieutenant at the station was willing to do the daily grocery shopping for two years was recently solved when he'd gotten caught nailing a produce manager at the Piggly Wiggly. But Tess had never been one of them.

"We'll take things slow next time." There was a liquid sound as he caressed her with a deep, rhythmic stroke. "Right now I just want to be inside you."

Heaven help her, it was what she wanted, too.

But she hadn't had sex in a car since she was eighteen. By the time she'd come home from college for Thanksgiving vacation her freshman year, Danny was already a probie, with an apartment of his own in town. No way was she going to risk getting caught in a compromising position by Brendan, or, worse yet, the beat cop who walked the harbor front.

Feeling more reckless than she ever had

charging into a wall of flames, Tess made her decision. "Take me home."

The Flamemaster hummed along with *The Ride of the Valkyries* blasting from the stereo speakers. "I love the smell of napalm in the morning," he quoted Duvall's famous line from *Apocalypse Now* as he soldered the wires of his latest masterpiece together. The design was ingenious, if he did say so himself. The first fuse, keyed in electronically by his cell phone, lit the sterno, which, after burning down, set off another, longer heat-sensitive igniter that caused the C-4 to explode. "It smells like . . . victory."

The Flamemaster had missed the pleasurable era of Vietnam napalm, but in just a few days the entire city would be breathing in the chemical aroma of his own victory.

They couldn't say he hadn't warned them. Any time now, another letter would be delivered to the paper. Which would, he suspected, immediately call in the cops. Not that they'd recognize him if he suddenly showed up at the police station and yelled, "Hey! Here I am, arrest me!"

He remembered reading that the Zodiac Killer had written notes to the newspapers saying "Stop me before I kill again."

What kind of suicidal idiot would do something like that?

He was too clever to be apprehended. He knew everything they knew. And more. Much, much more.

Some men were born saints.

Others sinners.

The Flamemaster was neither. What he was, what he'd been born to be, was a stone-cold killer. He'd had no choice; the decision had been made for him, woven through his DNA like a deadly, flame-red ribbon.

He began rolling the claylike explosive between his palms. He still had a lot of preparation ahead of him before the big show. Fortunately, The Flamemaster loved his work.

twenty-two

Later, Tess would try to remember how they made it from the Porsche to the front door of her house, and found that the short trip was still hazed in a fog of need.

As soon as they were inside, Gage kicked the door shut with his boot, spun her around, and pressed her against the stained-glass oval. He was between her thighs, rock hard, his fingers digging into her butt.

"This is your last chance." As she strained against him, he pulled back only far enough to allow himself to glare down at her.

There was no love in that gaze. Not even affection. It blazed with a dark and dangerous lust. Which was, Tess realized, exactly what she wanted. What she needed.

"If you intend to say no, this is the time."

Because she believed him, Tess felt a little braver. Bolder.

Gage O'Halloran knew things about sex she'd never even imagined. She could see it, in those smoky gray eyes that looked a hundred years old, she could sense it in the way he moved, a predatory male swagger that couldn't be learned but came from somewhere deep within.

She could taste it, in the tangle of tongues. And feel it in the hard, thick erection pressed against her belly.

She met his warning gaze with a level one of her own. "Someone once told me that thinking will get me in trouble."

"Ain't that the truth," he muttered.

His head swooped down. Teeth clashed as his mouth claimed hers in a hot, voracious kiss.

Showing a total disrespect for her uniform, he ripped her blouse open, sending buttons flying across the polished heart of pine floor she'd spent weeks refinishing.

Her heavy leather belt with the metal Maltese cross buckle was whipped through the loops and hit the wall six feet away.

She sucked in her breath, waiting for him to rip open the ugly black slacks she hadn't bothered to rezip, when he pulled her head back.

"Where's the bedroom?"

The power of his hand tangling in her hair was nearly her undoing. Tess managed to gesture toward the staircase. "Second floor."

She'd no sooner gotten the words out than he scooped her off her feet and tossed her over his shoulder in a classic fireman's carry seldom used anymore.

It might be worlds away from how Scarlett had gotten carried up those sweeping stairs of Tara, but the savage intent radiating from Gage was pure Rhett Butler.

"Which door?"

Being upside down was making her head spin. His broad hand on her butt had her so hot, she was amazed the polyester hadn't melted. "First on the left."

She bounced when he dropped her onto the flower-sprigged quilt she'd found at a yard sale in Charleston. Then cringed when he untied her ugly oxfords and pulled them off.

"Fuck-me shoes," she murmured, realizing she'd spoken out loud when he looked down at her, dark brow arched. She shifted beneath his steady scrutiny, feeling foolish for having brought it up.

"I was thinking I should be wearing a pair of sexy stilettos like Carrie always wore on *Sex and the City*."

Unfortunately, all the shoes in her closet were as practical and unseductive as her underwear. She had three pairs of running shoes, flip-flops for the beach, and two pairs of practical pumps with two-inch heels — one pair black, the other an even more boring taupe — for testifying in court.

"Never watched it." Now there was a surprise. "But believe me, baby, you don't need high heels to be sexy. I've been horny as a three-peckered billy goat since you bitched at me about breaching your crime-scene tape."

"So verbal abuse turns you on?"

"Never has before. But feel free to talk dirty when I'm inside you." He yanked her slacks down her legs.

Had she shaved them this morning? Or was it yesterday? Tess couldn't remember.

Black oxfords, white cotton underwear, and leg stubble. Was that what he was going to remember about her? And why did she care?

It was just sex, she reminded herself.

Lust.

No strings.

No promises.

She gasped when he whipped off her bra and panties with an expertise that told her he was a man who knew his way around women's clothing.

Equally efficient with his own, he shed

his jacket and shoulder holster, then jerked today's black T-shirt over his head. Tess's breath hitched at the muscled curves and contours of his broad chest. His skin was the color of polished walnut, which meant he spent more time in the sun than most cops she knew. Unless he went to a salon. *Yeah. Right.* She could more easily imagine O'Halloran facing down the Clanton brothers at the O.K. Corral than putting on white safety goggles and lying down in a tanning booth.

Her gaze followed the arrowing of dark hair to where it disappeared below his jeans. With his eyes on hers, he unfastened the silver rodeo belt she suspected might be a souvenir of his days in Wyoming, pulled off his boots, peeled his socks off his long, narrow feet, then shoved his jeans and briefs down his legs.

Breathe! Easier to think than to do, as Tess eyed the rampant penis that jutted aggressively out in front of him, even longer and thicker than in last night's fantasy.

Her throat tight with expectation, she swallowed.

"Maybe this isn't such a good idea."

"I gave you the chance to back out downstairs. You didn't."

211

Oh Lord, what had she gotten herself into? Tess wasn't naive. She knew about the dangers in hooking up with a stranger.

"You wouldn't rape me." That's probably what the girls who'd gotten in Ted Bundy's Volkswagen had thought.

"Hell no." Not only was he horny, now he was pissed off. *Not a good combination.*

He took her hand and wrapped her fingers around his length. He was hot, hard, and solid. And huge.

"I'm not into hurting women."

"That's encouraging."

"Nor forcing them."

He'd begun moving her hand up and down, in long, firm pulls. The power throbbing in the raised dark veins caused a gush of hot moisture to flood from between her thighs.

"So I'm giving you a second chance to change your mind." In contrast to the suede-soft skin beneath her fingers, Gage's voice was harsh with intensity.

"No." A pearl of moisture glistened on the tip of his penis. Tess had a sudden urge to lick it off. "I haven't changed my mind."

A slow, satisfied smile made an appearance.

"But I don't have any . . ."

Oh, God, she was so out of practice she

couldn't even say the word. She'd used birth control with Danny until they'd decided to make a baby. STDs hadn't been an issue.

"Did I mention I was a Boy Scout?"

She had come to the conclusion, watching him at the fire scene this morning, then talking to him in the Swan, that he was telling the truth about being here to track down her pyro. Still, although she had a hard time picturing him as a Boy Scout, when he retrieved the foil package from his jeans Tess had to give him points for being prepared.

She watched, mesmerized as he sheathed his heavy bulk in latex. Who knew condoms came supersized?

He leaned over her.

Tess held her breath.

His dark fingers toyed with the chain around her neck. "Take it off," he commanded gruffly.

"No." Tess's fingers curled around the St. Florian pendant.

"Look, sweetheart, I don't know what gives you the idea that I'm willing to share. There isn't room enough in this bed for three people. Especially if one of them's a goddamn ghost."

"What do you care? If it's only sex?"

Tess challenged. "No shackles or messy emotional baggage, right?"

His face was close to hers, his eyes narrowed in that Dirty Harry squint.

"Right. Okay, so keep the damn necklace on. And let's see which of our names you scream when I make you come."

"I never scream."

Gasped, maybe. Even whimpered. But scream? Not in this lifetime.

"Wanna bet?" Apprehension kicked in when he abruptly flipped her onto her stomach; she felt the weight of him as he mounted the bed and covered her body with his larger, stronger one.

Then his hand reached beneath her, stroking between her engorged lips, coaxing more hot juices to flow out of her, and she forgot to be afraid.

"You want me." His teeth nipped at the nape of her neck like a wolf staking claim on his mate.

"Sex," she corrected. "I want sex."

"Ask and you shall receive."

He lifted her up onto her knees and nudged her legs far apart. She was braced on her forearms, bare-naked ass in the air, and had never felt more vulnerable. More exposed. More excited.

Tess had never thought of herself as

weak, or submissive; she'd always had a reputation for remaining calm and controlled under pressure. She was an independent woman, a fire cop, for crying out loud, in charge of herself and any situation life could throw at her.

She'd proven that time and time again in a world populated by strong, macho men. But she'd never met anyone who wielded his male power, who made her want to surrender her self-control, like Special Agent Gage O'Halloran.

One large hand caressed her swollen breasts, pinched her stiff nipples, creating havoc on her body, while his other palm pressed against the small of her back, restraining her, not that Tess had any intention of going anywhere.

His penis was hot and heavy between her cheeks as he reached between them again and spread her wetness, his fingers working her, opening her, preparing her.

"So, how do you want it?" His breath was hot against her neck.

"The same way you do," she muttered into the pillow. "Fast and hard."

Tess cried out not from pain but passion as he surged into her, plunging to the hilt.

He stilled, allowing her to adjust to the erotic invasion. "Are you okay?"

No, she was not okay. *Don't stop now, dammit!*

"Just do it," she muttered.

Tess did not have to ask twice. He began to move, his rough thrusts so deep she could feel him pounding against her womb. His heavy balls slapped against her as he pumped into her, again and again, his ragged breath fanning the nape of her neck in sync with his strokes. Faster. Harder.

The pistoning hips driving her into the mattress were so strong, so powerful, Tess collapsed, falling flat onto her face, nipples scraping against the cotton bedcover.

Without missing a beat, he yanked her back onto her knees, his hands tight on her hips, balancing her as he drove them both toward release.

The friction was so hot it was nearly unbearable. Her breath was being ripped from her in broken gasps.

His fingers dug into her flesh. "Now," he instructed against the whorl of her ear.

The growled command was all it took. Tess came, not with a scream, as he'd predicted, but with a low, keening cry that sounded as if it'd been ripped from the throat of a wounded animal.

His hips jerked, every muscle in his body

tensed. His climax was as hard as everything else about the man. And utterly silent.

Which for some strange reason, as he collapsed onto her, made Tess want to weep.

twenty-three

While Somersett might admittedly be more laid back than a lot of northern cities or even Atlanta, with its gleaming skyscrapers, spaghetti knot of crowded highways, and sprawling suburbs, just driving past St. Brendan's Cathedral and over the bridge into the marsh was usually all it took to make Tess's mind and body unwind.

Of course, usually she wasn't tracking down a killer. Nor driving with a man she'd just had down-and-dirty sex with. She'd considered, when trying to make up her mind what to do about Gage O'Halloran, that getting involved might make working with him awkward. But she needn't have worried. It was as if he'd put that unnervingly distant persona right back on with his clothes.

To fill the silence, she played tour guide, pointing out various points of interest during the long drive that meandered on two-lane roads through fishing villages, past sweeps of blinding spring-green spartina grass, still black waters reflecting stark gray cypress, and crumbling, once magnificent plantation homes.

There was no quick or easy way to get to Savannah from Somersett. Actually, there was no quick, easy way to get to anywhere from her home city, which was just the way Somersettians liked it, because it meant that the reverse was also true.

Admittedly, some outsiders slipped easily into the slow, laid-back Lowcountry lifestyle, enjoying the food and friendliness enough to put up with the humidity and mosquitoes.

Mostly, however, outsiders brought change. And the one thing that the majority of the residents of the three-hundred-year-old city had in common was a bred-in-the-bone resistance to change.

And wasn't she the same way? Though she knew that she'd never be the same person she'd been before the mill fire, Tess had moved on with her life. She wasn't certain she'd ever be truly happy again, but at least she was content.

Or had been until Gage had arrived in Somersett, stirring up both trouble and her emotions. Bringing unwanted change.

Tess breathed a sigh of relief as they crossed over the Savannah River into the city. Although he hadn't seemed the least bit inclined to share any personal conver-

219

sation, just in case, wanting to avoid any discussion of their whirlwind sexcapade, her sightseeing spiel had become so damn chatty, she'd begun to drive herself crazy.

The offices of Mannington Development, LTD, located in Savannah's historic district, were housed in a French Empire Victorian with a view of the Spanish-moss-draped environs of Forsyth Park.

Belying Savannah's reputation as "Hostess City of the South," Donald Mannington was not the least bit welcoming.

"Back again so soon, Miz Gannon?" he drawled from behind a huge antique desk. Not only did he not stand up when his secretary led them into the office, he didn't bother to take his Gucci loafers off his desk. "I would've thought you'd be getting tired of making that long drive between Savannah and Somersett."

"It's *Inspector* Gannon," she reminded him, as she always did. He'd never granted her the title, but she was damn well going to continue to claim it. "This is Special Agent O'Halloran." She paused as his beady brown eyes narrowed. "From the Bureau of Alcohol, Tobacco, and Firearms."

"Alcohol, tobacco, firearms, *and* explosives, after the Homeland Security bill moved our law enforcement group over to the Justice Department," Gage said helpfully.

Tess nodded. "And explosives."

They'd gotten Mannington's attention. The shiny black alligator shoes dropped to the plush white carpet. He sat up a little straighter in the high-backed black leather chair.

His expression morphed from scorn to southern good-old-boy geniality. "If this is about those fireworks I set off last week —"

"We're not here about any fireworks." Tess cut him off.

"Well, I'm real glad to hear that." His smile was as false as the rug perched atop his head like a roadkill possum. "Since it was my boy's birthday and you know how young'uns enjoy their bottle rockets."

Bottle rockets had the unfortunate tendency to set neighborhood roofs on fire, but that wasn't the issue.

"It's about yesterday's fire in the apartment building you own in Somersett on the corner of River View and North Harbor."

He shook his head. "That was an unfortunate incident."

"That's not exactly the word I'd use

when a woman gets murdered."

"Murdered?" His brow lifted in an exaggerated show of skepticism. "While my insurance investigators haven't checked it out yet because y'all still have it sealed off —"

"As a crime scene."

"A *possible* crime scene," he corrected. "As I was saying, the insurance company hasn't been on-site, but I've heard, through the grapevine, that the deceased woman was the one who started the fire that sent so many needy people to homeless shelters."

"Needy people who just last week were protesting the fact that they hadn't had hot water or air-conditioning for weeks," Tess countered.

He shrugged shoulders clad in a blue-and-white-striped seersucker suit. "If you'd ever been a landlord, Miss Gannon, you'd realize that a few malcontents go with the territory."

"*Inspector* Gannon," Gage corrected, just as Tess had done earlier. The warning in his tone caused a little muscle to throb in Mannington's temple.

"Of course," he corrected. "I apologize, Inspector, and will confess to being a bit of a dinosaur when it comes to women's issues. After all, men of my generation aren't accustomed to southern ladies choosing to spend their days mucking around in wet ashes with dead bodies, rather than making a nice home for their husbands and children."

"Different strokes," Tess said mildly, refusing to let him know his words had pricked. Having his finger in so many pies all over the Lowcountry, he had to have known about the fire that had prevented her becoming a wife and mother. "Could you tell us where you were two nights ago?"

"Of course." Beginning to relax again, he folded his too-soft hands over his large belly. "My wife, Dolly, and I attended a UGA fund-raiser. I'm a Dawg."

Tess couldn't have said it better herself.

"The bulldogs are, of course, UGA's mascot," he explained to Gage. "I'm an alumnus."

"Good for you," Gage responded agreeably.

"What time did you leave?" Tess pressed on.

"Having no idea I'd need an alibi, I'm not certain. I'd guess about half past ten. Maybe eleven, since I stopped to chat with some folks on my way out. If you need a more precise time, perhaps you could ask your mayor. Since he was there."

The comment was meant to remind Tess of the old boy's club, to which he belonged and she didn't.

"I may do that," she said. "After you left, did you and your wife go anywhere else?"

"No. Dolly had a headache; she took a sleeping pill and went to bed as soon as we arrived home."

"But you stayed up?"

"The Dawgs were playing the Blue Devils on ESPN. I thought I'd catch the end of the game."

"So no one can verify you didn't leave after your wife went to sleep?"

He clucked his tongue. "I don't understand why you're constantly thinking the worst of me, Miss — I mean, Inspector — Gannon. I've always been a supporter of your fire department. Why, just last month I made a hefty contribution to the Firefighters Widows and Orphans fund."

"Yeah, you're a regular Mother Teresa." Tess didn't bother to hide her scorn. She stood up, put her palms on the glossy desktop, and leaned toward him. "Look, let's stop beating around the bush, okay, Mannington? I know you've hired yourself a torch in the past —"

"Suspectin' ain't knowin'," he interjected smoothly. "And knowin' ain't provin'."

"I'm going to prove it," she flared. "And believe me, if I find out you had anything to do with that woman dying yesterday, I will personally nail your balls to the firehouse wall."

He didn't appear intimidated. "Such unseemly language for a southern lady."

"I'm not a lady. I'm a fire cop."

"Your mama and daddy must be real proud." His tone said just the opposite. It also hit a raw nerve. "Too bad what happened to your daddy," he continued. "How's he adjusting to retirement?"

"Just fine," Tess lied through gritted teeth.

Doyle Gannon's ongoing fight to get put back on an engine after a five-member commission had forced him into retirement had been documented for months in Lowcountry newspapers.

The inability to work would have been bad enough for a man whose entire life had been about firefighting, but making the situation even worse was the cash-strapped county adoption of new disability regulations that no longer recognized a firefighter or police officer's "diminished future earning capacity." The resultant draconian benefit cut had many former first responders struggling to survive on incomes below the poverty level.

"Glad to hear it," Mannington lied with a weasel's sly smile. "The mayor and I were just talking the other night about how it was a real shame he came up with the short end of that stick in that final hearing."

Tess crossed her arms over the front of her chest and glared at him. No way was she going to discuss her family situation with this man. She also suddenly wondered how much Mannington had to do with the board's decision.

"Well, thank you for your time, Mr. Mannington." Gage unfolded his length from a leather barrel chair. "We'll be getting back to you when we've got more of a handle on the cause of the fire that damaged your building."

"Thank *you,* Special Agent O'Halloran." Mannington flashed the smile Tess figured he must use to distract politicians while picking their pockets for tax incentives.

He tilted his head and studied the ATF agent a bit more closely. "Would you be any relation to Doctor Patrick O'Halloran, at Emory University in Atlanta?"

"Patrick's a distant cousin on my father's side," Gage surprised her by saying.

"Well, now, isn't that a small world? Pat replaced my knee last year. The man's a genius. I was back to work in under a month."

"Cousin Pat's always been real handy with tools," Gage drawled. "He sells chainsaw animal sculptures on eBay as a hobby. If you're ever in the market for a life-size redwood grizzly bear, he's your man."

"Well, isn't that interesting?" The developer turned ashen at the idea of having been under a chainsaw sculptor's knife.

"All the O'Hallorans pride themselves on being Renaissance men." Gage shot a look at Tess. The western twang had morphed into something resembling a southern accent. Obviously he was playing good cop to her bad cop.

"Is that true?" she asked as she and Gage walked out of the building. It wasn't yet noon, but a ball of humid heat hit like a fist. "About that doctor and his chainsaw?"

"I've no idea."

"I figured it was a lie."

"The Supreme Court gave cops the right to prevaricate when questioning a suspect," he reminded her mildly. "Since we're not allowed to just take out our side-arms and shoot the bad guys for being pond scum, getting creative with the truth helps level the playing field. I made a personal connection with Mannington, which may or may not come in handy down the road."

"Are you and that surgeon even related?"

He shrugged as he put on those mirrored shades he'd hooked to his shirt pocket. "I haven't a clue. Like I said, there are a lot of O'Hallorans scattered across the country. That Atlanta sawbones might be a distant cousin. Or he might not be. My main objective at the moment was to get you out of there before you put your fist into the jerk's fat, supercilious face."

"He pisses me off."

"Why don't you tell me something I couldn't figure out for myself?"

"Did it show that he got to me with that crack about my father?" she asked as he opened the door of the Porsche.

"Let's put it this way. If I were you, I wouldn't plan on running off anytime soon to Vegas for the National Poker Championships."

"I hate poker." She'd never picked up a deck of cards again since the day of the mill fire. "And I hate Mannington."

"He's a scumbag. And I wouldn't be at all surprised if he pays hookers to let them tie him up. But it would've been a helluva risk to sneak out of the house and drive all the way to Somersett and back when there were just as many prostitutes to abuse in Savannah."

"He's more well known in Savannah. He'd have a higher risk of being recognized."

"He'd also know more escape routes here. Feel more comfortable in his routine. A lot of serials are, in that way, like everyone else. They like routine. Familiarity. And they don't like work commutes."

Giving him credit for having more experience than she did, Tess didn't argue. But she was still seething as they drove back to Somersett.

twenty-four

Trees lined the road, their leafy branches arching overhead so that it felt as if they were in a shady green tunnel.

"You want to tell me what went on back there in Mannington's office?" he asked after they'd been driving for some thirty minutes, the jazz keyboard of Thelonious Monk coming from the car's speakers filling in the silence.

"You were there."

She ignored his questioning look, her gaze directed out the passenger window as they passed a gray weatherworn house with a sagging porch, tar paper roof, and chickens pecking industriously in a scrubby dirt yard. A sturdy gray horse, known locally as a marsh tackie, stood patiently tethered to an abandoned and rusting tractor.

In contrast to the seediness, a deep purple clematis climbed the mailbox post and someone had planted what seemed to be a garden of colorful wooden whirligigs.

"Yeah, but I feel like I missed a couple chapters. Such as the one about your father."

"I don't want to talk about it."

"Okay."

Monk had given way to Coltrane, then someone else Tess, who'd always enjoyed jazz, couldn't recognize.

"Who's that?" She nodded toward the dash.

"Boney Jones."

Tess's CD collection was eclectic, but she didn't have a fan's depth of knowledge of any of the genres. She just knew what she liked. And she liked the steel drums adding a Caribbean touch to the blend of R&B and jazz.

"I'm a little surprised you listen to jazz."

He shot her a sideways glance. "You figured I'd go more for some twangy somebody-done-somebody-wrong song."

She shrugged, hating to be caught stereotyping. "The boots and the accent tend to point more toward Strait than Coltrane."

"Don't knock Strait. King George is a genius. And didn't they teach you at fire school that sometimes appearances are deceiving?"

"Of course." It was the same thing Bailey had reminded her last night. "They also taught me profiling."

"Which is a good tool," he allowed. "So long as it's kept in perspective."

It was her turn to shoot him a look. "Have I ever told you that I hate it when you're right?"

His lips quirked. "You don't have to. It shows. Right here." He reached across the center console and ran the back of his fingers up the side of her face. "You might have the worst poker face the guy upstairs ever put on a human being, but He was damn generous when he was passing out the looks."

She batted away his hand. "I'm not a suspect, so you don't have to lie to me."

He narrowed his eyes. "You don't see it, do you?" he asked, seemingly as much to himself as to her.

"See what?"

"What a man sees when he looks at you."

"You already got the sex without having to hand out the sweet talk," she reminded him, which in turn reminded *her* what her mother used to warn her about a boy not buying the cow if he could get the milk for free.

"Damn good sex," he agreed. "Though you realize by holding back that scream, you've just motivated me all the more to break through those barbed-wire barricades you've erected around yourself."

Thinking of what he'd said about not judging a cowboy until you'd seen him ride, Tess had to admit that Gage had been damn good in the saddle, but saw no point in boosting his already-inflated ego.

"You're a fine one to talk about barricades. Being how you're not exactly Dr. Phil yourself."

He didn't deny it. "Another thing we've got in common. And it's not just that your skin feels like flower petals, or that your breasts are a perfect handful — or mouthful —"

"Not that you'd know," she muttered.

"We were up against time constraints," he reminded her. "But don't worry, I plan to taste every inch of your long, slim body in round two. And to continue making my point, it's not just the fact that your eyes seem to take up most of your face. It's the intelligence in them that gets to me. The depth of emotion when you care about someone or something as strongly as you do, standing up for that woman some sick son-of-a-bitch turned into a charred corpse. Or nailing some crooked developer. You're an attractive female by anyone's standards, Tess Gannon. But it's your passion that grabs a man by the throat."

The words shouldn't have given her such a secret rush of pleasure. But, dammit, they did. "By the balls, you mean."

"Them, too," he said agreeably.

He took her hand from where it had fisted in her lap, lifted it, and brushed his lips across her knuckles.

The slow movement of those lips, which were usually grim and tightly drawn, was both arrogant and charming. The arrogance she could deal with; it was the charm Tess feared could be her undoing.

"I haven't even made up my mind if there's going to be a round two," she said.

"You also can't bluff worth a damn. If you're going to stay in the arson-detecting business, Inspector, you're going to have to find your inner poker player."

"I'm working on it," she muttered, knowing that once again, he was right.

"So your dad's a firefighter?" he asked casually.

"I told you I didn't want to talk about him."

"Family troubles?"

"Not the kind you're probably thinking."

Tess kept thinking back to what Mannington had said. Could he have influenced the committee who was, literally, holding her father's future in its hands?

Worse yet, was he keeping Doyle Gannon's disability from him to get back at her?

Do gators shit in the swamp?

"Turn here," she said suddenly.

Gage didn't question, just made a sharp right onto a narrow gravel road that cut through a stand of marsh grass.

"In about a quarter mile, you'll get to a strip of beach."

"Okay." Again, she appreciated him not asking why they'd taken the detour, or making some crack about sex on the sand.

The sun spilled over the still water, creating pools that sparkled like pale gold.

Just as she'd remembered, the road came to a dead end. Gage parked the car, pocketed the keys, and followed her along the narrow boardwalk that crossed mud and a low dune to the silvery packed sand.

The light wind coming off the Atlantic was a welcome contrast to the wet earth and rotting wood smell of the marsh. It cleared her head, cooled her temper.

Seeming to need to walk off her frustration, she marched along the water's edge. The tide was out; sea oats waved in the breeze and wet sand glistened like mirrors.

"Daddy joined the department right out of high school, when he was only eighteen years old," she said.

She edged around some tangled seaweed. A flock of seagulls, who'd been ripping apart a small, beached shark, took to the sky in a furious flapping of wings as she and Gage approached.

The circling gulls screeched at them furiously, then fluttered back to the sand after the intruders had passed, returning to their meal.

"He was a third-generation firefighter."

"Which would make you a fourth."

"My great-grandfather was in charge of the horses that pulled the pumper. In fact, the apparatus floor at my Harbor View station used to be the stable."

"That's quite a family history."

"If it's one thing we have a lot of down here in the South, it's history."

They walked a bit farther. A pod of pelicans flew by, skimming the waves, searching for fish in the surf.

"My parents didn't want me to join the department. They wanted me to go to law school."

"It's probably natural for parents to want a better, richer life for their kids. It's part of the American dream."

"It was *their* dream. My mother is constantly reminding me that my closest friend is an assistant district attorney." She stopped and looked up at him. "Tell me the truth. Can you honestly see me wearing a suit and pantyhose and pearls arguing a case in some courtroom?"

Gage would rather see her in just the pearls, with her smooth pale skin gleaming in moonlight.

"Absolutely." He raised his hand in a pledge when her expressive tawny brows shot down toward her nose. "If I were on the jury, I'd definitely vote to convict."

When she bent down to pick up a brown-and-white-speckled cockle shell, her dark slacks tugged against her butt. Even as ugly as they were, the trousers couldn't hide what he'd already discovered for himself — that the inspector had one very fine ass.

"What if I were on the other side? Arguing for the defense?"

"I'd vote your client innocent on all counts. But I'll admit it's harder to envision you on that side of the courtroom."

"Well, I can't envision myself on *either* side of a courtroom. So, as you apparently already know, I compromised on the college issue by getting a degree in fire safety and engineering technology, came back to town, aced both the civil service and physical firefighting exams, and joined the department."

"Which, despite his supposedly loftier dreams for his little girl, undoubtedly made your father proud."

"I don't know." She shoved a hand through her windblown curls. "He wasn't in the beginning. Mama worried I was a lesbian. Daddy was more succinct. He claimed that only dykes wear bunkers." It was one of the few times she'd ever seen her parents in full agreement.

"Want me to vouch for you?"

Tess laughed. Then was surprised that this man, of all people, could make her feel better.

"Thanks anyway, but I think I'll pass on the offer. Mama came around when I got engaged, and sometimes Daddy seems to be getting used to the idea of me being in the department. But he's not real good at showing emotion, so it's hard to tell."

"That goes with the territory. He's undoubtedly seen a lot of bad stuff. Civilians see the first responders show up in their shiny red trucks with sirens screaming and lights flashing and feel a rush of relief because it signals to them that everything's going to be okay. If a firefighter started crying once things go south, people'd lose confidence."

"I know. It's just that . . ."

She paused. Shook her head.

"Anyway, he started coughing a few months ago. He was trying to brush it off, but after he passed out and nearly fell off the roof at a house fire, the chief backed up Mama, who'd been trying to get him to go to the doctor for ages."

"Is it cancer?"

"No. At least not yet."

She'd witnessed too many cases of fire-fighters dying of cancers that were a result of years of breathing in chemicals. Especially among her father's generation, who considered themselves too macho to wear safety masks.

"But his lungs are so smoke damaged, three different doctors have predicted that if he breathes any more toxins, they'll shut down. One doctor wants to put him on a waiting list for a transplant, but he refuses to consider surgery because he intends to go back to work."

"Even though it could kill him?"

Tess looked out over the ocean, where a shrimp boat chugged along the horizon, trailing its long net behind it.

"He claims it's better than dying day by

day sitting at home watching soap operas and *Oprah*. Though he's too proud to admit it, I think part of the problem is that with the new disability regulations, he could die and leave Mama in debt with a mountain of hospital bills."

She sighed heavily. "For as long as I can remember, all he ever wanted to talk about were the fires he'd fought. Now his conversations revolve around lawsuits and how angry he is at doctors, and, quote, 'those goddamn pissant bureaucrats who wouldn't know a pike pole from their assholes.' Unquote."

"What does your mother say?"

"Nothing." Tess sighed. "She just bakes."

"Bakes?"

"You know, like pies, cookies, cakes. *Bakes*. It's her way of handling stress. When he was working, she'd spend nearly his entire shift in the kitchen. It's a wonder we kids didn't grow up looking like blimps. Most people would lose weight while they were recovering being blown out of a burning building. I gained five pounds." Tess shook her head. "These days, I think she's at the oven 24/7."

She turned and looked up at him. "And I have absolutely no idea why I'm telling you all this."

"Maybe because I'm safe?"

She barked a laugh. "You. Safe." Her thistledown curls bobbed as she shook her head. "Talk about your oxymorons."

"I'm safe because I'm an outsider."

"An 'away.' That's what we call nonnatives."

Although he'd lived in Los Angeles for more than a decade, Gage knew all about regional insularity. Hadn't his own father, somewhat justifiably, complained about all the Californians flooding into Wyoming?

"It's because I'm not from here, and will be going away once your torch is behind bars, that you can share things you wouldn't necessarily tell anyone else, since I'll be taking your secrets with me when I leave Somersett."

He had to steel himself against the emotion — sadness? regret? — that shadowed her eyes. Just a few miles offshore was a graveyard of sunken ships, whose captains had dared risk the warnings against sea monsters clearly labeled on ancient mariner's charts.

Here there be dragons.

The prudent thing to do would be to back away now. Before it was too late.

Like it isn't already.

"Tell me about McGee."

"Danny?" The shadow in her gaze was replaced with startled surprise. "Why?"

"Because someone might have wanted to kill him. And if we knew who that someone might be . . ."

She stiffened and threw up her chin. "No one would have any reason for killing Danny. Everyone loved him."

"Including you."

"Of course I did. I wouldn't have agreed to marry him if I didn't."

"But you *didn't* marry him."

"Only because he died before I could."

"But *you* didn't. Die, that is." Because it had been too long since he'd touched her, tasted her, Gage lifted her chin with his thumb. "And if the guy was as fine a man as you say he was, I have a hard time believing he would've wanted you to spend the rest of your life acting as if you had."

"I don't know what you're talking about!" She had to raise her voice over the thunder of two fighter jets from the Marine Corps air base in Beaufort roaring by overhead.

When she started to jerk back, his fingers tightened. "When was the last time you had sex?"

"A couple hours ago," she shot back. "And the fact that you seem to have already forgotten it certainly doesn't say much for my performance."

"I haven't forgotten a thing. Including how hot — and tight — you were. Hell, you had so much pent-up need inside you, sweetheart, I'm surprised we didn't set that pretty bed of yours on fire."

She didn't deny it. "There's more to life than sex."

"You might have been able to convince yourself of that for the past two years. But I think the genie just got blasted out of the bottle, so to speak."

Neither did she deny that, which was just as well, since the flush rising on those sharp angular cheekbones and the darkening of her eyes gave her away.

She'd just opened her mouth to respond when a tinny chime came from the cell phone hooked to her belt. Tess groaned when she viewed the caller ID.

"Oh, shit. Just what I need."

twenty-five

She flipped the phone open. "Gannon." It was half bark, half sigh. "I'm on my way back from Savannah. Yessir, I was interviewing Mannington. Yessir, I know he's a very influential man."

Tess exchanged a frustrated look with Gage, who knew exactly what she was feeling. "Yessir." She sounded as if she were choking down foul-tasting medicine. "Absolutely. We'll meet you there."

She slammed the phone closed. Stuck it back in its holder. Rubbed her temple. "That was the commissioner."

"I figured as much."

"He and Mannington's frat-brother mayor are pissed that I stepped on the bastard's Italian shoes." She was marching back toward the boardwalk, renewed frustration radiating from every pore.

"Not unusual behavior from politicians." Gage knew a lot about political pressure.

"I know. But that doesn't mean it doesn't piss me off. He wanted to know if I understood how important the port renewal project is to the city's tax base." She made a sound of disgust. "Like any of that money's going to go toward first responders."

"Probably won't."

"Would you stop agreeing with me?"

"Sure."

Tess rolled her eyes heavenward, as if praying for patience. Then muttered an earthy curse that probably wasn't featured in any southern belle's guide to etiquette but suited her situation.

"They're going to meet us at the station."

"If you're already going to get reamed out for stepping on the guy's toes, why don't we turn around, go back to Savannah, and I'll punch out Mannington for you?"

"You're joking."

"You know, I'm not sure."

Gage tried to tell himself that these feelings of protection he was experiencing toward the woman were nothing more than any other man would feel under the same circumstances. It was only natural, woven into the male DNA, going back to the beginning of time.

He imagined dragging a not unwilling Tess back to his cave. In his fantasy, she was clad in a sexy bit of animal hide so minuscule she might as well not have bothered with it. Then, because this was neither the time nor the place, and because she had an annoyance of politicians waiting for her back in the city, he brutally cut off the mental fantasy of peeling a skintight Betty Rubble dress down her body.

"I'm probably not," he decided. "Since federal agents aren't exactly known for their senses of humor and I don't recall being issued one with my badge."

Her strawberry-parfait lips quirked. "I really wanted to despise you."

"Yeah, I've figured that out for myself." He also knew the feeling, having despised himself ever since he'd let his obsession with The Flamemaster destroy the life of a woman he'd pledged to love and honor until death they did part. "But right now you're stuck with me, Slim. So you may as well make the best of it."

Her phone trilled again, forestalling any response.

"Damn, you'd think they could hold their water for just a few more minutes," she muttered. "Gannon."

"Oh, hey, Bobby. How did you do on . . . what?" The faint tinge of color the sea breeze and anger had brought to her cheeks faded. "Okay. Yeah, we're on our way back to town now." She closed the phone. "The Flamemaster sent another letter."

"To the press?"

"Yeah. He's claiming credit for yesterday's fire. And threatening a surprise finale for the Easter weekend."

"That's four days away."

"Gee," she said with a spark of that sarcasm that had amused him when they'd first met, "a Fed who can count." She shoved her shades onto the top of her head and pressed her fingers against her eyes. "Sorry. That was uncalled for."

"You don't have to apologize to me."

"Obviously you've never heard of GRITS."

"Not only have I heard of them, I've even eaten them," he reminded her.

"No, I'm referring to the other kind. Girls raised in the South. Politeness is one of the rules."

"Must be hard, for a woman who chafes against rules."

"While my mother's too well-mannered to say so, I think she secretly believes I'm a changeling."

"How do you view yourself?"

"I don't know." Tess shrugged her slender shoulders. "Most of the time, as a

strong, independent, smoke-eating fire
cop."

"And the other times?"

She folded her arms. "How is this relevant to our investigation?"

"Humor me."

"I thought that's what I've been doing."
She blew out a breath. "Okay. As a misfit."

"Join the club," he said dryly.

He'd never fit in — not as a rancher, not
in the regimental atmosphere of the air
force, nor in the Byzantine bureaucracy of
the ATF. Even after they'd been married,
Kim had accused him of being the quintessential lone wolf — a charge he couldn't
deny.

"And although you didn't ask for my
opinion, I'll give it to you anyway," he said.
"You're a good investigator, Tess; you're
smart, thorough, and although you've been
doing the job long enough to have learned
the ropes, you're still new enough not to be
too jaded to care."

"If I ever become jaded, I'll quit," she
said as she began walking again. "Because
victims deserve someone who'll fight for
them."

"Another thing we can agree on."

She looked surprised by that. Surprised
and a little suspicious, like a woman wait-

ing for a punch line. "Not that we're keeping score," she said.

"Of course not," he lied.

"I keep thinking about the possibility of a connection between my arsonist and yours, but if they're not related, that rope's one helluva coincidence."

"The guy's built quite a name for himself in pyro circles. Maybe he had a protégé while he was on the outside. Or an admirer."

Tess shivered. "Well, that's a pleasant thought."

"Anyone willing to use flame as a murder weapon is already hardwired different from the average person. Even the average criminal."

"Now that the stakes have just been upped, maybe we should go to California to talk to him," Tess suggested. "Grill him and see if he knows anything about my copycat."

"I doubt you'd have to do much grilling. If I show up at the prison with you by my side, he probably won't be able to resist trying to impress you. If for no other reason than to piss me off."

"I guess you're probably not his favorite person."

"He hates my guts. And the feeling's mutual."

"It sounds as if you know him well." Her tone invited elaboration.

"Yeah." She may not be as proficient as he at using silence as an interrogation tool, but since Tess appeared willing to wait until doomsday for his response, he answered the unspoken question.

"I chased the guy for three years before we nailed him. I spent a lot of time in his head."

"Too much," she suggested.

"Not enough, or I would have nabbed him sooner. Before —" He slammed his mouth shut so fast, the clash of his teeth reverberated like a gunshot in his head.

"Before what?"

"It's not important."

"Why don't you let me be the judge —"

Partly to shut her up, but partly because he wanted to taste her again, Gage curled his fingers around her upper arms, dragged her onto her toes, and captured her mouth.

Once again, heat flared instantly, like a match to dry kindling. She tasted like aroused female. Like hot, raunchy sex.

Gage had known that despite her initial prickly-as-a-porcupine attitude toward him at that apartment fire scene, Tess Gannon would be hot. But damn, the woman was definitely surpassing expectations.

She was certainly not prickly now; in fact, her body was melting against his like wax beneath a summer South Carolina sun.

The kiss ripened. Deepened. When her tongue thrust between his lips in a pantomime of what his stiffened dick wanted to do to her again, his balls tightened.

"Oh, baby."

Baby, baby, baby. The word resonated in his head like a mantra.

She clung tighter, her hardened nipples pressing into his chest like small stones. He could feel her heart racing like a rabbit's; his was pounding just as hard and every bit as fast.

He was accustomed to being the one calling the shots, setting the pace, wielding the power, and Gage's body was shouting at him to take command, as he'd done in the pretty, feminine bedroom that was such a contrast to her firefighting career.

Spin her around. Lift her up onto the hood of the car and take what you both want right now, right here, wherever the hell here *is.*

She'd be damn well satisfied.

But on *his* terms.

His time.

"You realize, if you keep moving against

me like that, you're risking getting some crushed shells in some very uncomfortable places."

"Not if I'm on top."

"Now there's an image."

Sweat beaded on his brow. Soaked the back of his shirt. Another minute and the metal buttons on his jeans would start flying all over this swamp.

Because if he started touching her in all the places he wanted to, he wouldn't be able to stop until they were both naked and risking a public indecency charge.

He wrapped his fingers around the back of her neck. This time the sound rumbling from his throat was half groan, half laugh. "Inspector, you are one damn hot woman."

The green pools of her eyes were wide and deep; he could have drowned in them. Willingly.

"I am, aren't I?" She sounded surprised by that idea. Making him wonder yet again what the hell was wrong with the males in South Carolina.

"Any hotter and we would have set this swamp on fire."

"Marsh," she corrected absently as her gaze drifted to his mouth. "It's a common misconception to mistake them for the same thing. But a marsh's vegetation is mostly soft, herbaceous plants, while a swamp has mostly trees or shrubs. They do both have alligators, though. At least down here."

"I suppose that's all the more reason not to get naked right now."

"Good point. Since I definitely wouldn't want you to lose any important body parts until I'm done with you."

The thought of losing his cock to some gator's teeth was enough to make Gage go limp. "Well, that sure as hell makes two of us."

twenty-six

The Harbor View firehouse stood guard over the lower harbor district. Originally built to protect warehouses filled with the valuable cash crops of cotton and rice, it had not been designed for looks. The stones used for construction had originally been used for ballast in the ships crossing the Atlantic to the early colonies. Since frugal first inhabitants of the city had believed in making over, making do, or doing without, the gray stones had been used for buildings, sidewalks, and roads.

Two stories high, the station had three big fire doors housing a ladder truck, a pumper engine, two sedans — one assigned to Tess and Bobby, the other to the battalion chief and his driver — and a plug buggy, a red pickup truck containing various equipment not found on either the hook and ladder truck or the engine. Above the door was a bronze plaque entrusting the safety of all within to St. Florian.

To the side of the building was a basketball court and enough of a backyard for the firefighters to hang out and barbecue on hot summer evenings.

The powers that be at city hall had been trying to seize the small walled yard by eminent domain in order to allow a franchise takeaway crab shack owned by — who else? — Donald Mannington. Thus far, every time the issue came up before the council, citizens — who tended to love their firefighters, especially after 9/11, then the fatal mill fire — opposed the restaurant so vocally, that city council members, aware that their livelihoods were dependent upon the endorsement of the voters, refused to allow the takeover.

Also aiding in the firefighters' cause was the fact that as Somersettians began reversing the suburban sprawl seen in so many other cities, they insisted on fire protection for the historic homes they were so painstakingly restoring.

A street vendor had set up a wheeled cart and was selling boiled peanuts and sweet tea beneath his green-and-white-striped umbrella, as he'd done every day, rain or shine, since Tess had worked at the station.

"Boiled?" Gage asked when she paused to buy a bag of nuts.

"There's some other way to eat peanuts?" she asked with mock surprise.

He eyed the soggy brown bag with suspicion. "This is a test, isn't it?"

"Geez, and here I thought I was being so subtle. You must be a detective."

"Cute."

"They go back to when the Confederate soldiers ate them during the war. They even sang a ballad about them. Now they're a comfort food. Like Moon Pies, macaroni and cheese, and cream cheese and pepper jelly sandwiches. When I was a kid, we used to put them in our Cokes."

"Why?"

"I've no idea." Tess had never given it any thought. It was just part of a Lowcountry childhood, like catching lightning bugs in Hellman's mayonnaise jars with holes hammered into the top. "Because we were kids, I guess."

"These here goobers are dried red," the vendor volunteered helpfully, obviously recognizing an "away" when he saw one. "The raw green are outta season this time of year, but I boilt this pot up overnight and salted it up real good."

"Go ahead and try one." Tess held the bag out to Gage. "Unless, of course, you're afraid to embrace your inner culinary risk taker."

It had gone from a test to a dare and they both knew it.

Gage plucked out a warm, soft, gray peanut. "It's wet."

"Perhaps that's why they call it a *boiled* peanut."

Still openly skeptical, he put it in his mouth, sucked out the salty water as he'd watched her do, ate the nut from its shell, and tossed the discarded, brine-drenched hull into the extra empty bag the vendor had given her.

"Must be another of those acquired tastes."

"Wait until we get to pickled okra." She handed him a napkin. Boiled peanuts were not the neatest food to eat. "I'll turn you from an 'away' to a Lowcountry man yet."

The words, which had flown from her lips like white doves from a magician's black hat, hung on the sultry air. Since she'd only make matters worse by attempting to call them back, Tess didn't try. And was grateful when Gage didn't point out the obvious — that he wouldn't be sticking around long enough to even think about giving up the surf and sand of California for the pluff mud and difficult history of the South.

Shiny red trucks may have replaced the

horses Tess's great-grandfather had tended to, and more and more women were joining the firefighting ranks, but in many ways, the firehouse remained a world apart. It was, as it had always been, a place of tradition, of camaraderie, of rich and loyal friendships.

Firefighters not only lived together, they partied together, worked on each other's houses — the men of Danny's North Harbor fire station had installed Tess's lion-footed bathtub, and when a tropical storm blew off half her roof, it had been her brothers from Harbor View who'd shown up with pallets of new asphalt shingles.

If they were dealing with a serial arsonist — and it appeared more and more likely that they were — it was apparent that the brass had not yet felt the need to share such information with the troops. Life was pretty much going on as normal.

Jimmy Marion and Joe Bob MacArcher, the station engineers, had just finished washing their engine; Jimmy was polishing the brass, while Joe Bob was on his back underneath, doing his daily brake check.

Ty, who'd been transferred from North Harbor shortly after the mill fire, greeted her as she passed the front office. "Hey,

Tess. How's it going?"

He was taking the blood pressure of an elderly woman Tess recognized as one of the scrounging ladies — a group of elderly women who spent their days pushing their purloined shopping carts through the streets and their nights huddled together beneath the pier.

Checking blood pressure was one of the services the firefighters offered the community; residents taking advantage of the opportunity tended to be prostitutes, the homeless, and some elderly people living alone on fixed incomes who seemed to enjoy stopping by the firehouse every day, having someone besides their TV to talk to.

Tess had enjoyed blood pressure duty; when she'd moved onto the hot squad, Ty had taken on the job, and it had escaped no one's notice that once the firefighter one octogenarian had described as "cute as a doodlebug" took over, scores of local females had taken a sudden interest in their health.

"Busy," Tess responded to Ty's question. She paused long enough to introduce the two men.

"O'Halloran." The firefighter acknowledged Gage with a brusque nod. His lack

of a proffered hand and his uncharacter-
istic curtness made Tess suspect that he
and Bailey had discussed the Fed's arrival
after she'd gone home last night.

"I need to talk to you," Ty told Tess after
sending the bag lady back out onto the
street with her daily Hershey's bar from
the candy machine. Granted, it wasn't the
most healthy snack he could have chosen,
but Tess wasn't about to begrudge any
woman chocolate.

"The commish is waiting." She cast a
glance toward the staircase.

"Yeah, yeah, I know." He plucked a
soggy nut from her bag. "With the mayor.
Bobby got here right before you two. But
this'll just take a minute. And it's important."

Tess was no fan of politicians. But
needing their cooperation if she was to reopen the investigation on the mill fire, she
wasn't about to piss them off, either.

"How about after the meeting?"

Ty didn't look thrilled by the compromise. "If I'm not out on a fire when you
come back down."

John Tyler was one of the most easy-
going men Tess had ever met. Which was
why the fulminating glare he shot Gage
surprised her.

"Then we'll talk when you get back."

"Fine." His expression suggested it was *not* fine at all, but he'd realized there was no point in arguing.

Fifty years of southern cuisine had given Mayor Talmadge Townsend III an even bigger gut than Donald Mannington's. His Scottish-Irish heritage had given him a head of hair that looked like a rusty Brillo pad. That same heredity, coupled with a serious fondness for single-malt Scotch, was responsible for the network of red lines crisscrossing his cheeks like a South Carolina road map. She suspected it was frustration that had his cheeks even more flushed than usual.

"What in the blue blazes are you going to do about this?" He was waving a piece of stationery like the surrender flag Lee must've raised over Vicksburg.

"This being the letter from The Flamemaster?" Gage asked.

"Who the Sam Hill are you?" Townsend bellowed, yet more crimson darkening his face. His piggy eyes were narrowed; all three chins jiggled.

"Gage O'Halloran."

"From ATF," Tess added.

"The Somersett Fire Department is always happy to help our fellow agencies," the other man in the room stated smoothly.

Rex Dunne, the former chief who'd risen to office on the fire that had taken Danny's death, was, outwardly, the antithesis of the mayor.

Tall, with silver hair and a deep tan from days spent on the golf course at the Admiralty Country Club, he, rumor had it, was eyeing the mayor's job. Since a budget crunch had the mayor recently introducing middle-of-the-night annexations to build revenue, the number of suburbanites who'd awaken one morning to discover their property taxes had increased, giving Dunne a lead in the popularity polls.

"Especially now, with this lunatic on our hands."

"The federal government is always grateful for local jurisdictions' assistance," Gage said. He ignored Tess's snort. "I assume you'll be calling a press conference in time to make the six o'clock newscasts?"

"Newscasts?" both Townsend and Dunne asked in one voice.

"It's the quickest way to inform the largest number of citizens," Gage said.

"Oh, now, we wouldn't want to get hasty," Townsend blustered.

"Haste makes waste," Dunne said, which

Tess thought strange coming from a man who'd been in such a damn hurry to abandon two firefighters inside a burning building.

However, despite the hypocrisy, it appeared on this, at least, the two men were in perfect agreement. Tess also thought the commish would have to come up with a much better bumper sticker slogan if he wanted to oust a man who was in bed with so many entrenched special interest groups.

"You're not suggesting withholding this latest letter?" Tess wished she could have been surprised.

"Every hotel and bed and breakfast in town is booked for spring break weekend," Dunne, whose mother-in-law owned one of those B&Bs, said. "The logistics of notifying everyone would be a nightmare."

Tess pressed her case. "Not nearly as much of a nightmare as having all those college kids go home in body bags."

"It's a formidable task," Gage agreed in a Joe Friday, just-the-facts-ma'am tone.

For the first time since she'd met him, he actually sounded like a special agent.

"But not impossible," he continued. "Since we're in a slow news cycle due to all the government offices being closed for the long weekend, reporters don't have any political media spin guys writing their newscasts for them.

"There are only so many stories you can write about kids getting drunk and falling off balconies, or wet T-shirt contests. Those television guys especially love flames because they look so sexy on the screen. Even better than those helicopter views of sharks offshore."

"Sharks?" The scarlet drained from Townsend's ruddy face. "I haven't been informed about any sharks."

"I believe Special Agent O'Halloran was speaking figuratively," Tess said.

"Exactly," Gage agreed.

"Sharks would kill the weekend," Dunne complained.

While political aspirations might have him not exactly rooting for the mayor, there was also the little matter of the beachfront kite and swimsuit shop his wife had recently opened.

Tess was beginning to feel a lot like Chief Brody in *Jaws*, when Roy Scheider's character was faced with not only catching the shark who was turning the townspeople of Amity into his own personal buffet, but having to fight all the slimy bureaucrats who didn't want to risk losing any tourism money by warning people they might be in danger of being eaten.

"A shark'd probably be easier to deal with," she said. "Since so long as a person stays out of the water he's safe."

"The problem with a pyromaniac is that there's no way to ensure that you'll be safe," Gage said, picking up her argument. "Not even in your own home. At night. When your family's sleeping."

"Sweet Jesus," Townsend breathed. He was now a decidedly sickly color of gray.

"The thing to do is to catch him before he kills again." Dunne had a talent for stating the obvious.

"We'll get him," Bobby said. "Especially once we've got everyone in town watching out for suspicious activities."

Townsend dragged a hand down his face. "This'll kill the season."

"Revenue might dip a bit over the weekend," Tess allowed, "but what if the guy's still setting fires come summer Buccaneer Days?"

"Surely you don't think that's possible?"

"That would spell disaster," Dunne said.

Gage was beginning to radiate impatience. "Why don't you set up the press conference," he suggested to Bobby through clenched teeth. "While Inspector Gannon and I go interrogate The Flamemaster."

"Wait a damn minute." Townsend held up a hand. "If you can interrogate the arsonist, why don't you just arrest him?"

"Because the one you're dealing with is a copycat. Who knows stuff he shouldn't. Which suggests they know each other."

Tess put in her two cents. "There's a possibility they met in prison."

"But we won't know for sure until we get to California and grill the bastard," Gage said.

"He's in California?" Dunne asked.

"San Quentin."

"Our budget's stretched at the seams right now. Can't you interrogate him on the phone? Or perhaps on one of those closed-circuit television setups?"

"If you think your budget's stretched now, just imagine how it'll be if your Flamemaster decides to take out the Wingate Palace hotel. I read in this morning's paper that there's a trial lawyers' conference there this week. Exactly how deep will city's pockets be when lawsuits start coming in because a bunch of bureaucrats decided tourism bucks were more important than the tourists themselves?"

"Shit." Now the commissioner looked ill.

"There's a connection." Gage turned to Bobby. "While we're out of town, why don't you go back and reinterview all the spectators at the fire scene and the other residents of the building. See if any have boats that might use high-end marine rope."

"High-end anything would seem unlikely in that neighborhood," Bobby responded.

"Which is why you're also going to check out whether or not any of them visit S&M clubs."

"S&M clubs?" Townsend grabbed his throat. He appeared on the verge of a stroke. "Surely we don't have any such thing in Somersett."

"Then you'd be the only city in the country that doesn't. Especially now that bored Boomers and GenXers have discovered recreational bondage."

The mayor folded his arms across his chest. "That's sick."

"Different strokes." Gage turned back toward Bobby. "You might want to go revisit that strip club that had the fire opening week two years ago. See if some of the clientele crosses over. Maybe some of the girls are moonlighting and have johns who'll pay to tie them up."

That comment had Tess thinking of

Donald Mannington again.

"Yessir." Bobby snapped a salute that bordered on cocky. It was obvious that he still wasn't wild about having a Fed steamrolling over their jurisdiction, but Tess could tell he was enthusiastic about this new path the investigation was taking.

Of course, a lot of men might be tickled pink about the opportunity to watch overly endowed women strip down to G-strings and pole dance, but since Bobby was gay, she suspected he may have been starting to buy into O'Halloran's theory.

The meeting wrapped up soon after that. As usual, the politicians had nothing of substance to contribute, Bobby was off to ask strippers about guys who might be into bondage, and while Gage made arrangements for their trip to California, Tess went looking for Ty.

She found him on the second floor, cleaning out his locker.

"Bailey told me what you and she talked about," he said without preamble. "About you having doubts that so-called Fed is who he says he is."

Tess wasn't surprised Bailey had shared their conversation. Wasn't that one of the perks of marriage? Having someone to talk about anything and everything with? Especially things that troubled you?

"I had my suspicions last night," she allowed.

"So you checked him out this morning?"

"I haven't had time." After watching his take-charge attitude during the meeting, she was also second-guessing her doubts.

"Well, Bailey made time."

"Oh?" Tess braced herself for the bad news she felt coming.

"He's not a Fed."

"He has a badge that says he is." A badge she herself had admitted he could have acquired in any number of ways.

"He *was* an ATF agent, working out of the San Francisco office," Ty said. "But he's not assigned there anymore. There's some argument about whether he quit or was fired, but everyone agrees he's on a vendetta when it comes to some pyro he arrested a couple years ago."

"Well." Tess blew out a breath as twin blades of betrayal and anger slashed through her. "I guess I'd better go have a talk with him."

"I'd say that'd be in order. You also need to tell Bobby."

"I intend to." She glanced out the window as the red car drove off the apparatus floor and onto the street. Then scowled at the Porsche parked at the curb.

"Your partner — your *real* partner," he stressed, "needs to know that the guy who's weaseled his way into your investigation is a fraud."

"That may be putting it a bit harshly." Her calm tone cost her. Oh, she was going to talk to him, all right, Tess thought furiously. And then she just might kill him.

Ty's eyes narrowed. "You're not getting personally involved with O'Halloran, are you?" Concern etched furrows in his forehead.

Involved? "Of course not," she said truthfully, looking him straight in the eye.

He was the first to break the gaze, his eyes drifting down to her lips, which felt swollen and a little bruised after this morning's hard, fast sex. His brows dove as he took in the dark hickey above her collar. The one she'd tried to cover with concealer before leaving for Savannah. Apparently she'd failed.

"Whatever ulterior motive he has for not being up front about who he is and what he's doing impersonating an active ATF agent, that hotshot cowboy's not the sticking-around type, Tess," Ty warned. "He'll get what he wants from you, then he'll be riding into the sunset back to California."

"Believe me, I intend to ask him about his status. But to be perfectly honest, Ty, I'd be willing to deal with the devil himself if he helped me stop this pyro."

The arsonist had already murdered at least one person Tess knew of in her jurisdiction. He was threatening to kill a lot more. She took that damn personally.

"And besides, if he's got information on the mill fire —"

"Dammit, that fire was faulty equipment!" he exploded. His hand curled into a white-knuckled fist; the ugly frustration on his face had Tess worried he was going to slam that fist into the locker door. "I was there; the place was an effing firetrap. It's a miracle it hadn't burned down decades ago."

"Just because it was a firetrap doesn't mean the fire wasn't arson."

Tess was getting weary of repeating herself. How strange that the only person who seemed to share her theory was the one person who'd just been proven untrustworthy.

"As for Gage O'Halloran riding off into the sunset, I'm not interested in any sort of personal relationship. I just want —"

"To get laid."

It was the same thing Gage had said. The same thing she'd agreed to. But it sounded, well, tacky, coming from Danny's dearest friend.

"I know you mean well, Ty. But you're also one of the people who's been telling me it's time to move on with my life. Maybe that's what I'm finally trying to do."

"By having sex with some liar who, for all you know, has a wife and six kids back in California?"

Oh, hell. Tess hadn't even thought to ask Gage if he was married. She wondered if that was another of the "need to know" items he hadn't bothered to share with her.

"No offense intended, but whether I choose to have sex, or who I choose to have it with, really isn't your business, Ty. Now, if you're finished with the morality lecture, I'd better get back to work."

He caught her arm as she started to leave the locker room. "Dammit, I'm sorry, Tess. You know I loved Danny like a brother, which makes you sort of the little sister I never had. And he always put you on such a pedestal, thinking of you with O'Halloran just seems like one helluva big fall."

"That's one of the problems with being

stuck on a pedestal. There's always the potential for a fall." It was also damn lonely. She patted his cheek and forced an aura of calm assurance. "It's okay. I'm a grown woman. I know what I'm doing."

He looked unconvinced. "Yeah, but do you know what O'Halloran's up to?"

"Not entirely," she admitted. "But I intend to find out."

twenty-seven

Gage was waiting in the Porsche when Tess left the station. She yanked open the passenger door.

"Why the hell didn't you tell me you no longer work for ATF?" The question exploded out of her.

He didn't seem surprised by either her discovery or her flare of temper. "Sounds as if Tyler has been doing a little investigating on his own."

"His wife, who happens to be an assistant DA, is the one who made the call." The call, dammit, Tess should have made yesterday. "They both care about me. Ty was Danny's best friend —"

"You sure about that?"

"What?" The question, coming from left field, took a bit of the furious wind out of her sails.

"I asked if you're certain that Tyler was your fiancé's best friend."

"Of course." His reasonable tone ripped at her last nerve ending, which was already hanging by a very frazzled thread. "They were like brothers." She held up crossed fingers to demonstrate how close the two men had been.

"So were Cain and Abel."

Shocked, Tess stared across the center console at him. She wasn't at all sure she could speak. "You can't possibly suspect Ty of setting that fire."

"He had the knowledge, the opportunity —"

"He was also up on that floor with Danny!"

"My point exactly."

"He could have been killed just as easily by the fire."

"Perhaps. But what if McGee was already dead when Tyler supposedly went to get help?"

"There was no *supposedly* about it," she said between clenched teeth. As annoyed as she'd been at Ty's interference in her personal life, there was no way she was going to buy into this outrageous allegation. "He *did* go for help. They just couldn't get back up there to the eighth floor before the chief ordered everyone out. And Danny couldn't get back down because the stairs burned up."

"Convenient."

Her eyes narrowed. "I'm going to give you a bit of a pass because you don't know

Ty." Hadn't she been taught not to overlook any possible suspect in a fire investigation? "But you're overlooking one important fact."

"What's that?"

"Motive. Ty wouldn't have any."

"There's you."

Her jaw dropped. Shock caused her earlier fury to drain out of her. "If this wasn't such a serious subject, I'd have to laugh. My God, he's happily married. You should see him and Bailey together. They were expecting their first child; they'd already started going to estate sales looking for antique furniture for the nursery, and two weeks before the fire, he'd painted the spare bedroom buttercup yellow so they could turn it into a nursery."

"Maybe he was jazzed about being a father. But that wouldn't necessarily preclude falling in love with his best friend's fiancée."

This time Tess did laugh. But it was strained. "Why don't you just go for broke and accuse me of conspiring with him to kill Danny."

"I thought of that."

"What?" She sucked in a harsh breath. Blew it out. Drew in another one. "You didn't trust me?"

"No, but don't take it personally. I hadn't met you yet."

"And now that you have?"

"Anyone who knows you knows that there's no way in hell you'd commit adultery. But that still doesn't let Tyler off the hook. You were getting married in four days. Maybe he figured getting rid of the competition would give you time to fall in love with him back."

She'd come out here to tear a piece off Gage for having faked his badge. Well, maybe not entirely faked, but he'd definitely committed what the nuns at St. Brendan's would have called a sin of omission. But somehow he'd turned things around, putting her in a position of having to defend one of her dearest friends.

"If you use that kind of flawed reasoning in your work, I'm amazed you've ever managed to win a conviction. The very notion's ridiculous."

"I don't know why. We've already determined you're hot. I can't imagine any man not wanting to have sex with you."

"That's because you have sex on the brain."

"Just because I want to have you in ways that are probably illegal in half the jurisdictions in this state doesn't mean that Tyler doesn't feel the same way."

"I don't want to be having this damn conversation." She shook her head, which was beginning to pound. "Good try at sidetracking me, O'Halloran, but what we *should* be discussing is why you chose not to share the vital bit of information that you were fired from ATF with me."

"I wasn't fired. I quit."

"*Before* they could fire you?"

"They weren't going to go that far. In fact, although I've continued to make it clear that I'm not returning to the job, they consider me on indeterminate leave."

"Why did you leave?"

"Because, the agency, in its bureaucratic wisdom, believed I might be on the verge of a meltdown and everyone wanted to make sure they covered their collective asses in the event I decided to shoot up some San Francisco courtroom."

"In order to kill that pyro you arrested?"

"The thought crossed my mind."

"But you wouldn't have really done that? Killed a man in cold blood?"

She was not encouraged when he didn't answer. But decided to skip over that for now. "Were you? On the verge of a meltdown?"

He shrugged. "Probably."

"And now?"

"And now I don't think about it."

"If that were true, you wouldn't be here. Since you're not with ATF anymore, there's no official reason you'd be pursuing a copycat arsonist." She paused, remembering the feelings she'd sensed while they'd been in that burned-out room together. "Unless it's personal."

"Murder's always personal to someone." He gave her one of those frustratingly enigmatic looks, then twisted the key in the ignition. "We'll stop by your house so you can pack; if we leave in the next hour, we should arrive in time to make San Quentin before lockdown."

He might think he'd dodged the question yet again. But he'd also given her more clues to work with. Obviously his meltdown was directly connected to his last case. Was he really interested in apprehending her apparent copycat? Or, since he'd been prevented from killing the man he'd put behind bars, was he using her in some twisted way to achieve some other, more complicated form of revenge?

Tess wasn't sure of much where Gage O'Halloran was concerned. But she vowed that by the time the plane landed in California, she was going to have pried the damn truth out of him.

They'd no sooner pulled up in front of the house than a woman burst out of the house next door carrying a brown pasteboard box. She was wearing a short red sequined dress that looked as if it'd been applied with a paint sprayer, high heels that brought to mind a pair of ruby slippers — if Dorothy of Kansas had favored glittery skyscraper spiked heels — and makeup that made Tammy Faye Bakker look like an Alpha Delta Pi sorority pledge. She was a good six feet tall, with a Diana Ross seventies Afro wig adding another five inches.

"Someone left off a present for you, girlfriend," the Amazon called out.

Instincts Gage had tried to forget he possessed kicked in. "Drop the box," he instructed.

"What?" Brown eyes, thickly lined beneath at least three pairs of spiky false lashes, widened.

"I said, drop the box, ma'am."

"Ma'am." Glacier-white teeth flashed in a complexion the color of café au lait. If she was at all threatened by the Glock he'd pulled from his shoulder holster, she didn't show it. She fluttered those lashes, which

280

glittered with some sort of sparkly dust. "Why, aren't you just the politest policeman."

"Savannah . . ." Tess murmured.

Ignoring both warnings, she kept sauntering toward them on legs that went all the way up to her neck, her sequined clad hips wagging a happy hello.

"And such a handsome brute, too. But more rugged than the men around here." Her smile widened to include Tess. "You hooked yourself a trophy cowboy this time, child."

"Ma'am," Gage repeated. "I need you to drop that box. *Now.*"

"Gracious." Savannah deftly balanced the box on the palm of a ringed hand. The other patted her breast. "You are so forceful you just make me feel like Ah'm fixin' to swoon."

"Savannah," Tess tried again. "Gage isn't kidding around. You need to drop the box. Now."

"And hurt this precious little kitty?"

Kitty? Tess and Gage exchanged a look.

"Some kid brought him by," Savannah explained. "He came over to my house when you weren't home. Said the kitty was rescued in that fire and you offered to buy him."

She tilted the box so that Tess and Gage could view the marmalade kitten curled up, oblivious to the trouble she'd almost caused.

"You owe me fifty dollars."

"Fifty dollars?"

"That's what the boy said you'd offered to pay. Personally, I think it's a little high, but" — she shrugged her bare shoulders — "I figured that was between you and the homeboy."

"I didn't buy any cat," Tess said. "In fact, I specifically told the kid I wasn't in the market for a cat."

"Well." A hand wearing a milky moonstone that covered two knuckles stroked the orange fur. "Seems you've got one, nevertheless, hon."

"I don't have time for a cat."

"You work too hard." Savannah extended the box toward Tess, who had no choice but to accept it. "Do you some good to relax."

"I relax."

"When?"

"I'm on my way to California as soon as I pack." Tess saw no reason to point out that it was work related.

Chocolate-dark eyes sharpened with interest, sweeping speculatively over Gage.

282

"Ooh, you lucky girl. The Pacific Ocean, bleached-blond surfers in those cute little baggy jams. Muscle Beach, movie stars.

"Tell me, darlin' " — her gaze narrowed in on Gage's groin — "you wouldn't happen to own a Speedo, would you?"

"Hell, no."

"My mama always said, 'If you've got it, flaunt it.' And sugar, for any man with a package like yours not to be flaunting it all over creation is a downright disservice to women everywhere.

"As for the kitty, you don't have to worry, Tess. You can take her with you. I saw this program on A&E. Or was it the Animal Planet?"

She paused, thinking that over. "Well, it doesn't matter which it was." Bracelets clacked as she waved the problem away with a graceful flick of her wrist. "All you have to do is give her some Xanax and she'll just sleep all the way."

"I can't do that."

"Oh, you don't have to give her a full dose. Just a teensy nibble, according to her weight."

"I don't have the foggiest idea what she weighs. And even if I did, I don't have any Xanax."

"Don't worry. I do." Savannah shot another quick glance at Gage. "Prescription, of course."

"Of course," he agreed mildly.

"I get a little stage fright every now and again. That little blue pill takes the edge off. But gracious, Ah'm forgetting my manners."

She flashed him the smile Scarlett O'Hara had used to beguile the Tarleton twins. She was the only person Tess knew who'd memorized every single one of Vivien Leigh's lines from that movie.

"I'm the Lady Savannah from Savannah. And what would your name be, Mr. Man?"

"Gage O'Halloran, from —"

"California," Tess said quickly before he could flash his mostly phony ATF badge. She liked her outrageous neighbor a lot, but the female impersonator was also the biggest gossip in the city.

"Well, isn't that just *fabulously* interesting." Her gaze turned avid as her attention went from Gage to Tess and back again. "You takin' our sweet Tess home to sunny California to meet your mama and daddy?"

"Actually, my parents live in Wyoming."

"Ah!" She arched a perfectly waxed brow. "The Equality State."

"Very good."

"I excelled in geography in school. Most people," she informed Tess, "get Wyoming confused with Montana, which, of course, is the Big Sky State." She trailed a pomegranate-colored talon the length of a switchblade down Gage's arm. "And Wyoming's definitely got more macho men.

"I played at this little hole-in-the-wall club in Laramie back when I was first gettin' started in the business. It had all these snarling stuffed animal heads on the wall and a hunky, make-a-girl's-mouthwater cowboy on every bar stool."

Jewels flashed like the aurora borealis as she fanned herself with her hand. "All those pretty tight butts packed into tight blue stacked Wranglers was nearly enough to make the Lady Savannah swoon. I swear, darlin', Ah thought for sure I'd died and gone to heaven."

Tess suspected Gage was not often speechless. He appeared to be now.

"That's — uh — very interesting. So you're a performer?"

"An impersonator, sugar. I have this club" — she reached into her cleavage and pulled out a gilt card embossed with hot-pink hearts — "Savannah's on the River. You should drop in when you and Tess get back from the left coast. I'll do Cher for you."

285

He'd begun to relax. His hand, which had gone for his gun, was now hooked in the front pocket of his jeans and his eyes had lost the Dirty Harry glint.

"I'll bet you're a dynamite Cher."

"Oh, honey, there ain't none better." She fluffed her Diana Ross do. "Why, even those cute boys from the Village People said they couldn't hardly tell the difference. Of course, I'm a lot younger than Miss Cher, which did give it away."

Having heard all this before, Tess let her mind drift from the conversation between her neighbor and Gage to the kitten curled up on what appeared to be a white cashmere hoodie. She didn't need an animal to take care of. Didn't want one.

Worse yet, was there anything more depressing than an unmarried woman on the cusp of the big 3-0 getting herself a cat?

Not that thirty was old, or that she should cave into her mother's fretting about the risk of all the good men being taken if she didn't jump back into the dating pool. But Tess hated thinking of herself as a stereotype.

Then — oh, damn — she made the mistake of trailing her fingers over the downy marmalade fur. The kitten's almond-shaped yellow eyes opened and looked right up into Tess's. When the cat yawned, Tess knew she was in deep, deep trouble.

"You're the one with all the hotshot suggestions," she said to Gage. "Do you have any good answer for this one?"

"Maybe Savannah can take care of it until we get back."

"I'll put the kitty in my show," Savannah agreed cheerfully. "Maybe have a fairy-tale theme night. Make her a little pair of leather boots and bill her as Puss in Boots. Everyone will just go crazy over her."

"Maybe too crazy," Tess suggested. "I'm not sure a bar is a good place to keep a kitten."

A chin shot up. Eyes flashed. "Savannah's on the River is not a bar. It's a *cabaret*. And my mama raised me in a Savannah whorehouse and look how good I turned out." She held out her arms and twirled around on her high-heeled ruby slippers, like a little girl showing off a new party dress.

"Maybe you could keep her in the dressing room," Gage suggested.

"I suppose that's better. Though she certainly would have been a hit. But I do still like the idea of a fairy-tale night."

Tess, with whom the impersonator had shared the planning of last year's Buccaneer Days Bash at the club, could see the wheels spinning in Savannah's clever head.

"Maybe I'll get a pair of boots for myself. Sexy lace-up suede ones that go up to here." She splayed her manicured nails high on one smooth brown thigh. "And make one of those fancy whiskered masks like from *Cats*. With those and a tiger-striped bra and G-string, I could bill myself as, ta-dah" — she flung out her arms, laden down with those sparkly bracelets, and Tess saw it coming — "Pussy in Boots."

"Sounds like a winner," Gage agreed. Damned if he didn't have a devastatingly sexy smile on those rare occasions he chose to use it.

"Doesn't it?" Savannah looked more than a little pleased with herself. "Here, hon."

She snatched the box out of Tess's hands. "I'll take care of little pussy here while you and your man go have yourself a romantic holiday. It'll be a nice change for me, sharing a bed with something warm and furry who doesn't keep waking me up for a blow job."

The situation settled, she sashayed back to her house.

twenty-eight

"Interesting neighborhood you've got here," Gage murmured.

"Savannah's one of a kind. Thanks for not freaking out."

"She seemed nice enough. And we have transvestites in California."

"How many in Wyoming?"

"There must be some, if what she said about playing a club in Laramie was true. Of course, they could've thought they were getting the real Cher," he said as an afterthought.

"Well, I'll bet there aren't any in ATF."

"You'd lose. I once worked with an agent who wore his wife's lacy panties and a bra beneath his suit."

"I don't think I want to know how you discovered that little piece of information."

"We went undercover one time to bust this wacko self-named patriot group who were operating a bomb factory outside Jackson Hole. At our first meeting, since we were the new guys, we had to strip to prove we weren't wired."

"You could have been killed."

"Could've. But we weren't. Though I think Leon damn near died of embarrassment."

"Speaking of dying, did you ever think that what you were doing was dangerous?"

"Sure."

"And it never bothered you?"

"Most of the time I just figured it was part of the job. Sometimes, when the adrenaline rush kicked in, it made up for the hours of sitting on my butt at stakeouts."

"Did you burn out because of the tedium?" she asked as they climbed the porch steps. "Or the rush?"

"Who said I burned out?"

"I believe you mentioned something about a meltdown."

This was not Gage's favorite subject. But because of what he was going to do to Tess, exposing her to the manifestation of pure evil, he figured the least he could do was be honest about this.

"I used to be a bit of a control freak."

She smiled a little. "Used to be?"

"You should've known me back then. Or maybe not."

It was a quintessentially southern porch, with a swing, a pretty little white wicker table, leafy green ferns hanging in pots from the eaves.

Just the idea of getting naked and making out with her on that swing beneath a full southern moon was all it took to make him hard as a brick. If only life were that simple.

"Anyway, I'd gotten used to seeing myself as the hotshot ATF Special Agent who closed all my cases, put the bad guys behind bars —"

"Outran speeding bullets, leaped over tall buildings, all while making the planet safe for helpless women and children."

It sounded foolish, even naive, hearing it out loud. But amazingly, stupidly, he'd believed it.

"I was good at my work. Then one day I wasn't."

"Meaning one day you discovered you couldn't control the world."

"Yeah. I guess that's one way of putting it."

"I know the feeling."

She sighed and unlocked the door.

"What the hell am I going to do with a kitten?" she wondered as they entered the house.

"You could always take it to a shelter."

"Right. Where they'd end up putting it to sleep because there are already a gazillion unwanted animals in the world."

She dragged a hand through her hair. "I don't have time for a damn cat."

"Cats are easier than dogs."

"Easy for you to say. Since I strongly doubt you have either."

"I did as a kid."

"Yeah, I know, the un-ranch-dog whippet. But that's different. Kids and animals go together."

"I suppose so."

The last time he'd been here, Gage hadn't been interested in anything but rolling around the sheets. This time he noticed the house.

Buttery-yellow pine floors gleamed a warm welcome. Walls topped with creamy-white crown molding had been sponge painted in soft shades of green and were adorned with pastel drifts of watercolor gardens. A small glass bowl of potpourri gave off the faint scent of roses.

"Kids are more high maintenance than pets," he said. "But I'll bet that didn't keep you and your fiancé from planning a family."

"Of course we wanted children. But things change. It's true, you know, what they say about life moving on. That was then. This is now."

She let out a long breath. "And would

you please stop me before I embarrass myself with any more hackneyed clichés?"

"Sometime life's a cliché. Two years ago you had yours all planned out. Things went south. And now you're afraid of getting emotionally involved. Of getting hurt again."

"Sounds as if you'd know something about that."

A heavy, overstuffed couch that looked perfect for watching Monday-night football covered in a well-washed, faded flowered slipcover sat in front of a fireplace faced with white brick.

He could tell he'd hit close to the mark when she began unnecessarily straightening a trio of fringed pillows lined up like soldiers awaiting inspection.

"I guess I would."

She didn't push for an explanation; he didn't offer.

"Nice place," he said instead.

"I like it."

From the sheen on the floors, that was an understatement. "And neat."

"You see enough houses at two in the morning, you decide you don't want to expose your private stuff to strangers. Even ones who might be there to help." She glanced around with obvious pride. "This place was a mess when Danny and I bought it, but it's coming along."

Another understatement. She might pride herself on the tough, no-nonsense fire cop image she portrayed, but here in the privacy of her own home, she'd definitely allowed an intriguing glimpse of a softer, feminine side.

"I won't be long. It should probably only take five, ten minutes tops to change clothes and pack."

He didn't doubt her. From what he'd witnessed thus far, she was as efficient as she was delectable.

"No jeans. Or white T-shirts. And don't wear anything blue, green, or yellow, or they won't let us in."

"I hadn't realized prisons had fashion police. Maybe they could do a *What Not to Wear* special for people going to the Big House. What with all the white-collar criminals getting sent away these days, it'd probably be a hit."

"There's solid reasoning behind the rules. The staff wears green and khaki. The inmates are assigned blue and yellow and the prison administration doesn't want to risk there being any confusion about who's who in the event of an escape or lock-down."

"Well, that's encouraging."

"It's not meant to be. This isn't Sunny-brook Farm you're going to. There's a reason inmates call it the Arena.

"Which reminds me," he said. "If you wear an underwire bra, the guards'll cut the wire out. Because it can be used as a weapon."

She shivered a little at some image in her mind; Gage knew the reality was probably worse than anything she could imagine.

It was just as well they weren't going to get involved. How do you explain to your grandchildren that Granny and Grandpa's first date was at death row in one of the roughest prisons in the country?

"No jeans, no yellow, green, or blue," she repeated. "No Wonderbra. Is jewelry allowed?"

When her hand went to her throat, he knew she was thinking of that damn saint's medal.

"It's never been an issue for me, so I couldn't swear to it, but I've seen women visitors with multiple piercings. So you shouldn't have any problems."

She nodded. "Good."

Gage debated following her upstairs, and regretfully remembered his vow that the next time he tasted the delicious Inspector

Gannon he was going to savor it.

The room was not only as tidy as a nun's cell, despite its femininity, it lacked the clutter most women seemed to accumulate. His mother, who was both one of the most practical and hardworking women he'd ever met, had crowded little Hummel figurines into nearly every niche and cranny of the cedar-sided house Gage had grown up in.

Kim had collected crystal. Gage could still remember the sound of all those shattered vases and bowls crunching like ice beneath his feet.

True to her word, Tess was back downstairs in six minutes. She'd changed from her uniform into a black pantsuit, and plain black pumps with two-inch heels. He suspected the damn saint's medal was beneath the white silk blouse.

It was not an outfit designed to stir a man's blood. But he seemed destined to be stirred whenever she got within tasting distance.

Gage put the issue of *Fire Engineering* he'd been leafing through back down onto the coffee table atop this month's *Southern Living* magazine, stood up, and reached for the small black canvas carry-on.

Her fingers tightened around the handle.

"I can carry my own suitcase."

"I've no doubt you can. But since there aren't any bullets to outrun at the moment, why don't you just humor me?"

He took the bag, slung it over his shoulder.

Tess muttered something beneath her breath. But as they left the pretty little house, Gage noticed she was almost smiling.

twenty-nine

"So, what time is our flight?" she asked as he pulled away from the curb.

"When we get there. The pilot was scheduled to arrive" — he glanced down at the dashboard clock — "ten minutes ago."

"You own a plane?"

"It's a charter."

"A charter? As in we're going to be the only people on it?"

"If your pyro's telling the truth in that letter, we're up against the clock," he said. "Commercial flights out of here would take too much time; we'd have to take a regional jet to Atlanta, then —"

"Believe it or not, although I've spent all my life, except the four years I spent in Kentucky going to college, here in Somersett, I *have* traveled. I know how it works; down here in this part of the country, people swear that even if you're going to hell, you have to trade planes in Atlanta.

"What I'm trying to wrap my mind around is how an ATF agent — especially one who hadn't been on active payroll for two years — can afford to hire a private jet."

"Maybe I was one of the crooked cops who took graft."

"No. You can be a real son of a bitch, O'Halloran. But you're not a bad cop."

"I'll take that as a compliment."

"Good, since that's how it was meant."

"It's games," he said as the car idled impatiently at a red light.

"Games?"

"I build computer games."

"Like Pac-Man?" There was an original Pac-Man arcade machine, dating back to the 1980s, at the fire station. It was a bitch to repair; it was also, she'd discovered the first day Brian had rescued it from a landfill, addictive.

"Sort of." He shrugged, clearly uncomfortable with the subject.

"I don't want you to take this the wrong way, especially when we're starting to get along, but it's a bit of a stretch to picture you playing computer games."

"It didn't start out as a game. I worked with a lot of computer stuff while I was a firefighter in the air force."

"You were in the military?"

"Got a problem with that?"

"Not at all. I personally hate weapons of

all kinds, but I also appreciate the fact that I can sleep well at night because of all those military men and women who stay awake. I just can't see *you* following orders."

"Neither could I."

"So you were kicked out?"

"Hell no."

"Quit before you were kicked out?"

"No." His jaw clenched. A dark and dangerous intensity was humming around them, but Tess believed him.

"All right. I apologize for doubting you."

"Apology accepted."

"So, after you got out, you started your own private rocket launching company?"

"Very funny." He was not laughing. "After I signed up with ATF, I created a program for investigating fire scenes. We used it in a couple investigations and it worked well enough that other agents in the service suggested I trademark it."

"Can you do that? Trademark something you created while getting a government paycheck?"

"Do you have to nitpick every little detail?"

She thought about that for a minute. "I think so. It's probably what makes me a good investigator."

"Point taken. And the law's a little iffy on the subject, but the agency's lawyers came up with an agreement offering a split royalty if I ever made any money on the deal."

"Which, given the rental Porsche and the plane, you obviously have."

He shrugged. "I've done okay. After I demonstrated it at a fire marshal conference in Miami one winter, this computer utility packager came up to me and suggested mass-marketing it to other fire companies around the country.

"I was skeptical, but the idea took off and pretty soon nearly every big department, and a lot of middle-size ones as well, had scooped it up."

"I saw something like that when I was at school."

She'd also wished Somersett had been able to afford one, but the city council had pointed out that the police already had a crime lab and there was no point in duplicating efforts. The fact that the police didn't have anything nearly as effective at predicting the effects of fire had not moved the council members.

"That's yours?"

"Yeah. It proved pretty popular, and, like I said, even giving the government its cut, I was making some nice money, but then firefighters started writing to the company, asking if they could reprogram it as a game.

"The company, in turn, asked me. I did some tweaking in my spare time, and although not much of the investigative part stayed in, I ended up with a computer game where players have to fight their way through increasingly hot flames and thicker smoke and potentially deadly chemicals on their way up the floors of a high-rise building."

"With extra points earned for saving women, children, and pets," Tess said as recognition dawned. "Ty brought that game down to the station last fall and everyone went nuts over it. It's called . . . Oh, my God," she breathed as recognition belatedly kicked in.

"Flamemaster," Gage said flatly. "Ironic, isn't it?"

"You don't think that's where the original Flamemaster, the one you put away, got his name?"

"He won't admit it. But since the game CD was found in his house, and several months of scores on his hard drive, I'd guess it's a possibility."

"Which is why it's personal on your part."

"That's one of the reasons."

Tess was remembering more details, including watching a segment on *Good Morning America* about Flamemaster being that season's "must have" Christmas gift for males ages eight to twenty-four. Like Cabbage Patch Kids and Talking Elmo after them, demand exceeded supply and Charlie Gibson had reported that a single CD had sold for ten times its retail price on eBay.

"You must have made a bundle."

"I do okay."

"Okay enough to be able to charter a plane."

"Well, it's not exactly a 747 jumbo jet."

Jumbo jet or not, Tess was still impressed.

After what he'd told her about his computer success, Tess should have been prepared for the sleek white Gulf Stream waiting for them on the tarmac at Somersett Admiralty International Airport.

She should have been. But wasn't. Gage, she noted, as they were greeted by the uniformed pilot, seemed to take the trappings of wealth in stride. Exactly how rich was he? Not that it mattered.

Except, she thought, as she settled into a

pewter-gray leather chair that was as soft as a baby's bottom, it did.

It wasn't that she envied Gage his money. Despite her parents' desire for her to establish a white-collar career, she'd grown up in a family where true richness had nothing to do with any bank account, but was measured by strength of character.

What it did was throw her off her stride. Tess didn't like being thrown off her stride. Not that she was the control freak he'd admitted to being, she assured herself. The hell she wasn't.

Gage was in the cockpit, conferring with the pilot prior to takeoff, when her cell phone chimed. Momentarily regretting that the damn thing had ever been invented, she pulled it from her bag.

When she saw the station number on the caller ID, she flipped the phone open, expecting to hear from Bobby.

"Tess, it's Ty."

Not now, she wanted to say. *I don't want to deal with this. Even if you are calling to apologize for insinuating yourself into my personal life.*

"Hey, Ty," she said neutrally.

"I know you don't want to hear anything negative about O'Halloran —"

304

"He already explained about his situation at ATF."

Since gossip spread like wildfire through fire stations and she didn't feel his story was hers to share, she kept what Gage had told her about leaving the agency to herself.

"Good for him. Did he happen to mention that he's done prison time?"

"You're obviously misinformed."

"Okay, maybe not prison," he backtracked a bit. "But he *did* spend time behind bars in the San Francisco County Jail. On a murder charge."

"I don't believe that."

She'd seen the hardness in Gage O'Halloran's eyes and suspected that he'd have no difficulty pulling the trigger of his Glock in a life-or-death situation.

But murder?

No way.

"He was arrested and charged with murder in the first degree," Ty insisted over static. He paused a heartbeat. "Of his wife."

Wife? "Obviously he was released."

"Only" — *crackle, crackle* — "technicality."

"What kind of technicality?" Damn. The call was breaking up.

Crackle crackle. "Ask him."

"I will."

She was speaking to dead air. The lack of bars on the screen showed no signal.

thirty

Tess had just tucked the phone back into her bag when the door opened and the man who, if Ty could be believed, had been a murder suspect came out of the cockpit.

Tess was not a nervous flier. It was only the takeoffs and landings that made her tense. Which is why she decided to wait until they were in the air to question Gage about Ty's call.

One thing she was sure of was that the man who'd reached over and taken her ice-cold hand in his as the jet's wheels left the runway and the city grew smaller and smaller in the oval window was no murderer.

"We've reached our cruising altitude of thirty thousand feet," he said when there was a discreet little ding. "The captain has turned off the seat-belt sign, so feel free to move about the cabin."

"Thank you, but I'd prefer just to stay where I am."

"Why don't you let me give you the grand tour? The bedroom is small and lacks a chandelier to swing on, but we'll make do."

"I'd rather talk."

"We can talk after." He unfastened his own seat belt, stood up, and opened a small glass-fronted cabinet at the front of the passenger compartment. "Red or white?"

"After what?"

"I told you the next time I'd touch you all over," he reminded her mildly. "Red or white?"

"Red." She had a feeling she'd need it to get through the conversation.

"Red it is."

He reached for a dark bottle. She changed her mind.

"No, white."

"Okay." A green bottle.

"Red," she said again.

"You sure?" The crinkling around his eyes suggested a smile.

"Positive."

"I was hoping it'd be the red." He chose an Australian pinot noir. "This'll make more of a contrast when I lick it off your body."

"That sounds messy."

"Don't worry." His gaze caressed her breasts, which swelled beneath her white silk blouse. "I'm real good with my tongue."

Despite her determination to find out the truth, Tess had to bite back a whimper.

How could she want to make love with a man one of her closest friends had just told her might be a murderer?

Because whatever rumor Ty had heard wasn't true. Besides, it was only sex, not love.

Sex with Danny had been easy and inevitable, like sliding into a warm bath at the end of a long day. They'd been best friends first, lovers later.

Sex with Gage had been hot and sudden, like a bolt of lightning from a clear blue sky. She hadn't had time to think about it. To worry about living up to expectations. He was from California, for Pete's sake. Where any man as dark and dangerously sexy as Gage O'Halloran would stand out among bleached-blond beachboys like a blizzard in July.

Were there even beachboys in San Francisco? Wouldn't the sharks that once kept all those prisoners in Alcatraz eat them?

It didn't matter. Gage was a strutting, breathing sex magnet who undoubtedly had his choice of women. Women who knew the same sort of things he did. Women who studied Tantric sex, memorized all the positions in the Kama Sutra, and had not only *found* their G-spot but knew what to *do* with it.

"We really need to talk."

"And we will. After we get to California."

"That's a four-hour flight."

He feathered a finger along her neck and set every nerve ending in her body to buzzing. "Exactly."

Did he actually plan to have sex for four hours? Was that even possible? What on earth did two people do for that length of time?

"It's too bad Griffith's not in prison in China," he said. "Then I just might have the time to do everything I've been fantasizing doing to you." He brushed his lips along her jaw; his teeth grazed her throat. "Things I've fantasized you doing to me."

There was no easy way to ask. Other than straight out.

"What happened to your wife?"

His mouth ceased its sensual caress. She could feel every muscle in his body tense as he drew back. "She died."

At least he hadn't tried to deny the dead woman's existence. "Was murdered," she corrected.

He dipped his dark head in acknowledgment. "If you know that, you undoubtedly also know that I was arrested."

"You didn't do it."

He didn't respond.

"Gage?"

"Do you realize that's the first time you've called me by my first name?"

"Do you realize you're dodging my question again?"

"It's a complicated story."

"As you said, we've plenty of time."

"I was going to tell you, *had* to tell you, before we got to San Quentin."

"So, tell me now."

He sighed. Pulled a corkscrew from a drawer. "You might want something stronger than wine. It's not a pretty story."

"I've been in the life-and-death business for a while. I won't wilt."

"No. You're definitely not a wilter."

He poured the wine into a stemmed glass for Tess, then splashed some Jack Daniel's into a heavy crystal old-fashioned glass and sprawled in the chair facing her.

Tess waited as he stared down into the amber liquor, as if seeking the words to begin what had to have been a horrific time of his life.

She found it sadly ironic that along with all the other things she hated to admit they had in common, the loss of a loved one was yet another.

"I didn't kill Kim," he said finally. "But I'm responsible for her death."

"News flash, O'Halloran. I'm capable of making an informed decision. So, why don't you just stick to the facts, and I'll sort them out."

His lips quirked just a little at that. Then the half-smile faded.

"I met her at a bar in Cheyenne, where one of the agents was having a bachelor party. She was a cocktail waitress. We hit it off, so I stuck around until closing, then went home with her."

Tess pictured some tall bottle blonde Barbie doll with scarlet gel nails wearing one of those corsets people were wearing on the outside these days, a sprayed-on micro-miniskirt, black fishnet stockings, and stilettos.

Then, remembering the woman was dead, Tess felt guilty for the jealousy the uncharitable vision invoked.

"We went out for a few months. Then she started getting a little clingy, so I decided, since I wasn't into any long-term relationships, to break it off."

"What changed your mind?"

"She got pregnant."

It was not the answer Tess had been expecting. "You have a child?"

"No. I had to go out of town a couple weeks after we'd eloped to Tahoe. She miscarried while I was gone."

Convenient.

"And you felt bad about that."

"Hell, yes. She lost our child."

So she said. "And that's tragic. But not everyone gets married when there's an unexpected pregnancy." Her parents had, but they'd been brought up strict pre–Vatican II Catholics. Not getting married would have been out of the question.

His jaw hardened in that way she was becoming used to. "I was brought up to do the right thing."

"Now we're back to those speeding bullets."

Frustration radiated from every male pore.

"Never mind," Tess said. "It's admirable, if a little outdated, but we're getting off track. Go on."

"The night we met, she thought my job was sexy. She didn't feel that way when she had to deal with it on a daily basis."

"She worried about you," Tess guessed.

He moved his shoulders. Took a contemplative sip of the whiskey. "Yeah, among other things. Especially with all the anti-government groups scattered across the West. One of the reasons she wanted me to take the transfer to San Francisco was that she thought it'd be safer."

"Was it?"

"For the most part, since instead of going undercover with those wacko patriot groups who fly the flag upside down and build fertilizer bombs, I spent most of my days chasing down clowns who torch buildings for the insurance money."

Since her father had gone to Oklahoma to help search for victims of the federal building, Tess had firsthand knowledge of how dangerous those homegrown terrorist groups could be.

"Things got better for a while. Especially after I sold that computer program and she could afford to start decorating the new house we'd bought. She seemed happy, even talked about going to school to get a degree in interior design."

Which, Tess considered, made her the mirror opposite of Kim O'Halloran. While she was proud of the work she'd put into her house, she'd certainly never had the knack for decorating that women like Bailey possessed.

"Then Randolph Griffith started his

arson spree, which pretty much sucked up all my waking and sleeping hours. Kim accused me of loving the job more than her."

"Did you?" Tess couldn't help asking.

"No." He scraped a hand through his hair, obviously uncomfortable with such a personal conversation. "Not really. The job was important to me." He paused again. Tess hadn't missed his use of past tense. "But so was my marriage."

He wouldn't be one to admit to failure easily, Tess thought.

"Still, it's hard, balancing the demands of work and family," she supposed, having never had to do so herself, thanks to Danny having shared her zeal for their work.

"Tell me about it. I must've failed at the balancing act, because she had an affair."

"That must've been hard."

"It wasn't much of an ego booster," he said dryly. "She wasn't real good at covering it up. I confronted her, she cried and promised that it was over. Which lasted about a week. That's when I decided to look the other way."

"It didn't bother you that she was sleeping with another man?" Tess immediately thought of what Gage had said about not being willing to share when he'd wanted her to take off Danny's medal.

"Hell, yes. But I had a guy out there on the loose killing people. To be perfectly honest, I figured once the pyro was behind bars, I could spend more time trying to patch up my marriage. Meanwhile, it was easier for both of us when Kim was getting what she needed, what made her happy."

"And you didn't have to deal with all that emotional baggage of her being jealous of your work. Or feel guilty that you weren't ever home."

"I guess you could put it that way."

"I just did."

It was not often Tess felt as if she had the advantage with Gage O'Halloran. That she did now demonstrated exactly how uncomfortable the man was with emotional situations.

"Then she decided that our problem was that our marriage had gotten dull. That things needed spicing up. That's when she got into this kinky stuff."

Tess wasn't about to help him out there by asking for his definition of kink.

"It started out with some light bondage. She told me she'd always fantasized about me using my handcuffs to lock her to the bed, then 'having my way' with her. That wasn't so bad."

One of those rare half-smiles lifted the corner of his lips. "She had this fantasy . . . you don't want to hear about it."

"Probably not. But you can't stop now. Not when things are just getting good."

"She liked to play a pyromaniac's hooker girlfriend. The scene was that I'd force her to give me information about her arsonist lover."

"I assume you're talking sexual force."

The dead prostitute in that charred apartment came immediately to mind. It was only a coincidence.

"It wasn't really rape." The scowl sent his brows diving down to his nose.

"Forced seduction isn't that uncommon a fantasy. Which doesn't mean a woman actually wants to invite real sexual violence into her life."

"Kim did."

Again, Tess wasn't about to touch that line.

"One time, I came home from Portland, where Donovan and I had tracked The Flamemaster, and she greeted me in black leather — boots, corset, the whole works."

"I've heard a lot of men like women in black leather," Tess said mildly. A biker's wet dream is how she'd heard it described around the station house.

"Not when it comes with a mask and flogger."

"That might be pushing the envelope."

"She told me she'd been a bad girl. And needed to be punished."

Tess was discovering that he wasn't the only one who didn't want to get into emotional baggage.

Dammit, this was too personal. They'd already been as physically intimate as two people could be. But when it came to psyches — or hearts — she was more than willing to leave the barricades up.

"I think I'm getting the picture. You don't have to tell me this."

"Yeah. Unfortunately I do, since there's a damn good chance Griffith will and I want you to hear the story from me first. Besides, since we're having this sex thing, you should know the truth."

Sex thing. Well, you assured the man you didn't need hearts and flowers. So, deal with it.

"I take it you stopped playing the game at that point?"

"My father taught me never to hit a woman. But the flogger was made of black satin ribbons, and . . . shit."

He dragged a hand down his face. "To cut to the bottom line, the next time the flogger was leather. With knots."

"A cat-o'-nine-tails," Tess murmured. "Hey," she said, when he looked surprised she'd know of such a thing, "Buccaneer Days is a big deal around here. People dress up like pirates and those are popular accessories."

"I wasn't going that far. If nothing else, I didn't trust her."

"Seems to me if a woman hands a man a flogger and asks him to tie her up, she's the one who needs to be able to trust."

"True. But only a few weeks earlier, she'd been talking about leaving."

"A divorce in California would have given her half your joint assets."

"That wasn't a problem. The money was incidental. I figured if I so much as left a mark on her, she might go running to some ambulance-chasing lawyer with an abuse claim. My public profile, from the news interviews about the serial arsonist, was already pretty high. Since some of the press had taken to calling me 'ATF's Millionaire Special Agent,' any accusations undoubtedly would've made the tabloids."

"The guys up the food chain at the agency probably wouldn't have been real happy when a story of one of their special agents tying up his wife and flogging her landed on the front page of the *Enquirer*," Tess guessed.

"I would've been canned. At the very least, put on administrative leave until I'd somehow managed to prove my innocence. The job was damn important to me. Not only because I was determined to catch The Flamemaster. It was something I knew how to do. According to Kim, the *only* thing I knew how to do."

"Kim was wrong."

If allegations of abuse could have ruined his career, surely the shit must have hit the fan when he got arrested, albeit temporarily, for murdering his troublesome wife, Tess mused.

"She wasn't pleased I wasn't going to play the game anymore. Seems she'd had a special weekend all planned — a little private session followed by a more public party at some pay-for-play dungeon in Marin County.

"After she was killed, I discovered she'd already been going to those parties without me. Sometimes with the guy she'd been having the affair with. The one who'd introduced her to the S&M scene. When firefighters made it into our house the morning after the fire, her body was still tied to the bed."

If he hadn't already gotten her attention, that statement would have done it.

"With marine rope?"

"Yeah."

"Are you saying . . ."

God. Tess had witnessed death, up close and personal. But never as personal as this.

"The arsonist you were tracking was sleeping with your wife?"

"Twisted, isn't it?" This time there was nothing sexy about his edgy tone. "When I started getting closer, he arranged to meet Kim; they began having an affair when I was out of town. In fact, he got her involved with the plan of killing her just to show me he could."

"And set you up to be blamed?" Tess was stunned that anyone could be so evil.

"He didn't do that bad a job. Like I said, our marriage had been in a bad way; I'd finally moved out a week before the fire, and Kim had filed for a divorce."

"Before my life had gotten obsessed with Griffith, I'd taken up sailing. He used my marine rope, and, of course, my fingerprints were all over the handle of that damn ribbon flogger. I've always suspected that he wanted me at that club that night to add witnesses to the frame."

"It's hard to imagine any human being that twisted."

"Wait until you meet Griffith. The guy's about as far from human as you can get. More like the shit they pump out of outhouses."

"I still don't see why you were arrested."

"Cops always look at the spouse first in a murder case, which makes sense since the majority of homicides are committed by a family member."

"But you were released." On a technicality, Ty had said.

"Yeah. When the woman I'd been with that night came forward and vouched for me."

"Came forward?" It was what he hadn't said that grabbed her attention. "You didn't volunteer the fact that you had an alibi?"

"She was married."

"You would have been willing to go to prison? And possibly be put to death, just to keep an affair secret?"

"It wasn't an affair. It was a one-night stand with a woman I'd met at a conference in Reno. She'd just discovered her husband had screwed his secretary. She was in the city on business and was looking for a revenge fuck. The next morning she decided she was going to go back home to Fresno and try to patch things up for the sake of the kids. I didn't want to mess up her chances."

"Talk about overplaying your Sir Galahad card."

"You don't get it, do you? I thought you might, having lost someone you love . . . I didn't have anything to live for. I was already dying a slow death knowing that Griffith never would have targeted Kim in the first place if she hadn't been my wife."

The banked fury in his eyes was raw. Raw and deep and laced with despair that she never could have suspected was lurking inside that cowboy who'd swaggered toward her crime scene only yesterday.

"If a jury decided to speed things up, I sure as hell wasn't going to stop them. For a while it looked like I might end up with someone up at San Quentin sticking needles in my veins, then Claren — that's the woman I'd slept with that night — saved my hide."

"Well, that's quite a story."

"It's the truth."

She believed him. And ached for him. Which was only part of the reason she leaned forward and lifted a hand to his cheek.

thirty-one

Gage went still. Caution, tension, and a humming sexual warmth radiated from every male pore.

"Did you say something about this plane having a bedroom?"

"I didn't tell you that sordid story in order to get a pity fuck."

"Pity's the farthest thing from my mind," she said mildly. She took his glass away, placed it on the table beside the chair, then laced the fingers of her hand with his and stood up, coaxing him to his feet as well. "Unless you're getting tired of me already."

"Hell, no." And wasn't that the problem? Two days and he was already having a difficult time imagining ever getting tired of this woman.

Taking her to bed had seemed a good idea. They could both satisfy their desires, which would allow them to move on with the investigation. And, as soon as her pyro was behind bars, their lives.

It had been a reasonable idea. A good plan. The problem was, if it was true what they said about the gods laughing while men planned, those gods must be roaring their goddamn heads off about now.

Gage's feelings, which he couldn't untangle, were getting messy. If he didn't watch out, they could get complicated. Or worse, she could get hurt.

Interesting. That he could even, on some distant level, be concerned about that. It had been a very long time since Gage had cared about anyone.

Wanting to regain some control of the situation, he slipped his fingers below the neck of her silk blouse and pulled out the white-gold chain he'd known she'd be wearing.

"I've already told you, I'm not taking it off," she said, guessing his intention.

He tugged lightly at the medal. "I could rip it off you."

"And I could change my mind about sleeping with you."

"Like either of us are going to get any sleep. You'll take it off, Tess. Not because I tell you to, but this time you're going into things with your eyes wide open.

"You're not going to be able to bury your face in your pillow and pretend that I'm having my wicked way with you. You're going to be an equal — and eager

— participant. It's just a damn piece of metal. An inanimate object. But if you keep it on, you'll feel like you're committing adultery. And you're not a woman to cheat."

"I bought it for Danny."

"Who's dead." Realizing he was coming dangerously close to being jealous of a dead man, Gage had to wonder what the hell Tess Gannon was doing to his mind.

"You make it sound so damn easy."

"I didn't say that. But guilt's a no-win deal. A self-defeating, dead-end trip." Hadn't he learned that lesson the hard way? He brushed his mouth against hers, then bit her bottom lip just hard enough to draw a gasp.

"Look at it this way," he suggested. "You're not falling in love with another man. Hell, most of the time you can't decide if you even like me. It's just sex."

She let out a long breath. "Just sex," she agreed.

Her eyes were dry but resolute as she pulled the chain over her head and slipped it into a zipper pocket of her bag.

Then walked into the bedroom, leaving him to follow.

The bedroom was decorated in masculine tones of rust and browns. The queen-size mattress dominated the small space.

"Why don't you sit down?" Seduction hummed in the throaty, magnolia drawl, contrasting with the fire-cop persona she wore like a second skin.

The woman had layers. Facets. And *complication* written all over her.

"Take your boots off," she suggested. "After all, it's a long flight." She splayed her hand against his chest and gave him a little shove. "May as well get comfortable."

"Comfortable is not exactly the word I'd use." He sat on the edge of the mattress. Now that he'd gotten what he wanted, he was willing to cede a little control.

She tilted her head, studying the throbbing hard-on pressing against the metal buttons of his jeans.

"Perhaps we can do something about that." She knelt at his feet and pulled off first one boot, then the other. Then, after toeing off her own black pumps, climbed onto the mattress.

"Lift your arms."

The last time a woman had undressed Gage, he'd been seven years old, sent home from school with chicken pox. Although he'd complained about being grown-up enough to do it himself, his mother had stripped off his jeans and the green and yellow T-shirt the John Deere dealer had thrown in when his father had bought a new hay baler, then proceeded to rub calamine lotion all over the round red sores that had suddenly popped out all over his body.

This was *nothing* like that.

Tess's hands, strong and capable, yet tender and seductive in turn, moved over him. Her mouth whispered against his warming skin.

She touched. Tasted.

Teased. Tormented.

His head fogged, as if they'd flown into a cloud bank, Gage reached for her, intending to rip open her blouse as he had in the foyer of her pretty little house, but she was quicker, just keeping out of reach.

"I want to see you," he complained as his blood rioted. "Touch you."

"Believe me, you will."

She climbed down off the bed. Gage was regretting interrupting the flow when she flicked open the buttons of the blouse.

"Well." It wasn't that he hadn't found her damn sexy in the practical white cotton she'd been wearing this morning, but the sight of that skimpy white ivory lace made his mouth water.

Manfully, he kept himself from leaping

off the bed and burying his face between her smooth, artfully lifted breasts.

"Was that a moan of approval?" she asked.

He'd already discovered that he'd under-estimated her when they'd first met. Now Gage realized that he'd definitely not real-ized exactly how seductive the woman could be when she put her mind — and that long, sexy body — to it.

"Bailey — she's my friend, the ADA with the fuck-me shoes? — bought it for me for Christmas last year," she divulged. "For when I started dating again. Not that this is officially a date, of course, but you know what I mean."

When she skimmed her fingers over one lace-covered cup, brushing against that nipple he wanted to take in his mouth, Gage bit the inside of his cheek.

"She said men would like it."

"I like what it's barely covering even better." He also liked that she'd actually changed before leaving the house with this scenario in mind. "I don't suppose she also bought a pair of matching underpants?"

"Hmmm." The murmured purr was ripe with invitation. "Let's see."

The panties did, indeed, match the bra. They rode low on her hips, were cut high on her legs, and were sexy as hell.

Then, although he wouldn't have thought it possible, things got better. She was wearing stockings after all. Not the dreaded panty hose, or a fantasy garter belt and nylons, but lace-topped ones that accentuated firm, smooth thighs.

"Nice."

"I have to wear some sort of stockings with those pumps or I get blisters." She trailed a nail over the lacy band. "I have very tender skin."

"I can see that." He also wanted to take a bite out of her thigh. Just above the lace, at the inside of her leg, where her flesh did, indeed, look smooth as ivory silk.

"But I hate panty hose."

"Join the club." He watched her caressing touch move upward and wondered how the hell he was supposed to be carrying on a conversation when even his damn balls were throbbing.

"And these are more practical." Her hand headed south again; his gaze followed, riveted by those short buffed nails making slow, seductive circles down the front of her thigh.

"Gotta love a practical female. Do me a favor?"

She cocked her head. Wet her lips with

the tip of her tongue. "What favor would that be?"

He wasn't surprised that she didn't just flat out agree without hearing the details. Nor was he surprised that his penis was now standing up like a flagpole.

"Keep those on."

The vixen smile that tilted the corners of her lips was another surprise. "I can do that."

With her eyes holding his, she reached behind her back, unhooked the bra, then held it against her breasts for a suspended moment before letting it fall to the floor along with her other discarded clothes.

"If you keep this up, I'll come before we even get to the good stuff. Not," he said quickly, "that this isn't damned good stuff already."

"I thought you said we had four hours."

"I did. But maybe you should come back over here. So we take the edge off."

"I wonder if that's even possible?" She shimmied out of the panties, leaving her gloriously naked, save for the lace-topped stockings. She bent down to pick up his jeans from the floor, giving him a mind-blowing view of her high, firm ass as she retrieved a condom from the pocket. "You and I ever taking the edge off."

"Maybe not." His mouth went dry, his tongue turned thick and cumbersome as she rolled the ribbed latex down his erect penis. "But I've never been one to back away from a challenge."

"Isn't that a coincidence?" He wondered how she continued to carry on a conversation in such a matter-of-fact way when seemingly every bit of blood he'd had in his head had shot down to more vital regions. "Since I'm the same way."

Her sensual touch, as she sheathed him, was nearly enough to make him explode. But apparently that wasn't enough for her, because she curled her fingers around him and began stroking him. Up. Down. Up. God help him, down again.

"Dammit, woman . . ."

"Oh?" She lifted a brow. Who would have expected that the law-and-order fire cop could be such a tease? "Did you want something?" Still holding his shaft, she positioned herself over his hips. "Perhaps this?"

She lowered her body just enough to brush against him, dampening the tip with hot, slick moisture.

"You're enjoying this, aren't you?" he said between clenched teeth.

"Absolutely." She lowered herself another

millimeter. "Are you saying you aren't?"

"That's definitely *not* what I'm saying."

"Good," she said smugly. Although he wouldn't have thought it possible, he swelled fuller, throbbed harder, when she began using his length to stroke her clitoris. "Because I wouldn't believe you."

If he thrust upward, he could end this erotic torment. But understanding her need to feel in control, Gage resisted the urge and did his damndest not to pant like the animal he was.

"I may not have been entirely up front with you," he said hoarsely. Although he knew he was risking blowing the mood, it was important that she trust him. "But I'll never lie to you, Tess."

She paused, not to tease him but to consider that declaration. Her suddenly sober eyes met his, looking hard. Looking deep. Then she nodded.

"I know."

Anticipation was running hot in his veins when she lowered herself the rest of the way down, bringing their bodies intimately together.

The sudden feel of hot flesh against hot flesh made him shudder.

From her sharp gasp, he knew he was not alone.

"Wow." Her eyes were wide, and finally, he noticed with satisfaction, unfocused.

"Yeah." *Fucking wow.*

She began rocking her pelvis against him, which put her breasts right in front of his face. He squeezed them together, licked them, rolled her nipples in his mouth.

As she rode him, taking every bit of him, he sucked a raspberry-pink nub hard enough to rip a strangled sound from deep in her throat.

He did it again and felt a corresponding tightening around his cock.

Neither of them said another word. There was only the slap of hot flesh against flesh, the dull, steady roar of the engines outside the plane, the sound of their breathing growing shorter, harsher, as the pressure built.

The voluptuous convulsions started deep inside her, clutching at him, then radiating outward like a tidal wave, a long, powerful crest that pushed her over the edge, taking Gage right along with her.

She'd leaned forward, crushing her mouth against his when she came, allowing him to taste the scream she still couldn't allow herself. But scream she would, Gage vowed as she collapsed on his chest.

Next time, when he had her alone with an entire night ahead of them and she didn't have to worry about anyone — like the pilot — overhearing her.

She'd surprised him. Despite her having agreed to his no-strings terms, at first he'd sensed that she wasn't the kind of woman who'd settle for sex without all the emotional ties.

He knew she'd started this latest round because she'd been shocked by his story and had wanted, in some way, to try to soothe the pain.

But what they'd just shared hadn't been pity sex. She hadn't sacrificed her own pleasure for his. Hell, the woman had nearly been drunk with power and passion, which was fine with him. In fact, there'd been a moment there, just before she'd come, when she'd closed her eyes, seeming to mentally disconnect with him in order to focus on her own body. Her own needs.

He could recognize the disconnect between the emotional and physical because he'd been doing it himself for years.

But strangely, as hot as it had been, now that the roles were switched, Gage found himself vaguely dissatisfied.

thirty-two

"You sure you're ready for this?" Gage asked after they'd returned to the outer part of the cabin. He'd taken several thick manila files from a briefcase.

"I've seen people incinerated," Tess said. "I believe I can handle a few crime scene photographs."

"That doesn't mean you should have to." He held up a hand, forestalling a response. "I'm not being chauvinistic. Personally, I'd like it just fine if no one, including me, ever had to look at these kinds of photos. If sicko killers like Griffith didn't exist."

"But unfortunately they do." Steeling herself for the contents of the files, Tess held out her hand. "Which is where we come in."

The photographs, shot in graphic, living color, were every bit as unsettling as he'd warned they'd be. But it was the details of the crimes, which he'd related in such painstaking detail, connecting a maze-like trail of dots as Randolph Griffith had hopscotched across the country, that were even more horrible.

"He set all those fires, killed all those women, for money?"

"That's why most crimes are committed."

"I know that. But even professional torches try to avoid killing people."

"Hard to stay in the business if you keep drawing attention to yourself," he agreed.

"It was like killing was just a job to him."

"The number guys ran his various bank accounts, most of which were in Caribbean banks, and came up with a conservative estimate that ninety-four to ninety-six percent of his income came from life insurance policies."

"On women who foolishly fell in love with him." She shook her head. "What were they thinking?"

"We'll never know, since they're not around to tell us. But the woman who let me wire her hadn't had real good luck with men. Griffith was the first one who, quote, 'took care of her.' "

"Yeah, with money from his previous victims' deaths. She's just lucky you found her in time. And were able to convince her to cooperate."

How difficult must it have been, she wondered, continuing to work these cases after losing his wife in such a painful way.

Then again, she supposed at the time Gage could've been running as much on the need for vengeance as for justice.

She stared at the stack of papers she'd just read. "It's amazing he was able to take on so many different identities. Pretend to be so many different occupations."

"I never said he wasn't intelligent. Just that he's a fucking twisted sociopath."

"Not all the fires were for money, though."

"No. Some were personal."

Like Gage's wife.

As much as Tess had struggled with survivor guilt over the past two years, at least she hadn't suffered the heavier burden of having been, in any way, responsible for Danny's death. No wonder Gage had seemed to know exactly what she was feeling when he'd convinced her to take off Danny's St. Florian medal.

"I still can't understand the link to the Somersett fires."

She was beginning to trust Gage's gut. Unfortunately, arrest warrants weren't issued due to gut instincts, but to facts.

"That's what we're here for," he reminded her. "To put the pieces together."

Tess certainly hoped so. Because if that latest letter was on the level, there were too many potential victims out there who couldn't afford for them to fail.

San Quentin prison was spread over more than four hundred acres on Point Quentin, in one of northern California's priciest — and most stunningly beautiful — coastlines.

"Talk about your contrasts," Tess murmured as she took in the red-roofed, creamy peach-colored fortress set on a promontory once known as the Bay of Skulls. "This isn't exactly what I think of when I think of Marin County."

Bailey, who'd attended a conference in San Rafael a couple years ago, had sent her a postcard showing stunning beaches, redwoods, and wildflowers.

"Prison in paradise," Gage said as they drove through a neighborhood of homes, several with signs stating PRIVATE RESI-DENCE, NO PARKING stuck into their front yards. "The ultimate gated community."

White sheets flapped in the breeze on a clothesline behind a Cape Cod blue house with yellow trim; next door a woman was planting perky red and white petunias along the sidewalk leading to the front door while her daughter, bundled up in pink fleece against the stiff ocean breeze, watched from a stroller.

Tess supposed most of the homes in the neighborhood belonged to people who worked at the prison and wondered if, in some way, they might be nearly as much prisoners to this place as the inmates.

Gage had picked up his car in the San Francisco Airport short-term parking garage. Now that she knew he was rich, she wasn't surprised that it appeared to be the same model of Porsche he'd rented in Somersett.

"The plans are to build a new death row, but most people around here would just as soon the entire place go away. Especially since it's one of the few spots left on the bay deep enough for a ferry port. Plus, they can make a lot more bucks developing it for resorts, homes, and shopping."

"But it wouldn't just go away," Tess said. "It'd move to somewhere else."

"Thus pissing off a lot of other folks," he agreed. "Unless they stuck it somewhere out in the desert, miles from nowhere, which would make it difficult to staff and encourage lawsuits by prisoner's rights groups who say inmates need to be near state supreme court offices. There's talk of moving death row to a maximum-security facility outside Folsom, but that's drawing a lot of opposition. Personally, I think they just ought to reopen Alcatraz, lock most of the inmates in this place away up there, then throw away the key."

"You're not serious." She glanced over at him.

"Wait until you meet Griffith."

He pulled into the visitors' parking lot, shut off the engine. When he looked over toward her, his eyes were that spooky ice color they got whenever the serial arsonist's name came up.

"The guy's a textbook sociopath who's missing a helluva lot more than a conscience. Randolph Griffith lacks a soul. The bastard's the personification of evil."

Even knowing Gage understandably had a personal ax to grind, from what she'd read in the arsonist's file, Tess, who'd been brought up to believe that there were no unredeemable souls, suspected he might be right.

As they walked past the prison fire department and gas station, which added to the impression of San Quentin as a village, Tess thought of the children in the tidy green yards and wondered what it must be like to grow up with a prison for a neighbor.

On the drive north from San Francisco, Gage had told her that San Quentin was built by convict labor in 1852. Although, from a distance, it had resembled a massive resort overlooking San Francisco Bay, up close the haphazard sprawl of weather-beaten buildings definitely showed its age.

One building even reminded Tess of a crumbling castle, but the barb and razor band surrounding it, along with the prisoners in Day-Glo yellow coveralls policing the area, took away from that romantic notion.

She knew, intellectually, that she'd be able to walk out of the fortified gates after her visit to Griffith. But that didn't stop the sense of loss when she was required to hand over her bag and ID.

What if there was a riot when they were inside? she worried as a heavy, bulletproof metal door slid closed behind her. The walls were covered with posters citing rules and regulations. How could she ever prove who — and what — she was?

Surprisingly, the guards were friendly, almost chatty, more like staff at that resort she'd thought the prison first looked like than at a maximum-security facility.

After making their way through the main

building, they were sent through another series of glass and metal doors.

It was about a five-minute walk to East Block, one of two death row sections. A tall metal chimney, dating back to the days before execution by lethal injection, when gas had been the State of California's method of choice, reached from the roof into the steel-gray overcast sky.

Next to the chimney were two lights; one was on, the other dimmed.

"The chimney was used to vent the gas," Gage said when she slowed down to take it in. "People say birds used to fall out of the sky whenever an execution took place. The red light still signifies that the death chamber's in use. It goes back to green after the prisoner's officially been declared dead."

He'd been right. This was about as far from Sunnybrook Farm as Tess would ever want to get.

She paused in front of a pocked wall. "Tell me those holes are from weather and faulty workmanship."

"Bullets," he said, confirming what she'd feared.

"Interesting exercise program. Dodging gunfire." She willed the knots in her stomach to unwind. "But I'm not sure it'll catch on."

"If you want to wait in the car, now's the time to do it."

"I'm fine." No way was she going to admit that her knees were shaking beneath her slacks.

"Okay," he said simply.

The cacophonous roar of too many men packed together like sardines was the first thing Tess noticed as she entered the stifling-hot East Block building. The second was the stench. The third was the machine gun–carrying guards dressed in full riot gear walking the upper gun rail.

Backing up the armed guards was a sign by the door advising NO WARNING SHOTS FIRED IN THIS UNIT.

Christ. What was she doing here?

Trying, Tess reminded herself, to catch a killer.

The building was dark, the small amount of natural sunlight slanting through the high windows obscured by dirt and oily grime coating the glass. Dust motes fluttered in the air like so many moths.

They went through yet another series of electronic doors, Tess's nerves growing more tangled as one after another slammed shut behind her. Their passes were checked by more friendly employees clad in green shirts and khaki slacks, all of whom, like everyone else Tess had met thus far, appeared to have attended the Stepford prison academy.

Finally, thirty minutes after arriving at the main gate, they were cleared to enter the visitors' area.

This room, even more dimly lit than the main cell block, was almost entirely taken up by a huge metal cage divided into two sections of much smaller cages, with armed guards stationed in the center. The guards were locked inside, which again made her wonder how they couldn't feel incarcerated, as well.

She imagined it must sound like bedlam when all the cages were filled with visitors, but because they'd arrived after official visiting hours, the others were empty. As they'd gone through all the security checks, Tess had begun to realize how much weight Gage must have once pulled to allow them this meeting.

A man, clad in a yellow jumpsuit, was already in the cage at the end of the first section of cells. As they approached, he was ordered by a guard — who was more grim-faced than any Tess had seen thus far — to put his hands behind his back and through a flap in the rear of the cage.

Another guard opened the door, allowing Gage and Tess to enter. It was only after the metal door was closed behind them that the first guard uncuffed the man.

Although there were many who'd called him the devil incarnate, Randolph Griffith had neither tail nor horns. His thinning hair was the color of weak tea and beginning to go gray at the temples, his eyes were a nondescript grayish-green hazel, his nose slender, his lips a bit thin.

He didn't look at all dangerous. Nor would anyone pick him out of a crowd. In fact, he looked exactly like the accountant he'd twice claimed to be.

"Well, well," he said. "Will you look what the cat dragged in." He grinned as if at a private joke. "What's the matter, Special Agent, have you missed me?"

thirty-three

Gage's face was as hard as the stone walls of the prison, his eyes steel. "Like I'd miss the clap. This isn't a social call, Griffith."

"Oh, dear." The other man feigned hurt. "And here I thought you'd brought your new girlfriend to meet me." His gaze shifted to Tess. "Hello. I'm Randolph. I'd shake your hand, but contact visits aren't allowed. Who are you, darling?"

Tess felt Gage stiffen and willed herself to stay calm. The one thing she didn't need was for him to feel the need to protect her.

"Fire Inspector Tess Gannon."

"Tess." Griffith rolled her name around in his mouth, as if tasting wine, and seemed to approve. "Like of the d'Urbervilles. That was one of my favorite movies. There are, of course some who were annoyed by Roman Polanski layering his own psychosexual impulses on Hardy's story, but personally I felt it made it much richer.

"Besides, what did they expect? Everyone knows that every film the man's directed since that messy little murder of his

347

pregnant wife has been about Sharon Tate and the Manson family."

He tilted his head, studied her. "You remind me of Natassja Kinski; you both have those amazing green eyes. Have you seen the film?"

"I don't believe so." Tess had grown up being asked if she was named for the doomed heroine of Thomas Hardy's tragic novel, but couldn't believe she was sitting here in one of the country's most infamous prisons, receiving a movie review from a cold-blooded pyromaniac.

"You'd remember it if you did. It was a riveting portrayal, though I've always thought Polanski made a mistake leaving out the pivotal part where Tess wakes up in the forest surrounded by all those wounded and suffering birds and breaks their necks, supposedly to alleviate their suffering, but I personally always thought that deep down inside, she rather enjoyed the power that comes with snuffing out a life.

"According to interviews, the director omitted the scene because it anticipated the ending. Duh." Anger suddenly slashed like a whip in his voice. "Does the man know nothing about foreshadowing?"

He sighed. Heavily. Drew in a deep

breath and composed himself. "Nevertheless, despite that obvious flaw, it's still an exceptional film. You must see it."

"I'll keep it in mind."

"Please do. Take care you don't mistakenly watch that torturously slow version made for television. The only bright spot in that version was Justine Waddell, who was as brilliant in her complex take on the character as Kinski.

"You're not from the Bay Area, are you, Inspector?" he asked, switching gears. "Your lovely voice has the melody of the Lowcountry."

His own accent slipped effortlessly into a cadence that would've fit right in on the streets of Somersett. He was a chameleon, Tess realized, able to appear to be whatever — whomever — he needed to be to win over his victims.

"I'm from coastal South Carolina."

"Of course you are. Which leads me to believe you must be here about those fires you've been experiencing in the lovely city of Somersett."

Tess resisted, with effort, from shooting a shocked look up at Gage.

The cage was small, no larger than four feet by seven feet, with barely enough room for a low table and two chairs bolted to the dirty green linoleum floor. Wanting to establish a connection with the man, Tess sat down across the table from him.

Gage remained standing, hovering over her like an overly vigilant Rottweiler.

"You've heard about those, have you?"

"Of course."

"From anyone in particular?"

"That's for me to know." He winked saucily. "And you to find out."

"That's what I'm here for. To discover what you know." Tess refused to return his smile. "Did you realize the arsonist setting those fires is calling himself by your name?"

"No." His eyes widened dramatically. "Really? Why, the nerve of some people."

He was faking. Playing her like a damn fish on a line.

"We were hoping you might help us find the person. Before he kills again."

"And I should care why?"

"Because if you don't, you'll be sent to the AC?" Gage suggested.

"Excuse me while I shudder at that prospect." Griffith leaned toward Tess. "The adjustment center is known, among other things, as the hole. It's where they put the most violent of the condemned. We all land there when we first arrive on the row, and it's not a pretty sight — all those bully guards strutting around in riot gear designed to make them look like manly men, carrying their little canisters of pepper spray as if it'd really make a difference when trying to subdue some of the insane inmates the system throws into this place.

"When I was there, I was told the Night Stalker was in the next cell, but of course I couldn't tell for certain if that was true since the AC cells are essentially reinforced metal boxes without windows. Such as where you might lock up a condemned dog that's waiting to be put down."

"Appropriate analogy," Gage muttered.

Whatever happened to making a connection? Tess wondered, remembering how he'd chatted with Mannington when she'd been wanting to punch the bastard's lights out. Unfortunately, the problem was Gage had already made a connection with Randolph Griffith. A tragically fatal one.

Tess understood that. Truly she did. But she couldn't allow his personal animosity to undermine what they were trying to do here — protect lives and, although the connection was still circumstantial, perhaps even find the pyro who'd killed two men she'd loved.

"Would you mind if we stepped outside

for a couple minutes?" she asked Gage with a calm she was a long way from feeling.

"Can't do that." The guard sitting outside the cage looked up from the *Car and Driver* magazine he'd been reading. "You leave the room and the visit's over."

Please, Tess's gaze begged Gage. *Play nice.*

Fuck this, his responded.

Her heart, which had begun pounding like a tympani when she'd approached the tall, crumbling walls of the prison, was now lodged in her throat.

Gage cursed.

The conflict raging in him was palpable.

Tess wasn't the only one who could feel it. "That crack was insulting and unnecessary," Griffith complained. "Apologize or I'll go back to my cell."

"You have an opportunity to make a difference," Tess told Griffith. "To save lives."

The curl of his upper lip was more sneer than smile. "You have an idealist on your hands, O'Halloran. Quite a contrast from that adulteress you were married to before."

Gage didn't clench his fists. Didn't reach over the steel mesh half-screen separating them and take the smaller, slender man apart. He composed his face into an expressionless mask and met his nemesis's mocking look with a level one of his own.

"This isn't about me," he said on an even tone Tess suspected took a Herculean effort after such a direct personal attack. "But if you can't help Inspector Gannon" — he shrugged — "we'll just have to try someone else. After all, even thinking that you might know anything relevant was a long shot." He turned his attention to Tess. "Let's go. This guy's been locked up so long he's out of the loop."

"That's what you think," Griffith said on a flare of temper.

Obviously Gage, who undoubtedly had a more intimate knowledge of this monster than most people, knew which buttons to push.

Regaining control, the killer wagged his finger at Gage. "That wasn't nice, Special Agent. Surely you don't think baiting me is any way to convince me to help your lovely friend?"

He leaned toward Tess. "You really are an attractive woman. I can't imagine what you're doing wasting your time with this burnout case. It can't be sex. Since his late wife told me he's a dud in bed."

Tess wasn't going to touch that statement. "I'd be grateful for any help you could give me."

"Of course you would. Which is why you're going to do me a favor in return. *Quid pro quo,* so to speak."

She'd suspected it wasn't going to be easy. "What kind of a favor?"

"For some unfathomable reason, your testosterone-driven friend here appears to have an in with the warden. Perhaps because she's a woman, though for the life of me, I can't understand the appeal of big overtly macho cowboys with bad attitudes."

He shook his head in feigned bemusement. "But that's neither here nor there. The point is that for some reason the warden likes O'Halloran. If he asks her to relax a rule, she undoubtedly will. Just as she let you both in here today, after visiting hours, without an appointment."

"What rule do you want relaxed?"

Tess could practically see her chance for any helpful answers flying away, and while she'd always hated violence, especially when wielded by those in authority, she found herself wishing for the "good old days" when blinding lights and rubber hoses were routine interrogation tools.

"I'm getting married," Griffith divulged.

"The hell you are," Gage returned.

"Jealous, Special Agent?" the killer inquired with a smirk. "Pamela Winters is an exceptionally remarkable woman. An art dealer who has a gallery in Cow Hollow. She handles my paintings."

"Paintings?"

"Serial-killer art is a hot commodity in the art world," he said. "Pamela's very impressed with my talent. She says I could even become the next John Wayne Gacy."

Ice skimmed Tess's spine and she couldn't hold back the shiver at the mention of the outwardly mild-mannered construction worker who'd dressed up like a clown to strangle young men he'd then bury in the crawl space beneath his house.

"Is that so?" she asked.

"Absolutely. Don't you want to know my subject?"

No. What she wanted was to get out of this place that smelled like mold and rot and urine mingled with death and despair.

"I'll tell you anyway," he said when she hesitated. He leaned toward her again, so close she imagined she could feel the evil emanating from his prison-white skin.

"I draw fires. Of course they'd be better if I had the proper oil paints, but Pamela assures me that the black-and-white charcoal drawings possess a raw energy. As you undoubtedly know, given your line of work, Inspector, fire is a primal force."

"You're a sick pervert, Griffith," Gage growled.

"Sticks and stones," the killer countered with a merry wink. Then got down to business. "You must understand my situation here," he explained to Tess. "I spend twenty-three hours a day locked in a four-and-a-half- by ten-foot cell in a relic of a building built during the gold rush.

"Do you know that they were executing inmates here in San Quentin before Abraham Lincoln was inaugurated?"

Taking it as a rhetorical question, Tess didn't respond.

"The entire prison should have been condemned fifty years ago," Griffith continued. "Our cells, which are overrun with roaches, consist of a steel-plate bed so short my legs hang over the end, a stainless steel sink, and a toilet. There are two showers for the entire cell block. They aren't even proper showers. They're merely refitted cells with pipes. The plumbing leaks, even when the pipes aren't stopped up by feces, the floor's slick with mold and mildew, and the stench is overpowering.

"An hour a day, when we're not in

lockdown, I'm allowed to go outside to the exercise yard," he continued. "But because they believe I'm a danger to others, I'm locked in yet another cage, not much larger than the one we're sitting in now, and allowed to pace like the wild animal our favorite special agent seems to believe I am."

"My heart fucking bleeds for you, Griffith," Gage said.

"You really must work on that inner rage, Special Agent," Griffith taunted. "Have you considered anger management therapy? There's a program here for repeat offenders that's suppose to be very helpful."

"What are you asking for?" Tess asked, wanting to get this visit over with as quickly as possible.

"I want a contact visit for my wedding."

"Not in this lifetime," Gage countered.

"You're the one who came to me," Griffith reminded them. "I was merely minding my own business, rehabilitating myself with my art, falling in love —"

"Rehabilitating yourself, hell," Gage said. "You're just running a scam with that gallery owner the same way you did all those women on the outside that you killed. As for love, scum like you doesn't even know the meaning of the word."

"And I suppose you would?" Griffith lifted a mocking brow, shook his head, then turned back to Tess. "You want information about the individual setting fires in your city. I want to be able to kiss my bride when we take our vows."

"Who's going to be your best man?" Gage asked. "Your friendly insurance man who's writing the life policy on your fiancée as we speak?"

Griffith ignored him. "It's a fair trade," he told Tess.

"How can I be sure you even know anything?" Tess asked.

"Good question." His smile caused another frisson of ice to skim up her spine. "Why don't I put a little sweetener into the pot?" he suggested. "He's planning something special for this coming Easter weekend."

"That could be a lucky guess," Tess said.

"Could be," he said agreeably. "Or not. It's your choice whether or not to believe me, Inspector."

Unaccustomed to making deals with stone-cold killers, Tess hesitated, trying to weigh all the possible consequences.

"I'll tell you what," he said. "Why don't you sleep on it and come back tomorrow."

He paused a significant beat. "Alone."

"No way, no fucking how," Gage said.

"Excuse me, O'Halloran, but I believe I was speaking with Inspector Gannon." Griffith bared his teeth and snarled, for a fleeting instant showing his true colors.

Then he shook himself, like a dog shaking off water from a bath. Closed his eyes. When he opened them again, they were filled with what Tess knew was phony remorse.

"I'm sorry," he said. "It's just that it's very stressful in here and I've been working overtime trying to meet the deadline for my gallery showing next month. Even Pamela, who understands artists better than most people, often forgets that creativity doesn't respond well to pressure and schedules. The muses, after all, must have calm. And time to spin their magic."

"Excuse me while I puke," Gage said.

"I'd expect nothing less from a philistine," Griffith returned. Then smiled at Tess, a smarmy, snake-in-the-grass smile she found more unsettling than his flare of temper. "I do hope you'll think my proposal over, Inspector."

He tilted his head, studying her with a renewed interest that made her skin crawl. "You really do possess excellent bones.

You could cut crystal with those Kate Hepburn cheekbones, and your lovely moss-green eyes are remarkably expressive. They're definitely windows to your soul. And to your clever mind, which is refreshing, since so few women these days are so open."

Damn. So much for her inner poker player.

"I believe I'll sketch you," Griffith decided. "Do you wear a helmet in your work?"

Tess could feel Gage seething again behind her. "Yes. When I'm at a scene."

"Good. It'll make a nice contrast, the stark masculinity of the uniform and the delicate lines of your face. I'll have the preliminary sketch waiting for you tomorrow. When you give me your answer. And I, in turn, will tell you who that faux Flamemaster may be. And where you can find him."

"I haven't yet decided —"

"Oh, you'll come, Inspector. Or live with the guilt of all those dead civilians on your conscience. And, as I'm sure Special Agent O'Halloran here can tell you, being haunted by the ghosts of those whose lives you could have saved is a very heavy burden to carry around. Very much like

Marley's chains, I suspect."

Another pause, rife with malice. "Has the special agent told you that he was arrested for the death of his wife?"

"That's it." Gage's fingers clamped around Tess's elbow hard enough to bruise. "We're getting the hell out of here."

"Time's up," the guard outside the cage said at the same moment.

Tess was torn. She hated to leave until she'd gotten the information she'd come all the way across the country to find out. But since she also suspected that there was no way Randolph Griffith was going to give up what he knew without making her work for it first, she didn't resist when Gage practically dragged her out of the visitor's room.

thirty-four

"You're not coming back here," he said. "And goddamn not alone." His voice was calm. His eyes were not. A storm raged in them.

"I'll admit it's not my first choice —"

"You don't have a choice, Tess. Not a first choice, a second choice, nor any other. You can't even get a visitor's pass without me. And I'm damn well not signing off on this."

"I don't want to argue."

"Good. Then it's settled."

Clouds had gathered while they were inside; the white-capped blue of the bay was now a misty, pea-green soup. The wind bit through her black blazer.

"I think this is where I remind you, yet again, that a partnership does not involve one person giving the other orders."

"Nor does it involve that other partner putting herself at risk."

"We were in a room with armed guards all around us; there's nothing he can do to me."

"Why don't you tell that to that woman

lying in a Somersett morgue?" he suggested. "The bastard's connected to those fires. I just haven't figured out how yet."

"Perhaps through that art dealer?"

"Once again we're back to being in perfect agreement. Since it looks as if we're going to be spending the night, you've got two choices. A hotel, or my place, which is down the coast a ways."

Tess, who'd only ever been to Los Angeles for a conference, had always wanted to see this part of California. She was also vastly curious to see what kind of home Gage lived in. Wondered if it would give her any insight into that inner self he kept so well guarded.

Unfortunately, this trip wasn't about her. "I suppose it would make more sense, given the time constraints, just to get a hotel room."

"It's your call." If Gage was at all disappointed in her response, he didn't show it. What else was new?

He glanced down at his watch. "Since this is your first trip to the city, perhaps I ought to play tour guide and show you some of the sights before dinner."

"Sights meaning Cow Hollow?"

"Good choice." His eyes crinkled at the corners as he smiled. The edgy, dangerous mood was gone. Tess knew they'd only postponed the inevitable argument about her returning without him to the prison in the morning, but was happy to put it aside for the time being.

Besides, if they were lucky, Pamela Winters might provide the answers they'd come across the country to seek.

During post–gold rush San Francisco, Cow Hollow had been a small valley of pastures and dairies. Cows had grazed the land between Russian Hill and the Presidio and laundry women had carted their dirty clothing to one of the few sources of fresh water in the city, which became known as Washerwoman's Lagoon.

These days the Victorian houses had been restored, the neighborhood boasted one of the city's densest concentration of upscale boutiques, cafés, and galleries, and shoppers had replaced the cows.

"So," Gage said as they paused outside the building housing Collectors Gallery. "How do you want to handle this? Want to play tourist? Or challenge her right off the bat?"

Tess liked that he'd asked her opinion. It was an indication they were back to being partners again.

"Let's play it by ear," she decided. "And

if we do end up grilling her, you can be the good cop."

"I usually play the bad cop."

"Really?" Her eyes widened. "Gracious, I never would have suspected that." She skimmed a look over him. "Pamela Winters is a woman. And despite her apparent lack of taste when it comes to men, all her strings will undoubtedly go zing when she gets a look at you."

He lifted a dark brow. "I do believe that's the first compliment you've paid me."

"A good investigator uses all the tools at her disposal. So, I'm using you."

"Inspector, you make me feel so cheap. Though" — he caught her hand as she reached for the door — "I certainly wouldn't mind if you wanted to use me later tonight."

There was no point in playing coy. Or trying to disguise the jolt of her pulse when he lifted the inside of her wrist to his lips.

"Count on it."

Entering Collectors was like walking into a meat locker. Having decorated her own home in the soft, natural hues of the Lowcountry, Tess found the glacier-white walls, broken only by oversize splashes of twisting, blue, red, and white — several of which looked as if Jackson Pollock might have painted them while on a particularly nasty acid trip — uncomfortably chilly.

Tess had never understood modern art, but she knew what she liked. And she didn't like these halogen-spotlighted paintings. But that didn't necessarily mean that they were done by a criminal, either. Unless vandalizing canvas was a crime.

A discreet little bell had rung when they'd entered the gallery. The woman who came out from an inner office also fit the art-world stereotype. Her silver hair was cut in a sharp, geometric bob, she was dressed from head to toe in unrelieved black, and her eyelids were shadowed in charcoal and lined in kohl. The slash of scarlet on her lips provided her sole color. She appeared to be in her forties, or, Tess considered, perhaps a very well-preserved fifty.

"Hello." She managed to smile without causing a furrow in her forehead. Botox, Tess thought cattily. "Welcome to Collectors." Her voice was carefully cultured, with just a tinge of a British accent Tess suspected added a good ten percent to her prices. "May I help you find something particular?"

"We heard you had a somewhat more esoteric collection," Gage said, glancing around the open white space. "Something a bit out of the ordinary. Edgy. Some might even say, outrageous?"

"Ah." Speculation sharpened with greed glittered in her icy blue eyes. "Yes. I believe I know what you're referring to." Her feline smile was sly. "Follow me."

She led them past two smaller rooms, one featuring a collection of black-and-white homoerotic photographs, the other with glass cases of gleaming gold and silver jewelry, enameled boxes, and what appeared to be, at least the pieces Tess had been able to glimpse as they walked by, erotic ivory netsuke figures.

Were it not for the small sign beside the door of the smaller gallery reading COR-RECTIONS ON CANVAS, Tess wouldn't have immediately realized that she was looking at art created by killers.

There were a trio of seascapes, the artistic quality along the lines of what you might find at a starving artists' amateur show at the mall. A glass shelf displaying origami floated on a white wall; nearby a grouping of sock puppets that could have been a kindergarten art project perched on a bloodred shelf.

"That's a very valuable piece," the woman said when she saw Tess's gaze light on one of the puppets.

"It looks pretty much like a run-of-the-mill athletic sock." Though, studying it more closely, she wondered uneasily if that wide-open felt mouth was meant to be screaming.

"To the untrained eye. Read the card."

The first thing Tess noticed when she read the discreet white card beside the puppet was the price, which was more than she paid for her first car. The second was the name of the artist.

"Is that who I think it is?"

"The Night Stalker," the woman agreed, looking more than a little pleased with herself. "He usually portrays more visceral work — demons, horned self-portraits, bloody knives, the type of art that reinforces his image as the poster boy for Satanists.

"This, on the other hand" — she trailed a French-manicured fingernail over a black button eye — "is far more innocent. As if he's allowed his inner child free expression."

"Lovely." *Not.* "Are you Pamela Winters?"

"Yes." The art gallery owner's gaze turned cautious. She took another, longer look at Gage. "I recognize you. You're the so-called millionaire ATF agent. The one who . . ."

Her voice trailed off, but she recovered quickly. "Ah," she murmured as the pieces fell into place. She folded her arms. "I understand how the idea of my giving the man who killed your estranged wife an audience for his artistic expression might be a bit uncomfortable for you —"

"It's a free country."

Tess, knowing how much the mild tone had cost Gage, jumped into the fray. "Which means people have a constitutional right to make blood money by giving some sociopath murderer ego gratification by treating him like a celebrity," she said.

"Art is about human expression," the other woman responded frostily. "Not what pleases others. There are those, admittedly, who see such pieces as tasteless or sensationalistic —"

"How about sick?" Tess suggested.

"There's a parallel between art and murder. While art is creation, and murder annihilation, they're both, in their own way, a quest for aestheticism. As Nietzsche says, 'There is music and poetry in the art of the ugly soul.' "

Her fire engineering class had never covered Nietzsche, but Tess decided that if

Winters was quoting him correctly, the guy must be full of shit.

"Maybe Nietzsche never had a loved one murdered in cold blood," she said. "Then was forced to stand by and watch people lining up to throw money at the killer."

"That's a very black-and-white way to look at the issue."

"Hey, what can I say." Tess shrugged. "I'm a black-and-white kind of gal."

"Yet the world is comprised of shades of gray. Of nuances. There's a long tradition of using savagery to make a point. Depictions of bloodied saints and human atrocities were a staple of the medieval art world and painters like Cézanne and Goya —"

"Never murdered anyone."

A silver brow arched. "Excuse me. I didn't catch your name."

"That's probably because I didn't throw it. Tess Gannon." Tess flashed her ID. "I'm a fire inspector. From South Carolina."

If she was at all flustered by a visit from a former ATF special agent and a fire cop, Pamela Winters didn't show it. Then again, Tess considered, a person would have to have ice water in their veins to spend any up-close-and-personal time with Griffith.

"You're a long way from home, Inspector."

"I'm here on a case. A case we believe might have ties back to your fiancé."

"Well, I don't know how that could be. It's not as if Randolph has the freedom to just walk out of that horrid prison and travel around the country."

"If he *were* a free man, he wouldn't be of much use to you, would he?" Gage asked dryly.

"Are you implying that I'm taking advantage of Randolph?"

Hell with good cop, bad cop. Tess shot a look at Gage. *Go for it.*

"I don't know," he said. "Nor do I give a damn. Though I have to wonder how you sleep at night."

"Like a baby."

"Good for you. Seems to me some people might have problems with the idea of revictimizing victims and their families."

"As a matter of fact, I've many family members who've signed up for my newsletter. They're often the ones who buy the pieces."

"To destroy them."

Her slight shrug was elegant. And dismissive. Tess decided she and Griffith deserved each other. "Fascination with death has always been a human pastime," Winters said. "Why else would people buy items with John Dillinger's blood on it, or bits of dirt from beneath John Gacy's house, or Ted Bundy's Volkswagen? What people do with an item after they purchase it is their own business."

"Unfortunately, that's true," Tess allowed. "But murder on paper is one thing." She gestured toward a triptych on an adjacent wall, the three paintings depicting a female corpse laid out on a medical examiner's steel table, each body showing an increasing progression of purple, green, and gray postmortem lividity. "Murder in real life is another kettle of canvases.

"So, to cut to the chase, since I'm sure we all have places to go, people to see, where were you two nights ago?"

Winters stiffened. Imperceptibly, but enough that Tess, watching her carefully, noticed.

"I was at a cocktail party in North Beach."

"How about later?" Tess asked.

"I had dinner with friends."

"They'll confirm that?"

"Of course."

"Could we have their names?"

Hesitation. "Is that really necessary? And do you even have authority here in California?"

"We can get it," Gage said. "And yes, it would be very helpful if you could give us the names. We'll attempt to use every discretion."

"Well." She blew out an annoyed breath. "I'll go get my book."

"What do you think?" Tess asked after the woman had left the room.

"I think any man who took that female to bed would risk frostbite."

"I wasn't asking for a sexual scorecard. I was asking what you thought about her and Griffith."

"She's got a lot to risk, getting mixed up in arson and murder." He glanced around the gallery. "But then again, galleries are a dime a dozen in this city. Dealing with the thriving serial-killer art market could give her a financial edge over the competition."

Tess couldn't imagine ever wanting money so badly that you'd willingly deal with murderers. "Gotta love free enterprise."

Pamela Winters returned with a list of names and phone numbers. "I'd appreciate discretion."

"We'll do our best." Gage put the piece of paper in the inner pocket of his jacket. "Meanwhile, you haven't happened to accidentally smuggle any messages out of prison for Griffith?"

"Of course not." She bristled. "That would be against the law."

"And we know what a proponent of law and order you are. So, what do you think about your fiancé's request to the warden regarding your wedding?"

"What request is that?"

"Seems your husband-to-be wants to kiss his bride."

The color drained from Pamela Winters's face, leaving her complexion as white as her stark gallery walls. "Randolph is on a no-contact order."

"Yeah, but he's willing to cooperate if I manage to get that prohibition lifted for the ceremony."

"You can't." Wavering ever so slightly on her high heels, Winters pressed the heel of her hand against her temple. "The warden would never agree to such a thing."

"I wouldn't wager your little freak show here on that," Tess said, beginning to enjoy herself for the first time since arriving in California. "As your pyro boyfriend pointed out when we paid him a little visit today, Special Agent O'Halloran has a special personal relationship with the warden."

Tess handed her a business card. "My

cell number's on this. If you think of anything that could shed some light on how your fiancé might be manipulating a crime on the other side of the country from death row, I'd appreciate your cooperation."

"I told you, I don't know anything about that."

"So you said. Just like I'm not going to know anything about the fire marshal paying you a surprise visit in the next few days to make sure you aren't violating any fire regulations here in your little shop of horrors."

"Are you threatening me?"

"Some might see it that way. Me, I view it more as keeping citizens connected with their government agencies. If you happen to think of anything, give me a call. In the meantime, if a salesman shows up at your door, I wouldn't go buying any life insurance right now . . ."

"Did you say something about dinner?" she asked Gage.

"I believe I mentioned it."

"Good. Let's go. I'm starving." Tess paused in the doorway and glanced back over her shoulder. "Call me." It was more order than suggestion.

Pamela Winters stood alone in the room,

listening to the silvery peal of the bell as they left the building. She made her way, on unsteady legs, to her office, which she'd decorated in muted shades of gray. Sinking down onto a chair upholstered in black-and-gray-striped silk, she braced her elbows on the black glass desktop and buried her face in her hands.

No! She would not give them the satisfaction of giving in to despair. If she allowed herself to crumble at the least little thing, she'd still be Chamber Anne Carpenter, a little raggedy-ass bastard girl who'd grown up on the wrong side of the tracks in Alturas, California, a mountain town whose sole claim to fame was the annual cow dog championships.

It hadn't been easy reinventing herself. But with hard work, education, and a fifty-thousand-dollar check from a rancher who was willing to pay to have her leave town — and his son — she'd made a damn good life for herself.

She didn't believe in all that crap she'd spouted to those two cops about the purity of prison expression, of course. But the art business, like any others, revolved around supply and demand.

Fortunately, there were a helluva lot of people — including some A-list celebrities who preferred to keep their purchases private — in the market for such macabre items. She'd even had a Golden Globe nominee tell her that he considered possessing objects killers had created, or even touched, to have a talisman effect, protecting him in some mystical way.

Which, of course, was bullshit. But it provided her a very comfortable lifestyle.

She took a deep breath, pushed herself to her feet, went into the adjoining bathroom, and splashed water on her face and the inside of her wrists. The little black dots swirling around her eyes vanished and it became clear what she was going to have to do.

With her head and focus clear, Pamela Winters returned to her desk, picked up the receiver of the sleek chrome and black phone, and placed a call to her "fixer."

thirty-five

"Wow." Tess took a deep breath of the brisk breeze blowing in from the bay. "That woman's a piece of work."

"She deals in blood money and is engaged to a serial killer," Gage said. "Can't really expect Mother Teresa."

"I suppose not." She looked out at the orange towers of the Golden Gate Bridge and wished she and Gage had come here for some — any — other reason. "I can't imagine doing such a thing for a living."

"Of course you can't." He shoved his hands into his pockets and stood beside her, staring out over the windswept bay. "The reason I left ATF?"

A bit surprised by the shift in topic, Tess glanced over at him. "Was because of what happened to your wife. It'd be understandable that would hit you hard."

"It did. But I probably would've gone back. Eventually. The reason I didn't was that I nearly killed Griffith."

Tess wasn't surprised. Because if she'd been in his shoes, she would've wanted to do the same thing.

"Define *nearly*."

"I beat the shit out of him, broke five bones, and put a gun to his head and threatened to blow him away."

Well, it appeared she'd been right on the money with that Dirty Harry image. "But he's still alive."

"Only because my partner yanked me off the scumbag before I pulled the trigger."

"You wouldn't have done it."

"That makes one of us who believes that."

"You value life, Gage. You wouldn't have spent all those years endangering your own and tracking down bad guys if you didn't. You wouldn't commit cold-blooded murder."

"My blood wasn't exactly cold at the moment."

"That's my point. *Of course* you wanted to kill him. Who wouldn't after what he did, not just to you and your wife, but to all those other families who'd loved his victims? But you didn't go through with it, *wouldn't* have, because it would've made you, at least in your own eyes, no better than him."

She lifted a hand to his chest, her eyes to his. "Do you know what I think?"

"What?"

"That you're a far better man than you believe you are."

"Maybe you *need* to believe that. In order to have sex with me."

"That would be selling us both short, don't you think?"

His laugh was a rough, harsh sound. But she detected a bit of warmth in it, as well. "Seems I've hooked up with not only an idealist, but an optimist as well."

"Hey, I've always felt that pessimists may be proven right in the end, but optimists have a lot better time on the trip."

"And I've always thought that a pessimist is merely a person who's had to listen to too damn many optimists."

A smile bloomed on her face and lit up her eyes in a way that had Gage wishing he believed in happy endings. "I guess I'll just have to change your mind about that," she said.

"Other people have tried."

"Ah, but those other people weren't me."

"You're not going to get an argument from me on that." Moved by the sweetness, the humanity, in her eyes, Gage brushed a windblown curl off her cheek. "Okay, practicing my optimism here, what do you say we go get ourselves a suite at the Mark

Hopkins and call down for room service."
Her cheek was gardenia-petal soft; Gage
knew the rest of her was even softer.
"Much, much later."

"I'd say I've changed my mind. If it's
okay with you."

"Sure." She didn't owe him anything.
Hell, hadn't he mistakenly believed that
once he'd had her, he could move on?

"Oh, don't be sulky." She took hold of
the hand he'd dropped to his side and
linked their fingers together.

"Men don't sulk. Brood, perhaps. But
we never sulk."

"Talk about splitting hairs. What I was
about to suggest, before you got all pouty
— uh, broody" — she corrected at his
warning glower — "was that if you don't
mind the drive, I'd like to take you up on
the invitation to spend the night at your
house."

"Works for me." He was surprised by
how much. Especially given that he'd never
invited a woman to his remote home before.

"Good. Because as lovely as this city is, I
think I'd like to get out of it tonight." She
glanced back toward Collectors and shivered.

"We'll come back another time," he suggested, conveniently ignoring the fact that he'd been the one to insist on no future. "I'll give you a proper tour."

"I'd like that," she agreed.

So would he.

thirty-six

It was a pretty little house. Charming, cozy, and it was obvious Fire Inspector Tess Gannon had done a lot of work on it.

It was the kind of house made for raising babies. The Flamemaster might not be the least bit paternal, but even he could picture a little girl dressed in pink ruffles, having tea parties with her dolls at the small wicker table in the front porch, and a rough-and-tumble boy digging up the backyard English garden with his Tonka toy bulldozer.

He climbed the stairs, wandered into the bedroom, and was nearly knocked over by the pungent odor of sex. Most people probably wouldn't even notice it. But The Flamemaster was very sensitive to his surroundings.

He ran his palm over the soft yellow quilt, imagined the two of them, rolling naked over the bed, greedy mouths eating into each other, hands grasping slick, hot flesh, engaging in ugly, filthy, disgusting acts no decent woman would ever allow.

Even worse, she'd gone off with that man

she'd been fornicating with, never mind that she'd only just met him. To San Francisco, and The Flamemaster was very angry about that.

Didn't she realize that her focus was supposed to be on *him,* on his threats of what he could do to the city, not on some has-been arsonist who'd been careless enough to land his skinny ass in prison?

The Flamemaster had no intention of going to prison. He was too clever, too good at his work. If they only knew how good.

A white frame sat on a table covered in a flowered cloth. He picked it up and felt a twinge of guilt as he took in the man's face smiling out at him. Danny McGee was standing next to his ladder truck, his arm around his fiancée, a huge, shit-eating grin on his face.

The Flamemaster rubbed his temples and struggled to stay focused. Thinking about the past only made his head ache.

The room began to spin. Acid roiled in his gut. His hands were trembling as he went to set the photograph back onto the table.

It fell to the hardwood floor, the crack of the glass sounding like a gunshot. He flinched. Covered his mouth with his hand.

When he bent to pick it up, a needle-sharp sliver of shattered glass punctured the tip of his finger. The poppy-red bloom of blood triggered memories locked deep inside him.

There was pain. Horrible, burning pain like the fires of hell. And blood, warm and scarlet and sticky. He'd had to scrub for hours to wash it away.

Just the memory of that night caused exhaustion to come crashing down on him like a sledgehammer.

He'd been weak. Weak and powerless.

The Flamemaster swayed as sobs echoed in his mind. He was breathing hard, his shirt soaked with acrid sweat. He *hated* it when this happened, when the horrible images reverberated in his brain!

Knowing that they wouldn't go away until he faced them, saw them through, he grasped onto the slender carved wooden bedpost and reminded himself what he'd come here to do.

He forced himself to pick the photograph up and managed to replace it on the table, refusing to meet the accusing look he knew he'd see in the fireman's eyes.

Back when the nightmares had kept him awake for weeks on end, The Flamemaster had visited an old Gullah woman who'd told him that when people died suddenly, violently, their souls, given no warning that would allow them to prepare to move on, got trapped between this life and the next.

He'd handed over a twenty-dollar bill in exchange for a spell to recite and a black candle to burn. The candle, which the woman had charged beneath a full blue moon, had flared the instant he'd lit it. Sparks flew upward like fireflies escaping from the melting black wax.

It was at that moment that the man he was today had been born. He'd seen his destiny in that flickering orange flame.

And destiny, he'd discovered, would not be denied.

He'd just opened his murder kit when the room was suddenly flooded with light. He froze, his heart pounding painfully in his throat, then realized it was only headlights shining on the closed shades.

He remained standing by the bed, still and silent as a mouse, listening to the slam of a car door outside. Then another. The lilt of a woman's merry laughter drifted on the night air, followed by the deep, rumbling baritone chuckle of her companion.

A hinge squeaked as a screen door opened. Then closed behind Tess Gannon's neighbor and whatever man the transvestite had brought home with her/ him from that club she/he ran on the river.

As the night turned silent again, The Flamemaster set to work.

thirty-seven

It had begun to rain. Tess was grateful when Gage didn't appear to want to engage in conversation on the drive down the coast. There were a lot of things they'd have to discuss before morning, subjects too complex to handle in a car speeding through the drenching downfall.

Such as Griffith insisting she visit him alone tomorrow, and what to do about Pamela Winters, who Tess was convinced was somehow involved in all this up to her neck. And how either one of them could possibly be connected to her fires.

"This is absolutely spectacular scenery," she murmured.

Even softly veiled in fog and rain, the view of the rugged cliffs — gleaming gold from their carpet of wildflowers — and wild, churning water was breathtaking.

"That's Devil's Slide." Gage pointed out a long, sloping shoulder of the mountain that jutted obstinately out into the ocean.

"I read about it in a novel once. The author called it the California equivalent of the Bermuda Triangle." The horror author had also blamed the many deaths in the book on the devil, an entity Tess had an easier time believing in since meeting Randolph Griffith.

"There are a lot of rock slides along this stretch of highway. The road's closed a lot. Once for nearly four months. A local medium has dubbed it the Bay Area trapezoid."

"Well, that's encouraging."

"Any woman who used to run into burning buildings shouldn't be nervous about a few rocks."

"The definitive words are *used to*."

Tess was grateful when he didn't press her to elaborate on the fear she'd kept to herself.

"There's been talk for years of building a tunnel, but it's recently been fast-tracked by the government, so maybe it finally will happen."

The sky darkened; the wind picked up, driving the rain against the windshield as Gage maneuvered the car around the tight narrow curves with easy confidence. Tess decided that he was definitely in his element here in this wild, untamed land.

He turned onto a narrow gravel road, stopping at a sign that read PRIVATE PROPERTY. NO TRESPASSING.

"Too bad you couldn't find a place with more privacy," she said when he returned to the Porsche after unlocking the heavy chain strung across the road. "What's the matter? Something wrong with your missile defense system?"

"Real cute, Slim. As it happens, I *did* have an electronic system, but the salt air corroded the contact points, so I decided to go with something more basic."

"Like anyone's going to find their way here in the first place."

They turned a sharp corner, coming to a dead end. Tess drew in a sharp breath as the house came into view. The hulking Gothic monstrosity, complete with a tower and widow's walk, clung to the rocky escarpment overlooking the crashing surf far below. Draped in deep purple shadows, it was no more welcoming than the angry sky behind it. The windows were heavily shuttered, the better, she imagined as thunder rumbled ominously overhead, to keep out prying eyes.

"Boy, I'll bet Dracula was ticked off."

"That reference escapes me."

"When you moved his home from Transylvania to here."

As if to accent her accusation, a bolt of yellow lightning streaked across the sky, washing the brooding stone building in a brief, stuttering light.

"That's what he gets for sleeping during the day."

The gargoyle door knocker was heavy and old and not the least bit inviting. Rather than offering a comforting sanctuary from the storm, the inside of the house was as black and silent as a tomb.

"What, no vampire bats?"

"They're probably out getting their nightly ration of blood."

He switched on a light, brightening the vast dark foyer. But not by much. Wondering how anyone could sleep in this unsettling home, which she suspected could well be haunted, Tess shivered.

"Come in the kitchen and I'll light a fire."

"I'd rather have a hot shower first."

Not only was she chilly from her brief run through the rain to the front door, the conversations with Griffith and Pamela Winters had left her feeling dirty.

"You." Gage ran his hands up her arms. "Me." Across her shoulders. "Naked and wet." His lips curved in a wicked, pirate's slash of a grin. "Inspector, that may just be the best idea you've come up with yet."

thirty-eight

Tess was relieved to discover that the bathroom had been modernized. A huge Jacuzzi tub large enough to swim laps in looked out over the water; the shower boasted six — she counted them — spray heads.

"Handy for orgies," she said as he pulled her into the magnificent tile and glass enclosure. The water from the sprays hit her body like vibrating fingers, front and back, against her breasts, her back, her bottom, stimulating skin already sensitized by his touch.

"Why in the name of heaven would I want any other women?" Water streamed over her. Over him. "When I have you?"

He picked up a blue bar of soap, rubbed it between his palms to create a lather, then began running his hands over her wet, slick body, spreading the fragrant bubbles.

Gage's hands were rough, but silky smooth with soap. When he cupped her breasts, they felt achingly full; his thumbs flicked over her unbearably sensitive nipples, dragging a ragged moan from deep inside her.

Steam rose, as warm as the mist that was clouding her mind, as his clever hands continued their sensual conquest.

His tongue slid lazily over her belly and made her moan. The nip of teeth against the wet flesh of her inner thigh created a jolt of heat.

"Gage." Sobbing out his name, she reached for him, but he'd already moved on, sliding down her wet body, creating a trail of havoc with hands and mouth from her thigh to the back of her knee, to her ankle, which she'd never suspected was an erogenous zone.

"Oh, God." The clouds of steam surrounded them, filling her lungs. Tess couldn't breathe. Couldn't think. "Please."

In response to the desperate plea that had escaped her parted lips, his mouth roved slowly, wickedly, back up her quivering legs.

Her body bowed as his mouth found her. Her head fell back against the black tile as she gave herself up to the voluptuous glory of being pleasured.

Awash in sensation, floating on soft clouds of seduction, Tess was not prepared for the quick, hard stab of his lascivious tongue that brought her to a swift, violent release.

It was stunning. Thrilling. Sublime.

Even so, she wanted — needed — more.

"Inside." She arched against him, urging him on. "Dammit, I want you inside me."

"Remind me, later, if the blood ever returns to my head, to tell you that I love it when you're bossy," he said against her quivering belly.

She fisted her hands in the wet silk of his hair. "You know that old saying about firemen finding a woman hot and leaving her wet?"

"I believe I've heard it a time or two."

"I have my own twist on that." She reached between them, circled his straining shaft with her fingers. If she could have forced him into her, she would have. But still he held back, driving her to distraction with his steely control. "A firewoman leads a man around by his hose."

She felt his deep chuckle as much as heard it. "Anytime, Slim." He continued to leave hot, stinging kisses up her torso. "Anywhere."

When his mouth paused long enough to clamp onto her breast, Tess instantly fell apart, with a ragged cry, a thrust of hips.

More.

"Now," she managed.

"Now," Gage repeated.

He lifted her, spread her, slid into the wet warmth, filling her in one smooth, wet, wonderful glide.

She wrapped her legs around his waist; he pressed her against the wall. But before he began to move, he pulled his head back. His gaze was as serious as she'd ever seen it.

"I need you, Tess."

She felt a burning in her eyes and tried to tell herself it was the sting of soap. *Liar.*

"I know. I need you, too."

He began to move, his strokes long and deliberately slow at first.

Harder.

Faster.

Tess pistoned her hips to meet each grinding thrust as he pumped into her.

He took her, she took him, they took each other, on and on and on, until the heat inside Tess burst into a blinding nova. And he followed her into the light.

"Oh, God," she moaned, her head buried in his shoulder, "I think you've blinded me."

"It's the steam."

Her back was pressed against the tiles; his body had practically collapsed against her, and if he didn't manage to force some starch into his wobbly legs, they were both going to slide down to the floor.

"It's like a fog bank in here," he pointed out.

"Oh." She sighed happily and pressed her lips against his neck. "That's a relief." Her voice was thick. "I was afraid I'd never see again. Not that it wouldn't have been worth it," she decided, slurring her words.

"Don't go to sleep yet," he said. He put his hands beneath her butt, lifting her up when she would have slid down to the floor. "Because I'm not done with you."

"Good. Because I'm not done with you, either."

He turned off the water, snagged a couple thick towels from the rack set into the tile, and wrapped one around her. Supporting each other, they somehow managed to make it to the bed in the adjoining room.

"You screamed," he said as they tumbled together onto the bed.

"So did you."

"Guys don't scream."

"Just like they don't sulk," she said, pressing her smiling lips against his. "But someone in that bathroom was screaming 'Tess, Tess!' And since I know it wasn't me, if the house isn't haunted by a ghost with an incredibly sexy voice, by process of elimination, that leaves you."

"Good deductive reasoning." He sucked in a sharp breath as she shimmied down the mattress, pressing kisses down his chest.

"Thank you." Her fingers curved around him with a silky but sure touch. "I am, after all, a detective."

"And, for the record, it happened to be a shout," he managed as the wet silk of her curls skimmed over his groin.

"Well, then." She brushed her smiling mouth against the tip of his penis. "Let's see if we can make you do it again."

Tess's mouth was warm and generous, savoring Gage as he savored her. His hands were patient and knowing, touching her in all the places he'd discovered she loved to be touched, loving her with a tenderness Tess wouldn't have believed possible only two days ago.

"You're crying," he said later, as they lay amid the tangled sheets. He touched a fingertip to the tear that had accompanied her last orgasm.

Firefighters don't cry. Tess was determined to be seen as one of the boys, and this had become her mantra over the years. But she knew she couldn't deny the depth of emotion their lovemaking had tapped.

"Only because it was so . . ." She was momentarily at a loss for words. Amazing? Mindblowing? "Perfect," she decided. "If I could just figure out how to bottle you, Special Agent O'Halloran, I could make a fortune."

He laughed, that rough, rusty sound that told her it was not something he did often. "It's you." He brushed some still-damp curls away from her face. Lowered his mouth to hers, kisses punctuating his words. "You're the perfect one, Inspector."

Her lips curved beneath his. It wasn't true, of course. But the words, coming from a man she knew was not one to easily bestow compliments, warmed her heart.

"It's us," she decided. "We're perfect together."

As impossible as he would have found the idea only days ago, as she snuggled up against him, Gage thought she just might be right.

thirty-nine

Although sex had always proven to be a sure-fire sleep aid, Gage spent a long, lonely night lying beside Tess, staring up at the ceiling.

Tracking down Randolph Griffith had, for years, been nothing less than an obsession. Having experienced one obsession, he could recognize another.

It was obsession that kept his mind wandering to Tess, even during that first night, when he'd lain awake in his hotel room wondering if she was lying alone in her bed across town thinking about him.

It was obsession that made him — even when they'd been locked in that suffocating cage on death row — want to drag her to the nearest hotel, where he could feel her hot and naked beneath him.

It was obsession that had his mind rerunning all the things they'd done together. And fantasizing about all the hot, erotic things he was still aching to do to her. With her.

Gage warned himself that he was rapidly approaching quicksand. A few more steps and he could end up in over his head.

And the strangest thing was, he couldn't even make himself care.

The evening rain had moved inland to water the grapes in the valley; moonlight and star shine streamed into the bedroom through the skylight some previous owner had installed over the bed.

Rolling over onto his side, bracing himself on an elbow, Gage studied her.

Her redhead's skin was as pale as porcelain. But, he knew, much, much warmer. Softer. The smooth flesh beneath her closed eyes was smudged with purple shadows. Her lashes were like gilt threads against her cheeks; her breath escaped from her softly parted lips.

Although he'd never considered himself a fanciful man, lying in his bed in the moon glow, she reminded him of Snow White, waiting for the kiss of her prince to awaken her from the evil spell.

The problem with that scenario was that while Tess might be a beauty, he was definitely no Prince Charming.

A fact underscored by the bruises on her arms. Her shoulders.

And Gage knew that if he pulled the sheet away, he'd be able to see the same marks darkening the silky skin of her inner thighs.

Annoyed at his lack of finesse and knowing he wouldn't be getting any sleep tonight, he abandoned the warmth of the bed and went down the hall and up a curving flight of stairs into the tower room he used as an office.

Just as he knew that Griffith was somehow involved in these latest fires, Gage had not a single doubt that the fires two years ago, one of which had killed Tess's fiancé, had been purposefully set.

He couldn't promise her happily ever after. Hell, he couldn't even promise next week.

But there'd been a time, before his life had gone into that downhill, self-destructive spiral, when he'd been the goddamn best in the fire-detecting business.

He sat down at the computer. A few quick keystrokes and he'd accessed the SFD files, which kept prefire blueprints for every commercial building in the city.

He pulled up the mill. Then, as the moon floated across the sky outside the floor-to-ceiling windows, Gage went to work.

Tess was not surprised when she woke to find herself alone. Disappointed, but not surprised. There are those who might think that sex is the closest two people could be, but she'd always thought the actual act of sleeping together was even more intimate. It was a time when barricades were lowered, vulnerabilities revealed, and not even the most rigid control freak in the universe could keep from revealing parts of themselves that they might not have even admitted to themselves.

Gage had shared far more revelations about his personal life than she ever would have expected. Then again, he really hadn't had any choice, given how his life and the case were so inexorably intertwined. But she knew she'd be expecting too much to wish that he'd lower his guard to spend the entire night with her.

"It doesn't matter," she reminded herself as she left the wide bed. "This isn't forever after you're talking about. It's about right now. It's a fling. As long as you keep that in mind, you'll be just fine." *Liar.*

Needing to go off by herself to think about Gage, to try to access her feelings, and, just as important, to figure out what to do about what Gage might be feeling toward her, she dressed in a pair of jeans and, having not packed anything warm, since she hadn't expected California to be so chilly in April, borrowed one of Gage's sweatshirts. It fell down to the middle of her thighs, and she had to roll the sleeves up, but it'd serve its purpose.

A bank of gray fog had come in from the ocean during the night, moving over damp sand like low-lying clouds, making ordinary things — rocks, driftwood, and the stunted trees clinging to the cliff's edge — seem dark and mysterious as she carefully made her way down the steep trail to the beach.

Despite the risk of hurricanes, Tess had always loved living in Lowcountry. She loved the still of the marshes, the tranquility of the endless tide, the brilliant expanse of sparkling, sunlit sand.

Although she'd never given it a great deal of thought, Tess had assumed California must be much the same. But she'd been wrong. There was absolutely nothing tranquil about this ocean. It stormed against the cliffs, carving away at ancient stone, before surging back to the sea.

In many ways, it reminded her of Gage. Strong and unrelenting.

Gage. She knew that despite his declaration about not becoming involved, he'd come to care for her. As she cared for him. Oh, neither of them might be ready to say the words, but the tenderness underlying his passion had assured her that she wasn't the only one experiencing something a great deal more than lust.

Something special.

But surely *not* love. Love, she knew from all those glorious years growing up with Danny, was built slowly, tenderly, on foundations of friendship and trust and common interests. It did not come bursting out of the sky like a bolt of lightning.

Did it?

Instead of ruffled surf and pale sands strewn with pretty pink and cream shells, rocks lined the stretch of beach between the surf and the jagged cliffs. Jellyfish, the size of marbles, shimmered on the wet gray sand between the rocks, small crabs scurried sideways back to the sea, and green kelp covered everything, like fishing nets left behind by careless fishermen.

The tide was coming in. She'd just warned herself to be careful not to get trapped down here when a voice said, "You're up early."

The fog's eerie acoustic quality made it sound as if the deep voice were right behind her. Tess spun around, nearly slipping on the rocks as she watched Gage emerge from the filmy gray shadows.

"It's the time difference." She didn't want to admit that a nightmare of Randolph Griffith had jolted her awake. "It's three hours later in Somersett. Besides, you left the room before I did."

Damn. Did that sound as petulant to him as it did to her? As if her feelings had been hurt?

"I've never been one for sleeping in," he said.

"Me neither. Which was handy in the days I worked a rig. There weren't many nights when I didn't have to jump out of bed and slide down the pole."

"I always thought that'd be cool. Back when I was a kid."

"It is. So long as you're awake. I knew a probie one time who was a sleepwalker. Ended up breaking both his legs when he woke up on the apparatus floor."

"Ouch."

"I wasn't there at the time, but according to reports, that wasn't exactly what he said."

"He was lucky he lived to say anything."

"Yeah. He washed out."

"Too bad."

"I don't know." She shrugged. "He became a cop and seems to enjoy his work."

A silence settled over them. The rock-strewn beach was deserted save for a few sandpipers skittering along in the frothy surf at the water's edge. They could have been the only two people in the world. The only man. The only woman.

"I owe you an apology," he said.

"For what?"

"Whatever you may think of me, I didn't mean to hurt you."

Tess looked out over the sea. "It's not every day I come face-to-face with evil. But if Griffith can tell us anything about my Flamemaster —"

"I'm not talking about taking you to the prison. I was rougher than I should have been last night."

"I'm not porcelain, Gage. I won't break."

He scrubbed a hand down his face. "I realize that. In fact, you're the strongest woman I know, but that's still no excuse . . ."

He took hold of her wrist, pushed the bulky sweatshirt up, revealing the reddish-blue fingerprints that marked her like a brand.

"I'm sorry."

"I'm not." Her smile hit like a sucker punch in the chest. "But if it'll make you feel better, after I finish up my meeting with Griffith —"

"Dammit," he cut her off again. "What part of 'That's not going to happen' don't you understand?"

"Oh, for . . ." She swiped a hand through her mist-dampened hair. "Did I imagine it, or did you just tell me that I'm the strongest woman you've ever met?"

"Yeah, but that's beside the point."

"Excuse me. That's precisely the point. And did you or did you not say we were partners?"

"You know I did."

"So, would you be having this argument with your former partner? The agent who pulled you off Griffith?"

"Hell, no."

"Of course you wouldn't." Scarlet flags waved in her cheeks, brightening last night's pallor. "So, would you like to explain to me exactly how this is any different?"

"Because I wasn't sleeping with my damn partner!" he roared.

Gage was frustrated she couldn't see the difference, but at the same time strangely relieved to be back to arguing with her again. This Tess he could handle. It was the other one, the soft and tender and, although she'd deny it, vulnerable Tess, that left him feeling confused, conflicted, and emotionally at sea.

"Speaking of being partners," he said, "I have something to show you."

She cocked her head. "I think I've already seen everything. But if you want to get naked again, I wouldn't mind a second — or third or fourth — look."

He laughed, feeling unreasonably free. And, amazingly after last night, horny all over again.

"Later." He put his arm around her and began walking back toward the trail leading to the top of the cliff.

"Promises, promises," she said happily, the brief flare of temper evaporating, like morning fog beneath a warm spring sun.

forty

"Wow!" Tess stared around the office. "The rest of the house may be channeling Frankenstein, but this is like the bridge of the *Enterprise*."

A bank of undraped, wall-to-ceiling windows offered a 360-degree view of what she had no doubt was some of the most stunning scenery in the world. In one direction, far below, she could see and hear the crashing of surf. In the other, woodlands gave way to tidy rolling hills dotted with cattle.

"This tower is the reason I bought the house," he allowed.

"I don't blame you." She sighed happily and sank down onto a bark-brown leather sofa. "It must really be something during a storm."

"It's pretty spectacular."

"I imagine. You must feel like Thor." She glanced around at the tall, freestanding shelves loaded with an eclectic mix of leather-bound books, three-ring binders, and computer manuals. "The question is how you'd ever get any work done."

"I manage." He sat down at the computer. "This is what I wanted to show you."

She left the couch and came to stand up behind him. Her eyes widened as she viewed the screen. "It's the mill." She'd recognize it anywhere. "Where did you get the blueprints?"

"From the prefire plan."

"You hacked into fire department computers?"

"I could have just asked for them, but given that the chief on the scene, who's the current commissioner, obviously benefited from claiming it to be faulty wiring, this seemed easier."

"And against the law."

He shrugged. "I could've gotten a court order."

"You don't work for the ATF anymore."

"Yeah, but my former partner still does."

She watched as he turned the two-dimensional blue-and-white plans into an amazingly lifelike rendering of the building right before it had been turned into a strange and foreign landscape of twisted steel, charred and smoldering wood, and melted plastic.

He zoomed in. Tess had an uneasy feeling of déjà vu when Gage made it seem as if they were approaching the main door. The heavy oak plank door she herself had entered with Jake. The one she'd later been blown out of.

"So," Gage said. "We start with the fire triangle."

"Fuel, plus oxygen, plus heat source equals combustion."

"Very good." His smile reminded her of the gold star Sister Magdalene had put on her spelling papers.

"It's basic Fire 101. I told you, I aced the state test."

"Then you recall the explosion triangle, as well."

"Fuel, plus oxidizer, plus ignition, equal — boom! — explosion."

"That's it." He continued to move the cursor, taking them inside the building.

Tess imagined she could smell the smoke, the acrid, bitter almond aroma from the hydrogen cyanide, the pungent odor of hydrogen chloride and the phosgene, which, despite its more appealing freshly mown grass scent, was every bit as deadly as the others.

Indeed, among all the chemicals used in the gassings of World War I troops, phosgene had been responsible for the most fatalities.

Her legs grew shaky at the thought. With that uncanny ability to read her thoughts, he stood up. "Sit down."

"I'm fine."

"You're as pale as water." He put his wide palms on her shoulders and pushed her into the leather chair. "We can stop if you want."

"Of course I don't want you to stop. I just sometimes have an overly active imagination." She took a deep breath. "So, how exactly did you hack your way into government property?"

"I've very clever fingers."

No kidding. If the ones massaging her shoulders got any more clever, she'd be melting into a little puddle of need right on the slate floor.

"Work," she reminded him when one of those cleverly wicked hands slid past her shoulder, down over her breast.

"Slave driver." He sighed. Then reached around her and began tapping the keys. "Here's the fire with a single ignition source under normal conditions, factoring in all the variables — ambient temperature, probable fuel load material in the building, fuel-air mix, et cetera."

Tess watched as a flame flickered in a corner of the first floor. A counter in the left upper corner of the screen showed elapsed seconds.

One of the things firefighters had in their favor was that despite the dramatic flashovers and backdrafts that Hollywood directors were all enamored with, fire actually underwent a relatively slow chemical reaction, which gave out a glow and usually only took place on the surface of burned substances. Pyrolysis — those flames that evidenced an irreversible change — only occurred when the fire had a continuous source of oxygen.

Which was why venting a building, often viewed by civilians as a good thing, since it allowed cooler air in, could prove fatal. Since a fire was always searching for air, every firefighter learned to vent windows ahead of the nozzle, and as near as possible to the fire itself, since the act of venting drew the fire toward the new air supply. If this air supply was behind the firefighters, you could end up with a disastrous situation. And a dead hose crew.

The fire spread slowly, lazily, creeping across the wooden floor. "Now we'll vent the roof," Gage said. As he hit another key, Tess imagined she could hear the grinding sound of the K12 overhead.

The fire, which had been snaking along

the floor, began to move faster, black smoke billowed upward as the dragon consumed fuel; a temperature gauge on the other side of the computer screen showed the temperature rising.

Still, the fire remained controllable.

"Now we'll add a little fireworks."

He pressed F12. Suddenly all eight floors seemed to ignite, one at a time, at lightning speed, like the bottle rockets her brothers used to set off on the beach on the Fourth of July.

"What on earth did you do?"

"Set off the Sterno."

"But how did you get them all to flare at once?"

"Ever hear of CHAOS?" he asked.

"Of course. It's an ecoterrorism group." The destruction of Dixie Petroleum's Somersett office building had been the first case she and Bobby had solved. Although they hadn't been able to tie the fire back to Cody Wunder, CHAOS's charismatic founder, they had nailed the torch, who was currently behind bars at the Wateree River Correctional Institute.

"Before founding CHAOS, Wunder belonged to the Earth Liberation Front, which officially merged with the Animal Liberation Front."

"I know that, too."

"Did you know that Randolph Griffith contributed heavily to all three organizations?"

"You can't be serious. I wouldn't have thought the man had a single philanthropic bone in his body." Not that the radical groups were worthy of support, in her opinion. Ironically, they seemed to embrace the same "win at all cost" philosophy as the industries they attacked.

"I think he mostly just got off on fires and things going boom in the night. ALF torched a slaughterhouse in Oregon by drilling holes in the walls, pouring thirty-five gallons of homemade napalm inside, then setting off three electronically controlled incendiary devices. The way I figure it, Griffith was funding his own research program."

"That's where he got the idea for the Sterno?"

"It's my guess he had the crazies try it out for him. It is, if you think about it, the logical choice. Unlike fertilizer, which would take an entire truckload to blow up a building, he can use less than a handful of C-4. But it's slow to ignite, which is why it was so popular in Vietnam. Hell, my dad did two tours over there and told me grunts used to use the stuff as a cooking fire when they were on patrol out in the jungle.

"And it's so stable, you can shoot it with a rifle and it won't explode. But hook it up to a detonator and all hell breaks loose."

She was, horrifyingly, beginning to get the picture. "The Sterno, which is slow-burning, gets the firefighters in —"

"The place is filled with smoke, so you've gotta vent, which makes the place go faster. Which, in turn —"

"Brings in more firefighters."

"Then, when you've got everyone just where you want them." He hit Enter. The screen seemed to explode in a blinding flash of orange. "Ka-boom."

She was taking all that in, realizing that not only had the mill fire undoubtedly been arson, but it had been set with the purpose of killing first responders, when Gage's cell phone rang.

"O'Halloran." He cursed. "Okay. Yeah. Thanks for calling." He ended the brief call. "Well, looks like we're not going to have to argue about whether or not you go back to San Quentin."

"We're not arguing because I'm going." She valued his knowledge, and his help, but she wasn't going to give in on this point.

"No need." His expression was set. Grim. "Because he's dead."

"Dead?" How could that be? She'd just spoken to him yesterday. "But he was surrounded by guards. He told us he wasn't even allowed to exercise with the other prisoners because he's considered a danger."

"Turns out he was the one in danger. He got a shiv in his gut on the walk to his pen. According to the warden, he was dead before the EMTs could make it to the scene."

"And the man who stabbed him? Surely they're questioning him?"

"Sure." Gage shrugged. "But he's already doing time for multiple murders now. Offing The Flamemaster just won him even more notoriety."

Her shoulders sagged. She pressed her fingertips against her eyelids. "What do we do now?" She'd so been hoping he'd be able to give her something — anything — tangible.

"We go back to Somersett. Start from scratch."

"Easter's two days away."

"I guess we'll just have to hurry."

forty-one

Tess was surprised when she got off the plane from California to find Bobby waiting for her at the bottom of the steps. With him was a homicide detective from SPD. Caitlin Cavanaugh had been Tess's brother's homicide partner.

"Heard about your murder," Bobby greeted her. It may not have been official policy, but he wrapped his arms around her and gave her a big hug. "Too bad."

"He was a horrid, evil person. But I do wish he'd managed to stay alive for a few more days, just to give us more of a handle on what's happening with our case."

Bobby exchanged a look with Cait. His expression was remorseful, hers insistent.

"About that." He sucked in a breath and looked as if he wished he were somewhere — anywhere — else than here. "Caitlin's ready to make an arrest on our hooker fire."

"Really?"

Tess was surprised. She'd been so sure that the perp who'd set that fire was her pyro. Then again, she thought, with a little spark of hope, although fires weren't the usual method of murder the homicide division investigated, sometimes everyone got lucky and the bad guys crossed jurisdictions, getting everyone involved.

"I haven't made the arrest yet, Tess." Cait's expression was grave. Almost, Tess thought, apologetic. "Because I was waiting for you."

Oh-oh. Internal warning sirens began screeching.

"It's Ty," Bobby said quickly, as if to spare her any more discomfort.

"Ty?" If there was anyone less likely to be her pyro, she couldn't think who it might be. "John Tyler? *Our* Ty?"

"Homicide's got an eyewitness who places him at the scene," Cait said. "Twice."

"That's impossible."

It had to be a mistake. What on earth would Ty be doing at such a flea trap? Gage's hand closed on her elbow, as if to steady her. Tess shook it off.

"It's the truth," Bobby said. His big brown eyes looked as disbelieving, as devastated, as she felt. "He was having an affair with the vic."

"An affair?" The idea was ludicrous. "With a prostitute?"

Gage entered into the conversation. "It's not uncommon."

"I know that." Tess turned on him, her tone sharp. This had to be a horrible mistake. "But Ty wouldn't sleep around."

"We had him in for questioning this morning," Cait supplied. "He admits to having a relationship with her, Tess. But he's not copping to setting the fire."

"Well, of course he didn't." Of this Tess had not a single doubt. "He'd never do anything so evil."

"I hope you're right," Cait said candidly, her expression grave. "I've always liked the guy."

"Everyone does."

"Like I said, he's a nice guy who's been through a lot, what with all that press and hoopla about the mill fire," Cait said. "But unfortunately that's all in the past. Yesterday's ball score, as they say.

"Right now we've got a woman who was engaged in a sexual relationship with a firefighter," she continued. "A woman who happened to die in an arson fire. Which, coincidentally, if you go by all the facts your new partner, O'Halloran here, has been compiling, could very well be connected to the fire that killed your fiancé."

She held the drawn-out pause with a homicide cop's renowned patience. Then said, "You know I wouldn't be doing my duty if I didn't check it out."

"I realize that." Cait was every bit as straight-arrow as Tess's brother Joe. "But you're wrong. About Ty's involvement."

The detective blew out a breath. Dragged her hand through her shoulder-length hair. "You've no idea how much I hope you're right."

Since Ty hadn't been read his rights and was, at this point in the investigation, a "person of interest," rather than an official suspect, he was being detained in a room usually used for prisoner interrogation rather than a cell.

When Tess arrived at the police station, he was wearing shorts, an SFD T-shirt, and running shoes. She knew how seriously the police were taking this when she saw that the cops standing guard outside the door had taken away Ty's shoelaces.

The public-relationship nightmare was going to be bad enough if a first responder turned out to be The Flamemaster. No one wanted a firefighter committing suicide while in police custody.

"Tess?" Ty looked up at her with bleary red eyes. Cait had told her that he'd been questioned all night and he looked like it. Actually, he looked as if he'd been on one helluva bender. "What are you doing here?"

"How could I not be?"

She pulled out a chair and sat down in front of him, their knees touching. She knew she had no legal right for a private visit and was grateful for whatever strings Cait had pulled to make that possible.

She also wondered if they were being watched. Was it even legal to videotape people without their knowledge? Tess didn't know. Nor had she ever imagined she'd need to.

"How are you doing?"

"I've been better." He attempted a smile that failed miserably. "How did things go in San Francisco?"

"Could have gone better."

"Bailey said Mercury's in retrograde this month. I don't have any idea what that means, but apparently it fucks things up. Guess you and I both got slammed."

"Guess so. Is it true? About the woman at the apartment?"

"I didn't kill Angela, if that's what you're asking."

"I'd never believe anyone who tried to tell me otherwise. But you did *know* her? Intimately?"

"Yeah." He dragged both his hands down his face. "We were kind of having a thing."

"What type of thing?" Although Cait had given her a bare-bones version of his earlier statement on the drive into town from the airport, Tess wanted to hear the story from Ty.

"You know. A damn thing. The kind a man has with a woman. Like you and that phony ATF guy."

The door opened in response to his raised voice. The cop stuck his head in. "Everything copacetic here, Inspector?"

"It's just fine, officer."

The cop shot Ty a warning stare. "Just so it stays that way."

"Like he would've given a shit about Angela when she was alive." Ty scowled at the one-way mirror. "The only time cops even notice women like Angela is when they want to roust them, turn them as informants, or get a free fuck in exchange for not picking them up on the hooker roundups."

"That's quite a sweeping statement," Tess said mildly. "So how did you? First notice her, that is."

"At the station. She came in to get her blood pressure checked. She was a little hypertensive."

"I imagine there's a lot of stress in her line of work." Dangerous johns. Greedy pimps. Jealous boyfriends?

"I guess so. We never talked about it."

"So, it wasn't exactly an affair."

"I don't know how the hell you define affair," he shot back. "We slept together. Correction. We only spent the night together once. Mostly we just had sex. Sometimes, when it was my job to buy groceries for the station, I'd get some for her. She liked to cook." He frowned. "Unlike Bailey, the takeout queen."

There was a deep vein of anger in that statement that Tess didn't want to risk tapping into in case they were being taped.

"That's why you were seen at her apartment, then?"

"Yeah." He paused, looking on the verge of saying something. "There's something else."

It was Tess's turn to glance up at the large mirror; she was becoming more and more uneasy about the idea of being watched and wished she'd at least called Joe on the way here to find out how things worked.

"Maybe you ought to call an attorney before this goes any further."

"Yeah, like I can afford a criminal lawyer

on a firefighter's salary. Maybe you haven't noticed that we haven't had a raise in two years."

"The union lawyer, then."

"I don't want a damn lawyer. I don't need a lawyer. Because I'm goddamn innocent!" He shot a look toward the door and immediately lowered his voice, leaned toward her, and took both of her hands in his. "I swear, I'd never kill anyone, Tess."

"I know that." She'd refused to accept the possibility when Gage had first professed suspicion about Danny and Ty going into the mill together and only Ty coming out alive.

He was squeezing her fingers hard enough to cut off her circulation. "But cops tend to think you're guilty until you prove yourself innocent," she said.

"So how do you suggest I do that? Ever try disproving a negative?"

"We'll find the killer."

"We both know it's Mannington. But I'd like to see you prove it."

"I'm working on that."

"You've been working on the guy for the past six months. Face facts, Tess. With all his connections, he's fucking Teflon."

"I'll get him."

She could not allow herself to believe

otherwise. She paused, then asked the question that had been bedeviling her ever since Cait had dropped her bombshell.

"Why, Ty? Why would you even sleep around when you and Bailey have such a great marriage?"

"Yeah, it looks like that from the outside, doesn't it?" he muttered bitterly. "Funny thing is, until a few months ago, I thought the same thing. Until . . ."

"Until what?"

"She started having an affair first."

"What?" Tess would have been no more shocked if Ty had accused his wife of being The Flamemaster. "Bailey adores you."

"That's what I thought, too. Until she started having this online thing."

"Are you saying you found emails?"

"No."

"Chat-room logs?"

"No."

"Then what gives you the idea —"

"She's never home."

"She has a high-pressure job."

"Like I don't? Never mind." He waved away her words. "I know, that's not the point. I was looking for some aspirin one day and went into her medicine cabinet, and guess what I found?" He didn't wait for her to respond. "Birth control pills!"

"She's been taking those pills for years."

"She wasn't supposed to be on them anymore. We agreed we were going to try for another baby. Shit." He raked a trembling hand through his hair. "No wonder she hasn't gotten pregnant."

Tess couldn't think of how to respond. She was surprised that her closest friend hadn't shared the decision to try to get pregnant with her. But then again, Tess hadn't felt the need to call Bailey and tell her about sleeping with Gage O'Halloran, either.

"I'm sorry." Even as she said the words, Tess knew how ineffectual they sounded.

"I know." He sighed and absently reached into the pocket of his T-shirt. "They took my cigarettes away from me. Can you believe the city council made all government buildings nonsmoking? Do you think you could go bum one from someone? It shouldn't be that hard. Cops all smoke."

"I'll give it a shot." She touched a hand to his shoulder and felt it tense beneath her fingers. "Be right back."

"Tess?" he called out as she reached the door.

She glanced back over her shoulder. "Want something else? Coffee, Coke?"

"No, I'm fine. Well, maybe not fine," he admitted with a faint grin that was a ghost of his usual endearingly crooked one. "I was just wondering something."

"What's that?"

"Do you ever wonder, if things had been different, and you'd met me before Danny —"

"You and I would have ended up friends. Just like we are now."

"Ever wonder if it could have been more?"

"No." She looked him straight in the eye. "I'll get your cigarette."

"How's he taking it?" Cait asked when Tess returned to the homicide bullpen.

"About as well as any innocent person would when they're dragged down to a police station and accused of murder."

"He hasn't been charged," the detective reminded her mildly.

"Then why is he here?"

"We're giving him some time to think it over. While we question a few of his neighbors."

"Why? Don't tell me you expect to find out he's been building incendiary devices in his garage?"

"No such luck. But we did learn one interesting thing."

Tess followed Cait's gaze to the one-way

mirror. Ty was sitting slumped in the molded plastic green chair, head down, hands hanging between his legs, looking like a man on the way to the gallows. Tess thought about what she'd experienced in San Quentin and knew that sweet, easy-going Ty would never be able to survive such a violent environment as prison.

"Are you going to tell me?" she snapped, losing patience with Cait, with Ty, with this entire situation. "Or are we playing twenty questions?"

"Sorry," Cait said. "I guess we're both not having a real good day. Sorry about you losing your source."

"I'll just have to find another. And what about Ty?"

"Seems his neighbor has a newborn. I guess they don't sleep much because the baby's got colic. Real bitch to deal with, the neighbor says. She's been spending a lot of nights walking the floor, trying to get the kid to stop screaming."

"That'd be tough."

"Yeah. Anyway, her bedroom window looks right into the Tylers' master bed-room."

"And?" Tess could see it coming. Like a runaway locomotive headed straight to-ward her.

"Seems while Mrs. Tyler was out of town last month, Mr. Tyler was entertaining friends. One friend, in particular. The neighbor was curious, since she'd watched the missus loading her suitcase into her car that morning. So, when she heard the front door open the next morning, naturally, she checked the visitor out."

"Naturally," Tess said dryly. Savannah would, of course, probably do the same thing.

"She identified a photograph of your vic as the woman who spent the night with Mr. Tyler."

"In the house?"

"Yeah." Cait flashed a grim smile. "I don't know about you, but if my husband ever pulled a stunt like that, I'd be pissed off big-time. He'd be lucky to escape Bobbittization."

The idea of Bailey cutting off Ty's penis was beyond even Tess's imagination.

However, she reminded herself as she drove out to the subdivision on the outskirts of the city, an hour ago Ty being involved in murder would have been equally as impossible to contemplate.

forty-two

Bailey was, to put it charitably, a wreck. Tess couldn't recall ever seeing her friend looking less than perfect. Or the least bit frazzled. Until today.

Her long dark hair was tangled, as if she'd been dragging her hands through it. Her red-rimmed eyes and blotchy face were evidence that she'd been crying.

"Can you believe it?" she wailed. "What was he thinking?"

"He didn't tell you?" Tess asked.

"He won't see me." Bailey pressed her manicured fingertips against her lips to hold back her sobs. "Detective Cavanaugh was here with a bunch of cops last night. They searched the house, the garage, everywhere."

"Did they say what they were looking for?"

Bailey arched an ironic brow and for a moment Tess was once again viewing ADA Tyler.

"Okay," Tess answered the unspoken comment. "I suppose they wouldn't share that information with you. Even if you do work for the prosecutor's office."

"He's my husband, Tess," Bailey said earnestly. "No matter what he's done. I love him and I'm going to use every ounce of my influence and every dollar I have to keep him out of prison."

"You're getting ahead of yourself," Tess soothed. Which wasn't normal behavior for the by-the-book Bailey.

Unfortunately, these were far from normal circumstances. Tess was beginning to feel as if she'd fallen down a rabbit hole into a strange and unpredictable parallel world. "He hasn't even been charged yet."

"Maybe not yet. But if he wasn't my husband, I'd start building a case."

"But he *is* your husband. And whatever else he might have done, you know he'd never take another human life."

"I also never believed he'd fuck a five-dollar whore!" Bailey screeched in a very un-Bailey-like voice. Then bit her lip. "I'm sorry."

"I know."

Tess drew her into her arms. Gave her another hug. It was strange to be the one comforting Bailey Tyler. Ever since the mill fire, it had been the other way around.

"He's been behaving so strangely lately." Bailey dabbed at her wet eyes with a tissue.

"So angry. And possessive." Her voice wavered. "Did he tell you that he even accused me of having an affair?"

Without having meant to, Ty and Bailey had put Tess on a razor-thin tightrope. Without a net.

"He mentioned you spending a lot of time online," she said carefully.

"Online?" Dark brows winged upward. Bailey's manicured hand flew to the front of her uncharacteristically rumpled silk blouse. "Oh, my God! Don't tell me he thinks I'm committing adultery by Internet . . ."

"He does!" she said disbelievingly when Tess didn't immediately answer. "I'm not talking with men on the computer. I'm researching old cathedrals."

"Cathedrals?"

"For my new antiquity line of jewelry. You know those pendants I made for you to give to your mother this past Christmas."

"Of course. The one that looks like St. Brendan's rose window." The same window that was featured on so many Somersett postcards. "My mother loves it."

"So she told me when I saw her wearing it in town a few months ago. That got me thinking that it might be fun to create an entire line of antiquities using other Gothic windows as patterns. Come see."

She led Tess into her dining room/ studio, opened a file folder, and pulled out some colored photographs. "This one, of course, is Notre-Dame, in Paris. This is Amiens." There were others, all stunningly beautiful.

Bailey reached into the top drawer of a small wooden cabinet sitting between a portable kiln and a container of PMC — precious metal gold, used to create her intricate designs — and took out a pendant.

"This necklace is based on Chartres."

Although personally Tess preferred simpler jewelry, the dazzling design of colored gemstones set in intricate white gold tracery was amazingly detailed.

"It's stunning. And must have taken you ages to make."

"Didn't it turn out well?" The distraught wife was gone, replaced by someone more familiar. "It's really not as difficult as it looks."

Bailey picked up a mechanical pencil and began to sketch on a white drawing pad. "I began with a circle, then constructed a square around it, then connected every fifth point to create this dodecagram, which is a twelve-pointed star, then . . ."

As she continued on and on about foils, and trefoils, and quatrefoils, and all sorts of other technical art and architectural terms, Tess began to understand how Ty could have misunderstood all that time his wife was spending online.

Bailey was obviously caught up in a passion that didn't involve Ty. But fortunately, that passion was for her creative expression, not another man.

When that idea brought to mind Pamela Winters's skewed description of killer art, Tess shuddered.

"Christ, listen to me," Bailey was saying, when Tess dragged her mind back to their conversation. "What kind of person goes on and on while her husband's locked up in jail?"

"A person who's passionate about her work." And who understandably might be in a bit of denial. "Besides, he's not locked up. Not really." Not yet.

The phone in the adjoining kitchen rang. As Bailey went to answer it, Tess studied a bracelet and pair of matching earrings, all featuring a brilliant rosette that appeared to be stained glass. They really were lovely.

"That was Winston White," Bailey announced when she returned to the dining room. "He's agreed to take Ty's case and said he'd meet me at the station."

Winston White was descended from one of the earlier Somersett settlers. Like so many in the city, he possessed privateer roots, and from what she'd read in the papers he'd continued his family's tradition of piracy.

The only difference Tess could see was that he used the law instead of a ship and cannon to acquire his wealth. Still, he won a great deal more cases than he lost, which, she figured, allowed him to get away with charging double the going rate for most attorneys in the Carolinas.

After her visit with Ty at the jail, Bobby had dropped her off at the Jeep dealership, where she'd picked up her Wrangler. Gage, having claimed he had some calls to make, had suggested meeting her back at her house.

As she returned to the city, Tess realized she'd forgotten to ask Bailey about the birth control pills.

Just because her case had dropped into Cait's lap, that didn't mean that Tess was going to just stop working on it. Especially now that her two best friends were involved.

It wouldn't be an easy conversation, but she'd ask Bailey tomorrow. After all, she decided as she pulled up in front of her house and felt a little spark of pleasure to see the black Porsche parked at the curb, one day wouldn't make that much difference.

forty-three

Unable to sleep, but not wanting to keep Tess awake with his tossing and turning, Gage decided to go running.

She murmured a faint, drowsy protest when she felt him leave the bed.

"It's okay." He brushed a kiss against her temple. "Jet lag," he said, using the same excuse she'd used for being out on his beach so early.

Christ, had that only been this morning? Gage felt as if he'd spent a lifetime with Tess. Exactly how appealing that idea had begun to seem to him was only one reason he felt the need to clear his head. Sort things out.

"I'm just going to work off some energy."

She opened one eye. "I can help you with that."

"I may just hold you to that when I get back."

"You've got yourself a date, cowboy."

She snuggled deeper into the pillow. The marmalade kitten, which Savannah had brought over earlier, was curled up beside her, purring like a small engine.

He was loath to leave her, but felt as if he were suffocating in the domesticity of the feminine room, the purring cat, the warm, sleepy, beautiful woman. He needed air.

He was on his third mile, running through the darkened streets, going over all the reasons why he couldn't love her. It was too soon.

Like there's a timetable for falling in love? a voice that sounded a lot like Donovan nagged in his mind. They'd been partners so long, they'd gotten like an old married couple, knowing what the other was thinking.

I knew the minute I saw Mel she was the one for me. Felt like I'd been pole-axed. The voice chuckled. *You can run, pardner. But you cannot hide.*

But that's what he'd always done. Run. If he hadn't run from the problems with Kim, choosing to count on her little affair running its course rather than take the time to work things out, his wife would still be alive. He doubted they'd still be married. They were, after all, too different. In the way they thought. The things they wanted. But however he tried to pretty things up, the fact was that he was responsible for her death.

So you've given yourself life without parole. Why don't you just put a gun in your mouth and end things?

"Been there. Tried that." His feet pounded the tabby stones as he turned the corner onto Harbor View. "Lacked the guts."

Sometimes it takes more guts to live. To keep slogging through the days, trying to get it right.

But that was the problem. Gage didn't feel like he was slogging when he was with Tess. He felt alive. And loved.

Not that he deserved her love.

Christ, you can be a pain in the ass. Sometimes a guy gets lucky. Sometimes the gods just decide to stroll down from Mt. Olympus and hand you a second chance. You toss it away and you'll piss them off. Big-time.

"Guy gets married and he thinks he knows everything about women and love," Gage muttered.

There's not a man alive who knows anything about women. That's what makes them such fabulous creatures. As for love, I may not be the kind of guy who writes sonnets and remembers to bring home roses on our sixth-month anniversary. But at least I'm smart enough to know that it's the only thing worth having. The only thing worth fighting for.

Gage hadn't fought for Kim. He wished he had, but truth be told, the bottom line was that he just hadn't cared enough.

While the idea of losing Tess ripped a hole in a heart he hadn't even been aware of possessing.

So, why don't you just go back and tell the lady how you feel?

"Why don't you just shut the hell up?"

But as he headed back to the cozy little Victorian, with the warm and welcoming woman waiting for him, Gage decided that wasn't such bad advice.

The last thing he expected to see as he approached Tess's house was smoke coming from the peaked roof. There was an orange glow behind the windows.

And not a bit of movement from inside the house.

forty-four

Why the hell hadn't the smoke detector gone off? Gage knew she had one; he'd seen it that first day. But as he raced into the house, it was silent.

The fire must've sparked right after he'd left. The downstairs was already filled with smoke, the floor hot beneath the soles of his Nikes.

Smoke clogged the stairway. As he crawled up the stairs, one at a time, feeling his way in front of him like a blind man, Gage made deal after deal with God.

If Tess would just get out of here alive, he'd call his mother every week, even if he didn't have anything to say.

He'd give every cent he'd made on that damn computer game to charity.

He might even, he considered rashly as he heard a rush of flames roaring through the attic over his head, go back to church.

Gage was struggling to come up with yet another bargaining chip when his hand came across something furry. And mad.

The kitten swiped out with a furry marmalade paw, leaving a bloody path. "It's nice to see you, too," he muttered to the kitten, who arched, orange fur bristling, and hissed.

Gage lunged for the animal, which deftly eluded him, disappearing back up the stairs into the smoke. Terrific. First he had to find Tess, who he knew wasn't going to be willing to leave without her goddamn overpriced cat.

His eyes were burning like hot coals and his nose was running as if someone had turned on a damn tap.

Someone had obviously called the fire in. He heard sirens wailing in the distance.

He'd made it to the top of the stairs and was inching along the hallway when he saw her crawling toward him, a wet washcloth over her mouth.

"I don't understand," she complained. She coughed. Violently. "Why the smoke detector didn't go off."

Gage had a few ideas about that. None of them pretty.

"We'll figure it out later. Let's just get you out of here."

"The kitten —"

"She'll be okay." It was a lie and they both knew it. "We can't take time to go find her."

"But she's what woke me up. She

jumped up on my pillow and kept howling in my ear. I can't leave without her."

"Dammit, Tess." She'd been a firefighter too long not to know that was a risky idea.

Fire roared overhead, in the attic, like a freight train.

"We're wasting time and oxygen. This place is about to blow."

"Don't say that." She did, Gage noticed, continue inching her way toward the stairs he'd just come up. "This isn't just some run-of-the-mill house." She coughed again. Harder. "It's my home. The home Danny and I . . ."

The rest of the sentence was lost in another racking cough, but Gage heard it loud and clear. The home she and her fiancé were going to live in. Make babies in. Probably have some huge dog that'd dig up her pretty little gardens and track mud all over the floors she'd refinished to a gleaming buttery shine.

That idea, which would have sounded like hell on earth even two days ago, seemed eminently appealing. It also left him, once again, feeling damn envious of a dead man.

The house could be rebuilt. Wallpaper could be found, new carpets and wood floors installed, antiques bought at those high-priced dealers he'd seen down on Heritage Row in the historic part of the city.

But none of that would mean a thing if Tess wasn't alive to live in it.

By Gage's calculations, they'd nearly reached the stairs. "Just a few more feet."

He'd no sooner spoken when a huge whoosh shook the second floor. A tower of orange flames engulfed the stairs, greedily ravaging the wooden banister.

Gage felt a thud on his back. Razor-sharp claws dug into his flesh through his shirt.

"Damn cat's got terrific timing." He reached behind him to pull the kitten off, but it only dug in deeper, refusing to be dislodged. "Looks like we'll have to switch to plan B and go out the window. You've got a portable ladder, right?"

"Of course," she responded. What firefighter wouldn't? "It's beneath my bed."

The spreading fire had caught onto the pretty rice bed she'd bought at an estate sale in Charleston, and flames were licking at the acorn finial. Tess knew they might only have seconds left before the room was engulfed in an inferno.

She reached to where she knew the ladder to be.

"It's gone!"

"Shit. I was afraid of that." Gage peeled the protesting cat off his back and buttoned her into his shirt.

"We'll have to jump."

"Oh, God."

"It's not my first choice, either." He went to lift the sash, unsurprised to find the window nailed shut. Someone had gone to a lot of trouble making certain Tess didn't escape this blaze.

"Here." Keeping the cool head he suspected had served her well as a firefighter, she handed him an upholstered chair, which he used to break the glass.

The pumper engine had arrived, strobe lights flashing. Gage guessed the siren in the distance was the ladder truck.

"We can't wait." He grabbed the quilt, wrapped it around his hand, and swiped out the jagged shards of glass that were still attached to the wooden frame.

"Ladies first."

He was relieved when she didn't waste time arguing. But as she swung her leg over the sill, she turned back toward him. "You probably don't want to hear this right now, but just in case, I want to tell you. I think I love you."

You feel lucky, punk? Gage heard Dirty Harry rasp.

You goddamn betcha.

"That's handy." He leaned forward and gave her a quick, hard kiss. "Since I *know* I love you."

The blissful pleasure that brightened her smoke-smudged face belied their potentially deadly situation.

"And now that we've got that settled," Gage said, feeling optimistic for the first time in years, "let's get the hell out of here."

"Good idea. Just one more sec." She crushed her mouth to his. "Meet you on the ground."

Gage held his breath as she leaped into space. Then felt his heart resume beating when she landed, feet first, on the ground. Her legs crumbled beneath her, but she was up in a flash, paying no attention to the firefighters racing toward her as she held her arms up toward him.

Holding the trembling kitten against his chest, Gage jumped.

Flashing red and white lights lit up the night sky.

Standing on the sidewalk outside, clad in the oversize T-shirt she'd pulled on after finding herself alone again, and a long, maribou-trimmed red satin robe Savannah

447

had brought her, Tess watched as firefighters fought to save her pretty, beloved house.

The excitement had brought out the curious and fire buffs who gathered on the other side of the barricades.

"It's just a house," she told herself. "It can be rebuilt."

"Absolutely," Gage said with a heartiness she knew he'd put on for her benefit.

"I mean, the important thing is that the three of us got out." The kitten was back at Savannah's, seeming none the worse for having just experienced her second devastating fire in the first six weeks of her life.

"Absolutely," Gage repeated.

There was a deafening crash as the roof caved in. Tess's heart hitched, and although firefighters might not cry, she was on the verge of giving in to the tears stinging at the back of her lids when she saw Bobby walking toward her across the hose-strewn yard.

Watching her dreams go up in smoke, Tess had thought it could not get worse.

She was about to be proven wrong.

forty-five

"You okay?" Bobby asked. His dark eyes looked more serious than she'd ever seen them.

"I'm fine." She managed a smile. "Thanks to Gage. The smoke detector never went off. I could've ended up like that woman in the apartment."

"Lucky thing you were here," he said to Gage. "Funny thing about the detector."

"Not so funny," Gage said. "I'll lay odds you'll find the batteries were taken out."

"Yeah, that was my first thought, too," Bobby agreed.

"Surely you don't mean —" Tess stared at them, her gaze moving back and forth from Gage to Bobby, then back to Gage. "It was him. The Flamemaster. He tried to kill us."

"That'd be my guess," Gage agreed. "Fortunately, he failed. This time."

"Which'll be the only shot he's going to get," Bobby predicted. He sighed. "Tess, this isn't going to be easy. It's about Ty."

"Oh, God." Tess pressed a hand against her chest. "Don't tell me they've charged him."

"They released him a couple hours ago."

"Then what's wrong?"

"He's dead."

"Dead?" She stared at him. Then gasped. "The Flamemaster killed him?"

"No." He shook his head. Looked as if he were on the verge of tears himself. "Tess." He took her hand, put it in both of his. "Ty *was* The Flamemaster."

Two days later, Tess still was having trouble grasping what Cait Cavanaugh and Bobby had told her. While she'd been lying in bed beside Gage, a fire had started in an abandoned building down by the docks. Just as it had happened in the mill, the fire had spread rapidly, forcing the firefighters to take a surround-and-drown defense.

When the smoke cleared, they found Ty, with a metal ring still clutched in his fist. Tests revealed the ring was from a can of Sterno.

Bailey collapsed when Tess, Gage, and Bobby arrived to break the news. Tess had never seen a woman more shattered. Knowing how painful it was to lose a loved one, Tess could relate.

But because of a journal found in a tool-box in a second search of the Tylers' ga-rage, it now appeared he'd been the one who'd set the fire that killed Danny, and a deep, wide chasm had sprung up between Bailey and Tess. Tess had, in one horrific night, lost two people she'd loved. One by death, the other by circumstances. But both losses hurt equally badly.

Tess was sitting on the balcony of a loft apartment over the Black Swan. The apartment, which had once belonged to her brother, and had been bought by Brendan as a real estate investment, was fortuitously between tenants.

Gazing out over the harbor, where white sails of a flotilla of pleasure craft fluttered in a dazzlingly blue sky, Tess was trying to find the words to ask Gage his intentions.

Not that she wanted to sound like her mother. But since, with Ty's death, The Flamemaster cases — both the ones from two years ago and the more recent ones — were closed, there was technically no longer any official reason for Gage to still be in town. In her borrowed apartment. And her bed.

Except for the fact that he'd told her he loved her the night her house had burned down. Then demonstrated it time and time again over the past two days, providing an anchor in the stormy tumultuous seas of her churning emotions. But with all that had happened, they hadn't had any time to discuss their future.

Tess had meant it when she'd told him she didn't need pretty words. Nor did she need a ring. After all, they were both strong, independent people. They shouldn't need the outward trappings of commitment.

Yet, dammit, apparently she was more old-fashioned than she'd thought. Because she needed the commitment.

After being reassured that she'd be fine if left alone, even for a few hours, Gage had gone fishing with her brothers and father. It was the first time in a very long while that her father had left the house for anything but to meet with attorneys and argue his disability case to the county commissioners, and Tess was grateful for anything that would take his mind off his frustrations.

She'd just decided to cook a romantic dinner, ply Gage with some very nice pinot noir Brendan had recommended, then ask straight out what his plans were, when her phone rang.

"Tess?" Bailey's voice sounded strained. As if she'd been weeping. Well, no wonder.

"Bailey." Tess exhaled a long breath. "I'm so glad you called." Tess had left countless messages. After all, Bailey couldn't be blamed for her husband's actions. In a way, she was just as much a victim as Tess. And all those others whose lives The Flamemaster had damaged.

"I know you must hate me," the other woman stammered uncharacteristically.

"Never."

There was a pause. Tess thought she heard weeping on the other end of the line.

"I'm so relieved to hear that. Do you think you could come out here? The funeral home just called. The coroner's office is going to release Ty's body tomorrow morning and you're the only person I can talk to about him. Who knows what I'm going through. Because of having lost the man you loved."

Tess saw no reason to point out that the man she loved hadn't committed murder.

"I'm leaving now." She glanced over at the clock. So much for a romantic dinner. Taking a page from Bailey's book, as she drove across the bridge out of town, she decided to order something from the pub.

Which was probably a better plan anyway. Since she was a terrible cook.

Bailey hung up the phone and spun around, tears streaming down her cheeks. She'd probably cried more in the past two days than she had her entire life.

Well, there had been that one night.

No! Having enough problems ripping apart at her, she closed her mind to the painful memory.

"There. I did it. I hope you're goddamn happy," she screamed.

She sounded like a fishwife. Probably looked and smelled like one, too. But her captor, who'd been keeping her awake since his arrival the night she'd gotten the news about Ty, had refused to let her bathe. She suspected it was a psychological tactic to keep her from anything that might calm her, in turn, to gain control over the situation. Over her.

It was working.

"Happiness doesn't enter into the situation," he said calmly. She'd never met anyone with so much ice in his veins. If she didn't know better, she'd think he was some sort of robot, some sort of killing machine. "Tess Gannon is a liability. She's an impediment. She's standing in my way. Which is why she needs to be eliminated."

"What about me?" Bailey shoved a hand through her filthy lank hair. "Am I an impediment? Are you planning to eliminate me, too? Like you did my husband?"

He looked up from attaching the wires to

the can of Sterno. The light from the window was hitting his eyes in a way that made them appear flat. And deadly. They reminded her of an alligator's.

"That depends solely on you," he said.

Bailey didn't believe him. He was going to kill Tess. Just as he'd killed Ty. And then he'd kill her.

And she had the terrifyingly sinking feeling that there wasn't anything she could do to save either one of them.

forty-six

Bailey looked even worse than she'd sounded over the phone. If Tess hadn't known better, she would have thought the other woman had suffered some terrible illness in the last few days.

She'd lost weight. The curves that had been the bane of her existence were, amazingly, gone. She was not only thin. But gaunt. How was that possible?

Her face was drawn. But it was her eyes that struck a note of trepidation inside Tess. They were red, and puffy, as she'd expected. But they were oddly, unnervingly distant.

"I'm so relieved you're here," she said, her voice as flat as her gaze.

"I'm relieved you let me come," Tess said as she entered the house. The drapes were all drawn, making the lovely home seem dark and closed in. "I've been so worried about you."

"About me?" Bailey looked puzzled at that idea. "Why?"

Why? "Because of all that's happened."

"Oh." She combed her hand through

hair that looked as though it hadn't been washed for days. The nails that weren't broken were bitten to the quick.

Tess would not have believed it possible for one person to change so drastically in such a brief time.

"I'm fine," Bailey claimed. Her lips twisted in an odd mockery of a smile. "Because I have a protector."

"A protector?"

"Me," the deep voice said from the shadows.

Shock mingled with disbelief shot through her as Tess found herself staring straight into the twisted, evil face of The Flamemaster.

Gage hated fishing. Always had. Probably always would. But when Tess's brothers had "just happened" to drop by the apartment and see if he wanted to spend an afternoon drowning worms with them and her father, he'd understood it was not so much an invitation as a command.

The three Gannon males, especially her former cop brother, Joe, had spent most of the trip grilling him on his intentions. Gage hadn't minded all that much, since it was exactly the same thing he'd do if he had a baby sister.

The trip had given him an opportunity to talk with her priest brother Mike about their father's problem and pass on the name of an attorney in the firm Gage used for his game business who was one of the best in the country at disability law. He'd already spoken with the lawyer; since Gage suspected the hard-edged former firefighter would never take charity, Doyle Gannon would be told that the case would be handled on a pro bono basis.

At the end of the trip, Gage had managed to catch a log, a boot, and a dead possum. On the plus side, he'd also had the best pecan pie he'd ever tasted. Tess was right. Her mama could flat-out bake.

Maybe, he considered, he could buy her the commercial stove she'd mentioned the country required her to have before giving her a permit to sell her cakes and pies to local restaurants.

"No point in having money if you can't use it to help people you care about."

All in all, the day had turned out a lot better than he'd thought when he'd allowed himself to be hijacked.

But as he approached Somersett, something was still niggling at Gage about The Flamemaster case. Something that wasn't ringing true.

The pieces all seemed to fit into place, including the fact that John Tyler's fire-fighter father had served in Vietnam and brought home three souvenir claymore mines, which had provided the C-4 his son would later use to blow up buildings.

Case closed.

Or so it seemed. But every instinct Gage possessed was telling him there was still a loose thread out there, just waiting to un-ravel.

The blazing sun was setting behind the towering twin alabaster spires of St. Brendan's Cathedral as he drove back to town. Tess had told him about Bailey's new jewelry line, and how her research had led Ty to mistakenly believe she'd been having an affair.

As he drove past the fire station, with its St. Florian plaque above the doors of the apparatus bay, the last piece of The Flamemaster puzzle fell into place.

forty-seven

"Bailey?" Tess stared at the woman she'd thought she knew nearly as well as she knew herself.

"Sorry." The Flamemaster winked. "But Bailey's gone back inside. She's never been able to handle stress very well. Which is why I was born."

"Who are you?" She couldn't believe that deep, masculine voice was coming out of Bailey's mouth.

"The Flamemaster, at your service." He bowed dramatically. "Of course," he said thoughtfully, "that hasn't always been my name. I only acquired that after she went to San Francisco last year and met Randolph Griffith."

"Bailey met Griffith? But he's in San Quentin."

"*Was* in San Quentin. But he became a liability. So, now he's in the cemetery. And the worms will eat him."

The entity that was not Bailey seemed to enjoy that idea.

"You had him killed?"

"Oh, not me. That was Pamela."

"Pamela Winters."

"Exactly. I take it you've met."

"I was in her gallery."

"Ah." The Flamemaster nodded. "Lovely place, isn't it? Especially that back room."

"Obviously we have different tastes." The thing to do was to keep him talking, Tess told herself. Until she could figure out what the hell was happening. What to do.

She reached out her hand, hoping some physical contact might reach her friend. "Bailey —"

The Flamemaster pulled back. "No touching!"

All right. Don't make him angry. Not when he's holding those contact wires. The wires were attached to a can she recognized as Sterno, which was, in turn, connected to a claylike lump that resembled the precious-metal clay Bailey used in her jewelry. But which, Tess belatedly realized, was in reality an explosive.

"When did you meet him?" she asked. "Griffith?"

"It was one of those lovely turns of coincidence." The Flamemaster bared his teeth in a smile. "Bailey was at a conference at the San Francisco Fairmont. Have

461

you ever stayed there?"

"No."

"You should. It's quite special. At any rate, she signed up for a tour of the prison. Sort of a field trip for prosecutors. Griffith spotted me as a soul mate right away, of course."

Having met the monster, Tess believed that.

"How were you able to meet?"

"Oh, we never actually spoke in person. That wouldn't have been allowed. But it wasn't difficult for him to find out who Bailey was. Given that she was wearing a name tag right above her visitor's badge.

"Pamela tracked her down for Griffith. Discovering that she was an artist was a stroke of luck, because that gave Winters an excuse to get involved with her. She sold some of her jewelry."

"I wouldn't think it would've suited her gallery's taste," Tess said.

"That's because you didn't see the ones she made when I was influencing her. They were really quite special. There was a pendant with Jack the Ripper's straight-edged razor, the Son of Sam's .44 handgun, Jeffrey Dahmer's stockpot, complete with a little skull in it, which was one of my personal favorites —"

"They must have sold well," Tess cut him off before he could describe any more gruesome murder weapons.

"Like hotcakes." His chest puffed out with pride. "Pamela couldn't keep them in stock."

"She carried messages for you and Griffith, didn't she?" Gage had suspected that all along.

"Of course. Griffith comprised a code he'd conceal in his paintings. Fortunately, none of those philistine guards knew anything about art, so they never caught on. Then Pamela would decode the message and send it to Bailey's and my computer in an email. Which, of course, I intercepted."

"Oh, God." Tess was shaking. She was also desperately trying to see some vestige of her friend somewhere inside that wan shell and couldn't. "You killed Danny."

"That was a mistake. I was attempting to kill Bailey's husband. Your fiancé was merely unfortunate collateral damage."

"Ty? Why would anyone want to kill Ty?"

"To protect Bailey, of course."

"She didn't need protection from Ty. He adored her."

"He was a man, wasn't he? With a man's ugly, disgusting needs. He'd gotten her pregnant. Just like before. When she was a little girl."

"Ty didn't meet her until five years ago."

"He wasn't the father. Not that first time," The Flamemaster said on a flare of frustration. "Pay attention!"

"I'm trying to," Tess said quickly, watching as the ends of those wires nearly came together.

"Bailey was only thirteen. But developed for her age, if you know what I mean."

Tess nodded. Bailey had told her she'd matured early. And had hated the attention her curves had garnered.

"Her father's brother found her particularly attractive."

"He molested her," Tess guessed with a sinking heart.

"That's too nice a word. What the man did was rape the girl. Several times. She tried to tell her parents, but they didn't believe her. Personally, I've always thought they chose to look the other way because it would have caused a scandal. It was only when she turned up with a bun in the oven that they were forced to face the truth."

"What happened to the baby?"

"They made Bailey abort it, of course. It was a brutal procedure." He shook his head. "She was so young. And there was so

464

much blood. She nearly died from fear. Which is when I was born."

"To protect her." Tess felt the tears begin to flow down her cheeks.

"To protect and avenge. That was the first time I killed."

"Her uncle."

"Of course. He drowned in his pool." The Flamemaster flexed his fingers. "With a little help."

"I'm glad he's dead." Tess could not be sorry. She also understood why protecting children was such an obsession with Bailey. Apparently she and the personality born from such physical and mental trauma shared that in common.

"Does Bailey know about you?"

"Of course not. Or at least she didn't until I killed her husband in that fire the other evening."

"Why?"

"Because he wanted her to have another child. Which would have been impossible. I couldn't allow that."

"Why not?"

"Because," he said, with a huff of impatience, as if even attempting to carry on a conversation with such a dim-witted person was an effort, "when Bailey's pregnant, she's forced to think about her body.

It gets fat. And ripe. And uncontrollable."

"Which reminds her of the rape and abortion," Tess guessed. Another time when poor Bailey's body would have definitely been out of her control.

"Exactly. The last time she was pregnant, the poor girl had nightmares for the entire first trimester. Things got so bad, I didn't know what was going to happen to us. Which was why I came up with the idea to kill her husband in that mill fire. But although he didn't die, all that stress caused her to miscarry. Which just goes to show that every cloud has its silver lining.

"Besides," his teeth flashed in another of those cold, eerie smiles, "as much as I came to enjoy setting fires, things were beginning to get complicated. I realized that when I was setting the charges in your pretty little house."

"You tried to kill me."

"You were going to try to kill me first," he said.

"I wouldn't have done that."

"You would have sent me to prison. Which would be the same thing. Besides, you deserved it. I'd always thought you were a nice, pure young woman. But the way you acted with that ATF agent . . . well, it was just disgusting."

He shuddered. Then regained his control. "I thought killing Ty would take care of things. Give the police someone to focus on so they could close the case and everyone could forget about The Flamemaster."

"You killed that woman in the apartment."

"Of course. In the beginning the idea was to frame Bailey's husband. But it was immensely enjoyable. And made the prospect of killing John Tyler even more appealing."

"How did you get him to the building where you killed him?"

"As soon as Bailey received his call saying they were letting him out, I left him a note to meet her at the office building. She had something important to show him. One thing about the man, he always came when his wife called him. He was better trained than a dog. I made certain he'd find the device right away. As a clever twist, I'd set that one to trigger as soon as anyone touched it."

He smiled reminiscently. "Ka-boom."

Not wanting to reveal weakness, Tess managed to keep from shivering at the matter-of-fact tone. "That was very clever of you," she said, even as her heart bled for

Ty, whose only mistake had been falling in love with such a tragically flawed woman.

"Wasn't it? But I'd miscalculated how much Bailey loved him. She was so heart-broken, something cracked inside her when that partner of yours came to tell her about his death."

"And in that crack, she saw you," Tess guessed.

"That's very good." Another smile. Colder and more treacherous than the others. "You're becoming a very good detective, Inspector. It's only too bad your career is going to be cut so tragically short."

"No!" Bailey cried out from somewhere deep inside the killer. "There's already been too much killing."

"Shut up," The Flamemaster growled. "This doesn't concern you."

"Of course it concerns me," Bailey screeched at him. Attacked him, clawing her own tortured face, leaving trails of blood on tear-stained cheeks. "Everything you do comes back to me."

"Everything I do is for you!"

"You murdered my husband!"

"He wasn't any good for you. He made us — you," The Flamemaster corrected quickly, "remember things that were better off forgotten."

"I loved him, dammit!"

"Bailey," Tess murmured carefully.

"Shut up!" The Flamemaster turned on her. "And stay out of this!"

"She'd be happy to." Another voice entered the conversation. Tess spun around. Gage was standing in the doorway to the kitchen, the ugly gun in his hand.

"Now look what you've done," The Flamemaster said accusingly. Tess was no longer sure if he was talking to her or Bailey. "You've involved someone else in our private business."

"Let Tess go," Gage said reasonably. "Let her walk away and we can end this. Here and now."

"End it by killing me, you mean."

"I don't want to do that. But I will. Without hesitation if you touch a hair on my woman's head."

"Maybe I'll kill you, too," The Flamemaster threatened. He waved the bomb that Gage had described so well. Having seen the computer model, Tess definitely didn't want to experience it firsthand.

"You set that off, and you'll go up, too," Gage pointed out. "Holding it like you are, there probably won't be enough pieces left to bury."

Tess could see the conflict in The Flamemaster's eyes. They circled the room, like trapped birds, looking for a way out.

Gage turned toward Tess. *On three,* he mouthed.

Tess gave an imperceptible nod.

One.

She took a deep breath.

Two.

Inched closer to the door.

Three.

She raced for the door at the same time Gage reached for her, grabbing her beneath her arm, dragging her out of the house.

The Flamemaster roared with rage.

They heard Bailey scream back.

The explosion rocked the neighborhood, throwing Gage and Tess into the air. They landed twenty feet away in the pond, amid the water hyacinths and koi.

Bailey's perfect house was ablaze; orange flames shot into the darkening sky.

"She stopped him," Tess murmured. There was not a doubt in her mind that Bailey had known exactly what she was doing when she'd sacrificed herself to keep her single-minded protector from ever killing again.

"That'd be my guess," Gage agreed as he gathered her into his arms and held her tight.

"How did you know?"

"Your St. Florian's medal."

Tess just stared at him.

"It was the same workmanship as those ones in the cases at Collectors."

Tess remembered glancing at some jewelry in the room with the ivory figures, but even knowing Bailey, the connection hadn't registered.

"You only could've glimpsed them for an instant."

"Yeah. But remember me telling you that one of my hotshot investigative talents is my photographic memory?"

"Sure. I just didn't believe it."

"Oh ye of little faith. Anyway, when I figured out the connection, I called the apartment and got the message you'd left on the voice mail about coming out here. I was afraid you might be in trouble."

"That's what I love about you, O'Halloran," Tess drawled. "You're the master of understatement."

"It's one of my many charms," he agreed. He skimmed his knuckles up her face. "You okay?"

Her two best friends were dead, she'd lost her home, she currently had water plants wrapped around her body, giant goldfish were nibbling at her legs, and ash

471

was dropping onto her head. But Gage's arms were around her. Which made all the rest bearable.

"I'm still not sure. But I will be."

"Yeah." With sirens wailing in the background, he touched his mouth to hers.

She would be all right, Tess told herself as he kissed her. Lightly. Gently. Tenderly. They both would be.

forty-eight

Just as Danny's had been two years earlier, John Tyler's funeral mass was celebrated at St. Brendan's Cathedral. A seemingly endless number of firefighters stood up to share intimate stories of their fallen brother. Strangely, the humorous stories proved the most emotion-provoking.

It had been raining earlier, but the spring storm had passed on when Brian Murphy piped Ty's casket out of the cathedral, and mourners were greeted with a vivid rainbow that sketched its way across a bright blue sky. The chrome of the washed and waxed red truck, which had been draped with red, white, and blue bunting, dazzled beneath a bright yellow sun. A black wreath had been wired to the front grill.

Going all the way back to the Knights of St. John, crusaders living on the island of Malta who'd begun firefighting in the 1200s after their enemies had started using naptha bombs as weapons, firefighters had always been a band of brothers. In more recent years the brotherhood had expanded to include sisters, as well, and members of that extended family had traveled from as far away as Seattle and Maine, and as nearby as Savannah and Charleston, to pay their respects to one of their own. The sweep of blue uniforms, badges covered with a narrow band of black tape, filled the tabby sidewalks for blocks on end. A sea of brimmed hats and helmets were swept off and white-gloved hands raised in a salute as the truck passed.

The route to the Queen of Angels cemetery took the funeral cortege past the site of the mill where Danny and Jake had died. In the early days after that fire, in a display of shared grief, Somersettians had adorned the fence with flowers, sympathy cards, and black-and-white toy Dalmatians.

Two years later, the rubble had been cleared away, and despite Donald Mannington and his cronies trying to get their hands on the property at fire-sale prices, public pressure had resulted in the recreation center that was now rising from the ashes. Future plans called for a bronze statue of firefighters to stand at the entrance of the adjoining park.

"I got a call from my former partner today," Gage told Tess after they'd returned to the apartment from the funeral supper. "About an arrest ATF just made."

"Oh?" she said absently, her mind, he figured, still on the funeral of her close friend.

"Seems a guy in Savannah offered to pay a torch two hundred and fifty thousand dollars to burn an abandoned theater building he'd bought in Charleston."

Her eyes widened. "Please tell me it was Mannington."

"Bingo." Gage grinned, more than a little pleased with himself. "Unfortunately the so-called torch was an undercover agent."

Her smile was dazzling. "It was you, wasn't it? The same way you got Daddy that lawyer and Mama her stove, you brought in the Feds to nail my nemesis."

"Since there aren't all that many tall buildings for me to leap around here, I figured it was the least I could do," he said. "I also got a job offer."

"You have a job. Making games."

"Yeah, well." He shrugged. "I just sort of fell into that. I've recently come to realize that perhaps I'm not as burned out as I thought I might be."

"You're going back to ATF?"

"Just because I'm not a meltdown case

doesn't mean I'm that fond of structured rules. This is for a private firm. The same one your brother Joe went to work for."

Hope fluttered its wings in Tess's heart. "Their home office is on Swann Island." A barrier island just two miles offshore, which meant that he wouldn't be leaving South Carolina. "Would you be working from there?"

"Since most of my work is computer oriented, your brother thought I could probably work wherever I wanted."

"Oh. Well. Flexibility is always a plus. Are you going to take it?"

"That depends on what my partner has to say."

"Your partner?"

"I told Joe that you and I are a team. Now, maybe I was taking too much for granted . . ."

Tess arched a brow. "Maybe?"

"Okay. I was. But here's the deal. We'd be doing the work we're both good at, we'd be free from political pressure, we'd make good money, and best yet, we'd be doing all that together."

"That *is* appealing." Especially the together part.

"So what do you say?"

"I'll have to think about it." She pursed

her lips in consideration. Stroked the kitten curled up on her lap. "Okay, I've thought about it. And I say yes." Her lips curved. "So, when do we start?"

"In a couple weeks. After we get back."

"We're going somewhere?"

"I figured, after all you've been through the past week, you could use a vacation."

"Vacations are nice." Tess couldn't recall the last time she had one. "Where are we going? Back to California?"

"Actually, I was thinking Wyoming." He took a deep breath. Rubbed the back of his neck. It was the first time Tess had seen Gage actually looking unsure of himself. "What would you say to meeting my parents?"

Having never been one to play emotional games, Tess refused to be coy. She flung her arms around his neck.

The kitten, squeezed between them, let out an irritated meow. Having a good idea what was coming next with these humans she lived with, she jumped off the couch and stalked from the room, orange tail swishing.

Tess pressed her smiling lips to Gage's. "I'd say yes."

About the Author

JoAnn Ross has published more than ninety novels, has been published in twenty-six countries, and is a member of the Romance Writers of America's Honor Roll of bestselling authors. She has won several writing awards, including being named Storyteller of the Year by *Romantic Times*. Her work has been excerpted in *Cosmopolitan* and featured by the Doubleday and Literary Guild book clubs.

With her husband and two fuzzy little dogs, she divides her time between the mountains of East Tennessee and the coastal lowlands of South Carolina.

Visit JoAnn on the web to subscribe to her electronic newsletter, at www.joannross.com.

The employees of Thorndike Press hope you have enjoyed this Large Print book. All our Thorndike and Wheeler Large Print titles are designed for easy reading, and all our books are made to last. Other Thorndike Press Large Print books are available at your library, through selected bookstores, or directly from us.

For information about titles, please call:

(800) 223-1244

or visit our Web site at:

www.gale.com/thorndike
www.gale.com/wheeler

To share your comments, please write:

Publisher
Thorndike Press
295 Kennedy Memorial Drive
Waterville, ME   04901

UNCARDED BOOKS

Paperback _____   Hardcover ✓ _____

(no c.l. ed.)